The First Stone

**Center Point
Large Print**

**This Large Print Book carries the
Seal of Approval of N.A.V.H.**

The A.D. Scrolls

BOOK ONE

The First Stone

THE DIARY OF
Mary Magdalene

Bodie & Brock Thoene

CENTER POINT PUBLISHING
THORNDIKE, MAINE

This Center Point Large Print edition is published in the year 2011 by arrangement with Bodie and Brock Thoene and www.FamilyAudioLibrary.com.

First Print Edition, August 2011.

The text of this Large Print edition is unabridged. In other aspects, this book may vary from the original edition. Printed in the United States of America on permanent paper. Set in 16-point Times New Roman type.

ISBN: 978-1-61173-157-6

Library of Congress Cataloging-in-Publication Data

Thoene, Bodie, 1951–
The first stone : the diary of Mary Magdalene / Bodie & Brock Thoene. — Center Point large print ed.
p. cm. — (The A.D. scrolls ; bk. 1)
ISBN 978-1-61173-157-6 (library binding : alk. paper)
1. Mary Magdalene, Saint—Fiction.
2. Bible. N.T. Gospels—History of Biblical events—Fiction.
3. Christian women saints—Fiction. 4. Jesus Christ—Fiction.
5. Diary fiction. 6. Large type books. I. Thoene, Brock, 1952– II. Title.
PS3570.H46F57 2011
813′.54—dc22

2011020398

Sing aloud, O daughter of Zion . . .
Rejoice and exult with all your heart,
O daughter of Jerusalem!
The Lord has taken away
the judgments against you;
He has cleared away your enemies.
The King of Israel, the Lord, is in your midst.

Zephaniah 3:14-15

Prologue

Old City, Jerusalem
Present-day

The line between servant and master had long ago been blurred and then erased in the Old City Jerusalem home of the Sachar family.

Alfie Halder, the aged giant once called half-wit and *untermenschen*, "subhuman," by the Nazis in Berlin, had escaped euthanasia to live out his days in reborn Israel. He had outlived those who plotted his death for the sake of the Nazi state. He had outlived the Muslim sniper on Jerusalem's walls who held the big man in his gunsight and pulled the trigger, only to have the rifle explode in his face.

For sixty years Alfie had lived as attendant and friend to Moshe and Rachel Sachar. He had outlived them both; grieved at their gravesides; then turned his attention to caring for their son, Shimon.

Now Alfie lay gray and weary in his bed like an elderly lion. His massive arms, once strong, twitched outside the blankets, unable to lift a spoon to his lips.

Shimon ladled broth into the old man's mouth. "There now, Alfie. You'll eat. You'll get strong again."

7

Alfie managed to shake his head in disagreement. "Almost home, Shimon," he whispered.

"Don't talk nonsense." Shimon grimaced. "What would I do without you?"

"Angels. All my life," Alfie wheezed. "They won't leave without me . . . almost home."

Emotion constricted Shimon's throat. How could he argue with angels, after all? Though he needed the old man's company, how could he forbid him from leaving a life lately grown as dark for Jews as it had in the days when Hitler came to power?

Nothing had turned out the way the first Israelis dreamed it would, back in 1948. The world had turned its back on the land of miracles. "Peace, peace," they cried, but there was no peace.

"Don't want to live no more, Shimon. Your mama and papa, they're lucky they left when they did. Lucky not to see what we seen. Happening all over again."

Shimon held the bowl of the spoon to Alfie's lips, urging him to swallow just one more bite. The old man resisted.

"For me, Alfie," Shimon urged.

The old man hesitated. "Because it makes you happy." He swallowed, then turned his pale eyes toward the window. A flock of blackbirds flew toward the Western Wall. "Your mama always says the birds remind her of old rabbis, flocking to pray inside the Old City. Your mama . . . she lived through so much, so you kids could be born—have a homeland, Israel." He sighed. "Always loved your mama. See her soon, too." Alfie closed his eyes. A single tear escaped from beneath his eyelid and trickled down his cheek. "America. They have forgot. The young ones. Forgot everything. Forgot why Israel must live."

Shimon could not reply. It had come to his mind as Alfie began his decline that perhaps despair was killing him. "Alfie. Old friend."

Alfie's eyes fluttered open. "Your mama and papa told me . . . Alfie, give the first story to Shimon when it's time. The first story your papa read to me . . . the old man, your grandfather, laid it out for your papa, see? And then your papa copied it word by word to send to your mama to read so she would know . . . her past don't matter. What happened to her don't matter to Jesus."

"Sure." Shimon rubbed Alfie's hand. "Sure, Alfie. Don't worry about it."

"But now . . . the end. I want to go back, Shimon. Back to the beginning. My favorite story . . . the stones that almost killed her . . . would you read it to me?"

What was he talking about? Shimon wondered. The Chamber of Scrolls was beyond Alfie's ability to reach now. It was forbidden to bring the scrolls up beyond the boundary. "What is it you want, old man? How can I help?"

"Your papa copied word by word. We lived on peaches and tins of bully beef. The stars on the ceiling . . . and then Eben Golah came to us in the chamber."

"Eben Golah?" Shimon leaned nearer to Alfie, trying to hear what he was saying. "You mean Eben Golah came to the Chamber of Scrolls?"

Alfie nodded. "Sure."

"He knows the way?"

"Sure. Eben knows all the streets beneath Jerusalem."

"And . . . and . . . you say he brought something to my mother?"

Alfie smiled weakly. "I gotta say stuff more than once? Your papa . . . he read me the first story. Maybe weeks he spent, writing a copy down for your mama. Eben came . . . your mama was pregnant. Eben brought out to her the copy."

"But . . . do you mean Eben? Jerusalem, 1948?"

"1948. All the Lamed Vav was here. They was waiting for it."

"And there is a copy of a scroll? Papa sent Mama a translation of a manuscript?"

"Shimon!" Alfie's eyes flashed with irritation. "In your papa's file. Top drawer. Back . . . get it. Read. My favorite, see? Find it."

Shimon left Alfie's room and strode quickly to the dark-paneled library. Nothing was actually filed in the red oak file cabinet in the corner; everything was simply crammed into the drawers. They were bursting with a jumble of Moshe Sachar's old notes, yellowed personal correspondence, and news clippings.

After Moshe died, Shimon never found the time or the courage to completely sort through his father's papers.

Pausing for an instant, aware the file drawer had not been opened since Moshe was alive, Shimon drew it back. The unorganized mess he remembered was revealed.

Could anything of such enormous value be stashed within?

Pawing through stacks of letters, Shimon came upon a tied-up bundle of sympathy cards sent when Rachel had been killed by a terrorist bomb in the Old City. Shimon thumbed through the cards. So many old friends who had battled beside Moshe during the War for Israel's Independence. Now most of them were gone too.

Shimon fought emotion as he remembered the stories of 1948: how Moshe and Alfie escaped into the tunnels beneath the Old City as the Jewish Quarter fell to the Muslim hordes. Then Shimon's mother, Rachel, with her brother and grandfather, were driven out of the burning Jewish Quarter among 1,200 Jewish refugees.

Rachel was pregnant and left on her own in Jerusalem for many months, not knowing if Moshe still lived. Was there more to the story that had not been told?

"Eben Golah?" Shimon spoke the name of the enigmatic elder in wonder. "Papa's friend, Eben, in Jerusalem in 1948?" This piece of the puzzle seemed beyond imagination.

Lifting stacks of papers, Shimon uncovered a brown paper package inscribed, *For my beloved Rachel and our child, from Moshe, November, 1948.*

Shimon withdrew it, holding the envelope reverently in his hands. Drawing his breath slowly, he peered inside at a handwritten manuscript inscribed by his father, with notations on the margins clearly written in Yiddish by Rachel.

The first page of the manuscript was a letter of introduction.

My beloved Rachel,
Our friend Eben Golah brings this gift to you
as the day draws near when . . .

This was followed by a dated journal entry— his mother's account of the day she received the gift and news that Moshe still lived.

November 13, 1948 . . .

Shimon blinked at the letters:

Today a man . . . named Eben Golah . . .

So it was true.

Shimon carried the package to Alfie's room.

The old man opened his eyes as Shimon entered. Alfie managed a smile. "Good boy. So. Now read. You read to me like your papa used to . . . the story, the beginning . . . almost to the end."

Alfie sighed with contentment as Shimon sat beside the bed and rustled the pages of the manuscript. "Wings of angels. Hear them? This story brought your mama peace sometimes when she remembered what happened when we was kids. Your papa would read it. And, you know, angels gather to hear and remember. Look, Shimon—listen to their wings." Alfie fixed his eyes on the space behind Shimon. The old man seemed to be focused on someone, hearing a voice Shimon could not hear.

Shimon felt the powerful presence of the unseen guest.

Alfie nodded with approval and spoke softly. "Shalom, yes. Back where we started, eh? Almost home, eh?"

Shimon began to read. . . .

Rachel Sachar
New City, Jerusalem
November 11, 1948

My heart sees light and color, though a gray pall lays over Jerusalem. From the window of my

13

tiny, one-room flat I can gaze out the window across No Man's Land toward the burned-out synagogues of the Old City. I remember the day my dearest friend, Leah, gave birth to her beautiful daughter and died, leaving the baby in my care.

As I write this, Tikvah, nine months old, sleeps in a wooden crate I painted pink and adorned with tiny red roses. Sweet baby. Little Tikvah looks so much like her mother that my heart finds joy when she smiles up at me. Though I am pregnant with Moshe's child and without my friend to talk to, even so, I feel as though Leah is beside me every minute. The Old City where Leah and Shimon lie buried is closed to all Jews now. The Muslim soldiers of Jordan prowl the parapets of Jerusalem's walls and sometimes shoot at Jews here in the New City in the west. Leah is buried in the Jerusalem of Jordan's King Abdullah and we cannot say *kaddish* at her grave. I am determined that Tikvah will know the story of her mother's life; always hear Leah's voice in the music of the cello.

Perhaps one day Tikvah and I will carry roses to Leah's grave and say *kaddish* over her.

I make this vow: "One day, Leah, I will bring Tikvah to visit. One day Jerusalem will no longer be divided."

Soon I will give birth to Moshe's baby. As I

write, the baby dances in me and taps the message of Shalom.

"Blessed are you, O Lord, who has not left me alone . . ."

My hand caresses my stomach and I send my love to the baby who shares my heartbeat. I wonder, *Is Moshe still alive? Is he still living in the hidden chambers beneath the ancient Temple Mount?*

"Blessed are you, Lord, who has given Moshe a child, though he may never see him. Blessed are you . . ." My whispered prayers falter, and I fall silent in the face of the daunting possibility Moshe is never coming back.

I count the weeks back to the last time I saw my beloved. Six long months have passed since the Arab Legion breached the defenses of our besieged Jewish Quarter. Two hundred Haganah defenders fighting tens of thousands of Jihad Moquades simply ran out of ammunition and food. Supplies for 1,200 Old City Jewish civilians ran out. Surrender was the only possibility for survival. As 3,000 years of Jewish residence came to an end, only Moshe and Alfie Halder had managed to escape into the labyrinth of tunnels beneath the city.

Now the Gates of Zion are closed to us. We are in exile. The Quarter where my ancestors lived for thousands of years is off limits. King Abdullah of Jordan, it is said, will soon annex all

Jewish land captured before the truce. Old City Jerusalem is now controlled by the Hashemite Kingdom of Jordan.

The charred arch of the Great Hurva Synagogue towers over the deserted stones of the Old City—a stark reminder that death is the fate of any Jew who dares to enter the Old City.

As the baby grows within me I have not received even a whisper of hope Moshe survived the desecration and burning of the Jewish Quarter. I remember long ago horrors. Just as my home and family in the Warsaw Ghetto were destroyed by Nazis, five nations of the Arab Legion have vowed to finish in Israel what Hitler began in Europe.

Was Moshe among the last to die when Jerusalem fell?

I know the venom of the Nazis. I am a woman well acquainted with sorrow, escaping the gas chambers only to exist as a prostitute in an SS brothel.

After the war the rebirth of the nation of Israel gave me a true home; a place where we Jewish survivors could truly say to the world: "Never again!"

"Never forget!" became our battle cry. We are the Jewish survivors returning to their ancient homeland as the Prophet Ezekiel predicted we would. But for me the shame of remembering the past made surviving the present almost unbearable. I am haunted by this memory sometimes in the dark of night when I reach out and Moshe is not with me.

But then I remember only God's love, and the love of Moshe Sachar, turned my life back from the brink of self-destruction.

Now the imminent birth of Moshe's child gives me the will to live and fight on for Israel and my children. I know well that if there had been a Jewish homeland in the 1930s, perhaps the Holocaust would not have happened. My mother and father would be alive. My brothers. My soul would not grieve for the purity I lost at the brutal hands of demons who lived in the flesh of men.

Since I came home to Israel the five Arab nations that swarmed over the mountains of Israel with the aim of driving us into the sea met with a supernatural opposition. The God of Abraham, Isaac, and Jacob fought for us. The reborn nation of Israel has miraculously survived these six months. And I, survivor of the Holocaust of my people, have also survived. I believe that Israel, the apple of God's eye, will live, and grow, and thrive, like the child I carry, who is soon to be born in freedom.

Will I ever see Moshe again in this world? I cannot say. But I will live and Israel will live, and our child will have a nation to call home. I must trust the Lord, who has brought me this far and who promises He will never leave me or forsake me.

• • •

November 13, 1948

Something remarkable happened this morning.

It is proof that the Lord has heard and answered my fervent prayers.

A flock of birds flew over the Old City. I said to the Lord, "The birds are like a rabbi's prayers. My prayers. They are flying home to pray beside the Western Wall."

I clearly saw the Arab gun emplacements on the parapets. They were aimed across the gulf into our Jewish New City.

"Never again," I whispered my prayer. "Shalom Jerusalem, please, Lord."

It came to me as I watched the black birds that the Arabs believed no Jews remained in the Old City. But perhaps they were wrong. I wondered, what if Moshe and Alfie survived? What if they were still there? Perhaps the two men lived far beneath the rubble that had been home to Jewish hearts since Abraham had offered his son upon the mountain. And then a single bird flew across the sky, and I felt Moshe's prayers flying toward me.

I turned from the window and put the kettle on the hissing Primus stove. Brewing a cup of tea, I savored the aroma. English Breakfast tea made with tea leaves used only a dozen times. Such luxury. I sat beside Tikvah's crib and sipped the hot, thin liquid.

"Blessed are you, O Lord, King of the Universe, who grows tea leaves and makes them last and last . . ."

Suddenly I heard the crunch of gravel in the narrow alleyway leading to my flat. Soft rapping upon the door followed.

Tikvah stirred at the unwelcome sound. Two steps and I was at the door.

"Who's there?" I asked.

"A friend," a man's voice replied cheerfully in Hebrew. The words were spoken in the musical cadence I remember from the Ashkenazi rabbis' accents of my childhood—Old Hebrew, not like the modern tongue Israeli *sabras* speak. The man said in a voice like a cantor's song, "I bring a message for Rachel Sachar. A gift."

I unlocked the door and opened it, leaving the chain lock on. I peered out to see the smiling, bearded face of an Orthodox Jew in his midthirties. He held up a package wrapped in brown paper. "Shalom. Rachel Sachar?"

"Shalom," I greeted him and placed a finger to my lips. "The baby is sleeping, you see. Yes, I am Rachel." I knew he would not expect to be invited in to the flat, but I unchained and opened the door. "Shalom!"

His face was young, but his eyes seemed very old, as if he had seen much sorrow. "Shalom! I am Eben Golah," he said quietly, taking note of

19

the sleeping baby. "I am an old friend of your husband. Of Moshe."

"Moshe? He isn't . . . he is not here."

We remained separated by the door's threshold, as is proper. Cold winter air drifted in, stealing the warmth of the little room. I stepped out and closed the door behind me.

Eben said, "Moshe not here. Yes, I know. Was not expecting him, you see."

I explained, "I don't know when he will return. Or if . . . I have not seen my husband for six months, you see. Not since the day the Jewish Quarter fell. I am sorry, Mister Golah."

"Moshe and I fought together. The war. El Alamein. And in London. The Blitz. He was at Oxford and I was . . . ah well. It doesn't matter, Missus Sachar. Your husband and I . . . we go back a long way. Very long."

"Yes. Wonderful. I only wish he was here and I could invite you in for tea. How I would love to hear the stories of the two of you together in the war. In London. I know so little. Moshe and I, we met only a year ago and then . . . well, you can see. Here I am, and a baby soon. A miracle."

"It has been a year of miracles. Indeed." He fingered the package and looked around. "I have brought this for you, you see?" He held it up and placed it in my hands.

I blinked down at the familiar handwriting and gasped. "Moshe?" My legs felt suddenly weak.

The package was from Moshe. Eben Golah was the messenger. "He's alive?"

"Yes. Yes. Missus Sachar . . . Rachel . . . do you need to sit down?"

I sank onto the step. Tears stung my eyes. My heart praised God. "He is alive?"

"Yes. Alive and well." He gazed down at me with concern. "Are you all right?"

I began to weep as I held the package to my cheek and kissed the handwriting. "Alive."

Golah remained standing, speaking in an urgent whisper. "It was difficult to find you. He did not know where you were living. Perhaps even Tel Aviv, he thought. But you are here."

"I would not leave. I had to stay, you see? Close to the place where I saw him last. In case he were to come back . . . but please, Mister Golah, where is he?"

"Call me Eben, eh?"

"Eben. Where is he?"

"Where you last saw him."

"Still? There?"

"Yes."

"And Alfie?"

"With him. They are safe. He wanted you to know. He was concerned about you. The baby. He knew. The time for you to deliver the child is near."

I gazed up at the stranger. "You've seen him? But I thought . . . I was told no one knew . . ."

"An old friend, as I said."

"But . . . how did you? I mean, I thought that only my grandfather and Moshe and . . ."

"All is not as it seems, Rachel, daughter of Rebbe Lubetkin. Granddaughter of Rebbe Lebowitz."

What was it about Eben Golah's face? His skin had an almost luminescent quality, as if he carried a light within; as if he could be seen even in a dark room.

"Tell me."

He hesitated. "This . . . it is Moshe's first manuscript translation. Your grandfather set an order of reading for Moshe. This was the first. The original scrolls may not be brought to the surface, for they will crumble if they enter the world. What you hold is a translation. Written in Moshe's own hand, you see. He wanted you to have it . . . to know he is thinking of you as he works. And you must keep it safe until the day when it will become known."

I gazed in awe at the brown wrapping then untied the string. The paper rattled as I pulled back the outer layer, revealing a handwritten manuscript.

"All these months," I breathed.

"One more thing." Eben held her in his gaze. "He is coming home to you."

"Moshe. Home?" My tears fell freely.

"Soon. The baby, you see." Eben smiled. "He

22

said he was afraid Tikvah would not know him and that perhaps you should have him near you. The baby . . ."

"And he sent you."

"It is important, Moshe felt, that you read the story of a woman like yourself—a woman whose heart was broken—to know the truth of the task Moshe has been given . . . for such a time as this."

"I have not questioned the Lord in my husband's absence. I only longed to know, prayed for an answer, to know if Moshe is still living."

Eben Golah bowed deeply and backed away. "So I was sent to bring you word. You must read her story, Rachel, for then you will know the true story of Israel's fall and her redemption. You will see . . . your story is her story. God's love and redemption for Israel. It has all been chronicled, recorded, and stored until now; the time just before *Or Olam*, the Everlasting Light, returns to Jerusalem. The God of Israel has seen and heard your prayers . . . He sent first to Moshe and now to you. Look for your beloved to return. Believe it. Shalom, shalom, Rachel, beloved and righteous daughter of Zion."

Eben's eyes twinkled with pleasure as he turned at the end of the alleyway and merged into the crowds on the main road beyond.

I stared after him in wonder, then caressed this

23

precious document; Moshe's gift of hope to me. Slowly rising, I returned to the warmth of my tiny flat and to the cup of tea. Now I will open the first pages of the manuscript.

I no longer feel alone. I will savor each word. I will ration myself and read only small portions as if I am tasting a great delicacy. Perhaps I shall read only ten pages a day. Then Moshe will come home to me . . . and I will see his face and feel his arms around me once again.

"Blessed are you, O Lord, King of the Universe, who has let me live to see this day!"

The Story of Mary Magdalene,
First Century, A.D.
Translated by
Moshe Sachar, Old City, Jerusalem, 1948

My dearest Rachel,
Beloved wife and friend,

I send you this greeting and gift as proof that my heart still beats for you, and that my every thought beneath the ancient stars of Jerusalem begins and ends with you.

Alfie and I are well. There are supplies laid in for us to last many years; this by the wisdom and foresight of your grandfather.

My heart yearns for you as I yearn for sunlight. Each hour I remember that the birth of our child must be very near. It is my prayer that I may be with you and hold our child in my arms on that day. But I have translation and preservation of the first flight of manuscripts which I must complete. This was the task laid out for me by your grandfather and I know you honor the urgency and importance of my assignment.

My old friend, Eben, has carried this manuscript through much danger to you in order that you may know and have comfort in the hope that I will soon be with you. How he came to be with us is a story I will tell you when we meet again face to face. By sacred vow he cannot speak to you of all he knows. The day will come when I may share all, as I am not constrained by the same vow as Eben Golah.

This manuscript is the first of all my work which I have translated. Your grandfather, Rabbi Lebowitz, guardian of the chamber, laid this document out for my reading first as he passed the duty on to me for protecting all that lies beneath the ancient city. I believe Rebbe Lebowitz placed this document first in my care because of its great message of HaShem's redemption and love for a woman who thought she could never be forgiven, and who lived her life in despair until she met Yeshua face to face.

This is but the first section of her memoirs, which is broken into three scrolls or shares. Ancient history gives her name in the first part, Amarum mare, or Mary, which is translated "Bitter Sea." Her story of redemption begins at the edge of the bitter sea.

As I read and translated her story my memory was filled with the moment of our first meeting. I first saw you that night of such danger aboard the little vessel Ave Maria, filled with illegal Jewish refugees seeking to enter Eretz-Israel. We were seeking to avoid capture by the British patrolling the waters along the shore. As we sailed through the dark and bitter waters toward the shores of Eretz-Israel the lights of a British gunboat came toward us and you thought to end your life rather than be captured and imprisoned again.

In the very first words recorded by Mary—"Amarum mare"—I remembered how I saw you slip over the side of the boat to end your suffering. I remembered how, without thinking, I dove after you. As we swam through the turbulent sea I tired and almost gave up. I fought to stay afloat and focused my mind on life. There came to my mind at that moment the memory of a miracle associated with Mary, which is recorded in the thirteenth century by Jacobus de Voragine in Legenda Sanctorum.

In 1260, a ship crowded with men and women was swamped on the sea and sinking. A fallen woman who was pregnant and drowning called out to the Lord and to the great witnesses in heaven. She vowed that if she lived, she would live like Mary lived . . . at the feet of her savior and choose the better part. And if she had a son she would dedicate his life to the service of God's kingdom. At once a woman of noble visage appeared to her, held her up by the chin and, while the others drowned, brought her unharmed onto the land. The woman gave birth to a son, and the vow was fulfilled.

I never told you before now. On that night, my

dearest Rachel, as we both came near to drowning, I felt a hand holding my chin above the water. I was given strength to swim for us both, though you had given up hope. After many hours we came into the safety of the Promised Land together. Thus, our story, like the story of Mary, begins in the bitter sea of sorrow but must end with salvation.

So the story begins.
Your loving husband,
Moshe

Chapter 1

Bethany, in Judea
First century, A.D.

My beloved friend, Claudia,

I pray that you and your honored husband are well by the grace of God.

I rejoice that your heart is being enlightened by the hearing of the words of the Hebrew Prophets and fear of the One True God of Abraham, Isaac, and Jacob.

Many months have passed since Maximus first brought me your letter, requesting me to set down the facts of how and why I have become a follower of Yeshua of Nazareth. Since then I have daily attempted to write down the record of my journey from darkness into the First Light of Morning which has dawned upon the earth.

Words cannot convey how near the abyss I stood or how great is the Gift of Life and Freedom Yeshua has given to me. Others around me, who also lived lives of dissipation and despair, now also cling fast to the truth, and follow after the One whom we know is Truth.

But there is great envy and hatred building in Jerusalem's corridors of power. The shepherds of my people, rather than welcoming Yeshua, seek how they may destroy Him.

You say your honored husband, as a servant of Rome, wishes to understand from the testimony of a Hebrew why Yeshua is so hated by Jewish rulers, while common folk risk everything to follow after Him. I can only answer for myself in this account. Each other life He has touched and changed must give his own testimony. Our rabbis say, "Every life is a book yet to be written." This book is my life until today.

The prophetic word in Torah is made firm by the fulfillment of every detail in Yeshua's life up to now. As it is written, He has healed the sick. The blind can see the lame as they dance. The deaf can hear as the dumb sing songs of praise. With my own eyes I saw my brother, dead four days in his tomb, returned to life with his family at the command of Yeshua. Many witnessed this miracle. Many thousands flock to Bethany to see my brother, El'azar, and hear his stories of who and what he saw beyond this life when he embarked on his journey into the kingdom of olam haba.

Yeshua gave back to El'azar this life. The people know that no ordinary man could perform such a miracle.

Today, outside our gates, hundreds of pilgrims are camped in hopes of seeing Yeshua when He arrives here at our home.

We do well to pay close attention to all these things, as to a lamp shining in a squalid and dark place until the First Light breaks through the gloom and the Morning Star rises in our hearts.

The story of my journey into the light is a tale of darkness and despair. You knew me in those days when we banqueted together at the royal palaces of Galilee. Sorrow surely echoed in my laughter in those days.

We fear for the safety of Yeshua as plots against Him grow more intense by the hour. Yeshua says plainly that His kingdom is not of this world. My brother, El'azar, who returned from that place, confirms that heaven is very different from earth. El'azar has seen the kingdom into which Yeshua promises to bring us. As He has said many times: "In my Father's House are many rooms. If it were not so, would I have told you that I go to prepare a place for you?" [John14:2]

When Yeshua will return there, or how, is a matter of much speculation among His followers. We all fear for His safety this Passover. Perhaps, wise and kind friend, you will read my testimony and know Yeshua means only goodness and joy for every man, woman, and child who lives upon the earth.

I send this by the hand of Centurion Marcus Maximus, as you have requested. Maximus has promised he will answer any questions you may have after reading.

Here then is what I have witnessed until today.

I remain your true friend,
Mary

Chapter 2

Magdala, Galilee
Reign of Emperor Tiberius
First century, A.D.

It was like this in the beginning. I was lost before He found me, though I did not know it.

That night I stood alone on the balcony of my estate house. The Sea of Galilee stretched out before me. The half-moon illuminated a highway of liquid silver on the water, urging me to come.

I felt as though I was being drawn to destruction by an invisible hand. Stripping from my clothes, I descended to the shoreline and stepped into the warm water. I pushed forward till the water was above my waist. Lanterns of distant fishing boats bobbed on the waves. Within a few steps the bottom would drop away into the depths of the Galil. I could swim toward the moon.

A whisper spoke to me on the breeze, *"Swim! In the center of the light your mother awaits!"*

Mother! How I missed her! Longed for her! Yes! She was waiting for me on the other side of life. She would embrace me! Comfort me! I would drift away with her into peace and eternal sleep. Every sorrow in my life would come to an end!

"Why not?" I asked myself.

I had heard the whisper call me a thousand times. Each night the desire to leave life was stronger than the last.

What was it that kept me moored to earth? Was it Maximus? There was no one else I cared about. Nothing of consequence to keep me from taking my own life as my mother had done in my childhood.

Powerful though he was, yet Maximus meant little to me. He was an amusing diversion from my desperate, empty hours. His strength and need for me was my opiate that dulled the pain of living.

The image of Maximus was clear in my mind as I stood rooted on the brink of death. I suddenly knew it was not love that held me back, but fear of what dying might bring.

I asked the voice, "Suppose the sleep I long for is only a door into a darker dream? Suppose what is beyond the shore is more horrible than this existence?"

And the voice answered me, *"Mary! Mary! Finish it. You have no reason to live. Unloved. Unhappy. There is no hope for you here. No hope . . ."*

Yet I hesitated. I had no fear of God, for I knew I would never see God, who must be a merciful being. I did not belong to God, but to the other creature that opposed Him. I feared the unknown evil I sensed existed just beyond my consciousness.

"Why do you speak to me?" I asked the voice. "Why do you require my life from me? As you must have taken my mother's life?"

The thing did not reply. I told myself the whisper was imagination borne from my loneliness. The course of all life followed a series of accidental twists and turns. Eventually every path led to the grave. Better to enjoy the journey than be burdened with empty religion. I had lost my way. Only once had I truly loved a man. He had married another, yet even in that moment I thought of him and plotted how I might win him back from his wife and family somehow.

Meanwhile, Maximus was amusing company. Maximus did not require love, only companionship. Perhaps it was enough.

Speaking aloud, I banished the voice. "Not tonight. Soon enough, but not tonight."

Hesitating a moment longer, I returned to the

shore and dressed in a saffron colored shift. I plaited my dark hair and returned to my bedchamber, where Maximus slept.

The air was still. Through the open windows the lake was a mirror reflecting the sky and hills of Galilee. A thin golden line on the far shore separated heaven from earth.

Winter was past and the rains of spring had ended. Northward the wheat fields were months away from harvest. Leaves had just begun to bloom on the terraced grapevines. On the hills and rocky ledges acres of red anemones and blue lupines blended with thousands upon thousands of golden flowers. The scent filled the air. I wondered briefly why I found no joy in this change of seasons.

It was the twentieth day of Iyyar, the day after my twenty-sixth birthday. I was the widow of old Yosef ben Reu, a wealthy landholder. He died childless, and I was his last wife, inheriting vast estates in Galilee.

What had been the kingdom of Israel in Solomon's day was now carved up into small provinces and governed by glorious Rome. Herod Antipas, corrupt son of Herod the butcher king, governed Galilee as Rome's puppet. The new Roman governor, Pontius Pilate, controlled Samaria, Judea, and Jerusalem.

Maximus, a centurion of Rome, slept in my bed, unaware how near I had come to ending my life. He was a great hero in foreign wars. Son of a princess of conquered Britannia, Maximus was a man of legend who saved the Roman army on the Northern frontier. I had seen the *corona obsidionalis* he won on that field. But without his armor and his crown, he seemed no more fierce than any other man. He was uneasy among my people, the Jews. He held a quiet disdain for the High Priest Caiaphas, who had been appointed by Caesar and remained in power by Caesar's will.

An uneasy peace existed between Jews and our Roman overlords, but at my lakeside villa, I made certain that Rome and Israel united in the harmony of a secret pact.

Maximus was stationed nearby at Tiberias, the Galilean capital of Herod Antipas. Living only four and a half miles from my home at Magdala, he was my frequent guest, arriving after dark and leaving before sunset. We were discreet, but rumor of our affair reached even to my brother in Bethany.

That morning in the first light of dawn I knelt at his head and studied his features. At thirty years old he was the battle-hardened *Primus Pilus* of the First Cohort. Senior officer over five hundred mercenaries in the pay of Rome, he was known to his men as "First Javelin."

Stocky, muscled, and strong as a bull, his sun-bronzed body bore the scars of a dozen wounds. Offspring of a British captive and a Roman officer of the equestrian order, he was not handsome. His nose had been broken. Russet hair was cropped close and I could just see a touch of gray. Dark, brooding eyes and a hot temper betrayed his Celtic ancestry.

I stroked his brow with my fingertips and whispered his name.

He opened his eyes and exhaled, then grasped my wrist, pulling me down beside him.

"Mary . . . where were you?"

"Swimming."

"You're chilled."

"Warm me then."

He kissed me and whispered some phrase of poetry he knew. *"He watches, a vigilant guard, and once you're captured, he never lets you lift your eyes from the ground . . ."*

"Poetry again?"

"Don't interrupt. Where was I?"

"I am captured."

"Ah, yes. *'But then, if you sin, he is a placable god, provided only he sees your prayers are heartfelt.'"*

He held me tightly and I struggled, pretending I wished to escape. "I pray. Let me up."

He kissed me. "Mary."

"It is almost light. You must go."

"I'm ready for battle or for breakfast. It is up to you. Either will do."

"I will neither serve you nor serve under you

this morning. It is morning, you see. And we have a bargain, Maximus, about you being here after daylight."

"Tonight then." He began to get dressed.

"Strength and courage, Maximus. I'll be in Cana for three days."

He pulled me down onto the bed. "Then I'll have you now."

I worried about the servants, but he wrestled with me, playfully pinning me as he quoted poetry. *" 'Stern old men may denounce these carousals of yours: only let us, my life, wear out our purposed way. This is the spot where you, skilled flute, shall sound . . .' "*

I smiled up at him, glad I was still alive. "Is it music you want from me? Then you'll have a song for breakfast."

"Mary. Mary. Should I be content to live with only one girl?"

"And a Jewish girl at that. What would Sejanus say?"

He smiled at me as he considered Sejanus, Caesar's most trusted commander. Sejanus hated Jews.

Maximus answered, "I would tell him you are fair to all the gods. You worship each equally. You worship nothing."

"I worship only one," I answered between kisses, almost loving him. "You are the god of my idolatry, Maximus. My morning sun."

And perhaps he almost loved me. "May I always rise to your expectations."

Maximus stayed late with me that morning. Light drenched the hills as I watched the Roman and his young servant Carta slip out through the orchard gate.

Fishermen, farmers, and merchants were already about their business. It was hopeless to imagine that the people of my village would not notice a Roman centurion riding from my estate. Maximus took to the road, but it was I who had lost my way from among my people. I no longer cared if the rumors about me were proven to be true.

Closing the curtains, I lay in bed and told myself that it did not matter what anyone thought of me. My reputation had long ago been destroyed by the town gossips. What did it matter if Maximus had been seen? It simply confirmed what everyone knew; unlike my righteous brother and sister in Judea, I cared not at all for appearances.

I heard the footstep of my aged nurse, Tavita, as she limped toward my room. The door hinges groaned as she opened the door. I turned my face to the wall and pretended to sleep. The aroma of breakfast filled the room. As Tavita slammed the tray of food onto the low table, I could not pretend to sleep any longer. She flung the curtains open, flooding the room with glare.

"I have a headache," I told her.

She mimicked me, "I have a headache."

"Tavita, please! The light hurts my eyes." I sat up and gave the toothless old woman my fiercest look. "Leave the tray."

Tavita was not intimidated. She filled a cup and handed it to me. She would not leave until she told me the gossip. "The little boy, Taddi, delivered milk to the kitchen this morning."

I remembered the little crippled boy. "What of it?"

"He brought the milk and gave me the news straight. He would not give me the news unless I answered his question."

"Which was?"

"Who were those Roman fellows coming out of the gate? The centurion on the black horse and the red-haired youth who ran along before the horse."

"And what did you tell him?"

"That they had come early to inspect the orchard. They had bought the next harvest of figs and pomegranates for the soldiers stationed at the Palace of Herod Antipas in Tiberias."

"My clever Tavita. Fruit from my orchards savored by Rome. The nuance of it is food for gossip. The boy's question is no doubt a feast for the village."

"I won't lie for you again. All these lies on my soul. You lie where you will. Lie with whom you will. But I will not lie for you again." She clucked her tongue at me as if I was a child. "And your poor husband not even cold in his grave these four months."

"My husband was cold for a lifetime before I married him. And he was cold in our bed for ten years before he died."

"He's not been dead long enough."

I was shameless in my answer, defying her attempt to shame me. "You're right. I would have buried him sooner if only he had cooperated. He was dead before he stopped breathing. Three other wives before me and no children. That is proof enough of his deadness. Our bed was a tomb."

"A kind old gentleman. Deserving of your honor."

"He, at sixty-nine, bought my honor when I was a girl of sixteen."

"Barak had your honor before that."

At the mention of my first love, my temper flared. "Enough! For the holy estate of marriage I endured, I deserve the estate I have inherited. I will enjoy my freedom after so long a time in the prison of a celibate marriage."

Tavita would not be silenced. She was my conscience. "You knew no one in Judea could take you or your brother or your sister in marriage with the stain of your mother's suicide upon your family. You should be grateful."

"My mother's madness branded us. El'azar and Marta accept loneliness. But I won't live by their rules. You may think my orchard satisfies the orchard of the centurion, but I am the one with an appetite to be satisfied."

Tavita covered her ears. "When the old man made offer for your hand, your brother thought it a great opportunity for you."

"To be rid of me. He knew I was in love with someone else."

We both fell silent as I remembered Barak and what I had wanted most out of life.

The old woman puckered her face in disapproval. "Your brother, Master El'azar, was wise. You could not have married Barak bar Halfi. His father would not be convinced madness did not run in the family. That your children might not inherit the desire to die as your mother."

I had never told anyone about my mother's demons or the voice that spoke in my head, urging me to death. I drained the cup. "It doesn't matter. The one I loved now has wife and children and debt and care. He is indebted to my estate. I am his landlord, even though I am not his mistress. I hope his father is well pleased with Barak's life. I know I am better off. From now on I'll only attend weddings that are not my own."

Tavita was pleased with my reasoning. "Just so."

I announced the news. "Therefore I am going to Cana."

"No! You can't!"

"I am going to the wedding."

"You will not be welcome."

"I'm invited!"

"Invited because your dead husband owned the orchard."

"Now I own it. I am cousin to the groom by marriage. My late husband would not have me neglect my duty to his kin."

"His kin hate you with great pleasure."

"Wait till they see my gifts."

Tavita changed her tone, seeking to cajole me. "I nursed you. Rocked you to sleep. Mary! It was I who heard your first word, which was NO! And I heard every defiant word after. You were always a stubborn, wicked little girl. Going to the wedding because Barak will be there. So you can show him how well things are for you. Rich and fine and beautiful. You will flaunt yourself before his poor wife."

"I have business to discuss with him. And my brother and sister will be there too."

"Yesterday you told me we would not go."

"I have changed my mind. I wish to see El'azar and Marta. My brother and sister. All the way from Bethany. Did you think I wouldn't go?"

Tavita grew fierce. "They will not wish to see

you. And now the gossip about the centurion will reach Cana ahead of you."

"Then I'll catch up with it. I wouldn't miss it. A reunion."

"It is Barak you go to see. Please! Send the gifts and stay home."

"An ounce of saffron and one of cinnamon for the bride and groom. Two jugs of the best olive oil. They won't refuse. I am going, Tavita. I'll wear the thing Yosef brought me from Alexandria. Gold embroidered. You know the one . . . pack it. Tell Freeman to prepare for our journey."

Freeman prepared for our journey under the disapproving eye of Tavita. I wondered what Maximus would say if he knew my true purpose in attending the wedding.

Perhaps he would not care, I reasoned. After all, I believed that Maximus cared little for anyone but himself. We were alike in that aspect of our lives.

His thirteen-year-old servant, Carta, was a possession; like Maximus' horse. Maximus had affection for his horse and his servant, but I believed it was the affection borne of ownership. Perhaps he felt the same about me. I was conquered territory, belonging to him as long as I suited his needs and gave him pleasure.

This was a man who would never be ruled by

love for any woman. We did not share love. Desire, certainly. Passion, yes. But Maximus would never be enslaved to a female or anything that implied weakness or frailty. Maximus owed allegiance only to power and unchallenged dominance. Rome ruled the world. Therefore Rome ruled Maximus. The all-powerful force of the state was the only thing worthy of his devotion. For love of Rome, Maximus had saved the army at Idistaviso. For love of Rome he fought and attained the highest battlefield crown. There was no other claim upon his heart that could be called love.

Although Tavita disapproved of my silence, it never occurred to me that I owed Maximus an explanation of my childhood love for Barak. After all, I did not ask if he enjoyed the company of other women in distant cities. I did not ask him if his heart had ever been broken. Nor did he ask me if I had ever truly been in love. Our relationship was a conveniently selfish arrangement, requiring no emotional effort on my part or his.

In contrast to Tavita's constant haranguing, by which her every thought emerged from her mouth, Freeman's leathery bronze face betrayed nothing. Trudging ever higher into the pass west of the Sea of Galilee, he led the pair of donkeys bearing Tavita and myself in stoic silence.

Our destination was the town of Reeds, a

day's journey from my home in Magdala. Cana, it was called, where nothing exciting ever happened. A dozing village of fewer than a thousand souls, it lay beside a swamp between the hills. Flax grew there, and sheep grazed there amid fig and walnut orchards. Cana's sole claim to fame was that King Herod once slept there with his army.

Freeman raised his chin and sniffed the air like a faithful hound. Then I caught it too: the aroma of meat roasting on a spit for the wedding feast. Joining the enticing smells on the swirling breeze were sounds: piping flutes answered by deep-voiced drums. Other roads coalesced with ours and with them flowed streams of other guests. The villagers were all dressed in their cleanest homespun garments. Their clothing was almost interchangeable: shades of brown and yellow set off by an occasional headscarf in dark red. This was what passed for finery in the Galil.

I despised all the rustic farmers and their squawking broods, but despite all my resolve, my heart leaped as I scanned every young, bearded face. Somewhere in this gathering throng was Barak.

Tavita gave me a shrewd and shrewish glance as if she could read my thoughts. I struggled to control my emotions and adopted an air of cold unconcern.

It was not easy to accomplish. Almost at once I spotted Barak's father, Halfi, in the crowd. It was he who had come between his son and me a decade before, after he caught us in the barn together. More concerned about his precious Levite purity than about love, the priest moved his family all the way from Bethany to Cana to remove his son from further temptation.

I bit my lip. Halfi was nothing to me now, but the sight of him caused unwelcome warmth to rise in my cheeks. The involuntary reaction made me angry with him, at Barak for deserting me, and at myself for still caring.

I preferred to believe the pink tint of my face was born of annoyance and not shame. For perhaps the thousandth time I instructed myself that Barak's family had no right to look down on me. Poor tenant farmers that they were, they subsisted on my husband's property.

And since my elderly husband died, now I was Barak's landlord. It was my fields over which Barak labored as his back and shoulder muscles strained to heft the shocks of wheat. Plowing my furrows caused the sweat to course down to the ends of Barak's jet-black hair.

A delicious shiver coursed through me.

With the longing for his touch came again the old curse with which I sentenced Barak bar Halfi. I prayed, if such a wish could be called prayer, for him to regret the loss of me and miss me desperately. I wanted visions of me to haunt him, waking and sleeping.

Not that he had ever shown any sign that my spell had effect. Whenever he came to the counting house, whenever I encountered him working in the fields, he kept his chin tucked down and his speech properly respectful.

Barak had to be somewhere among the wedding guests. He and his plump little wife and their plump trio of cow-eyed daughters must be nearby. Was he searching for me as I was for him?

I felt many eyes on me—all of them disapproving. I was rich, and I took lovers. From Judea to Galilee my reputation was discussed.

I put ice into the glare I bestowed on those around me. In a voice loud enough to be overheard I ordered Freeman to unfold my pavilion in my walnut orchard as locating it in my fig grove did not suit me. Let these rustics be reminded who controlled their lives. They had better stifle their thoughts.

My tenant farmers paid a large share of their income to me each year. They had no choice in the matter, because if they balked at my terms I would turn them out, and they knew it. Even those who owned their own small holdings were dependent on my good will, since I had the connections with the Roman authorities. A word from me about traitorous Jewish sentiment—just a hint that some grower held Zealot sympathies—and such a man would be lucky to keep his head, let alone his business.

Was it any wonder they hated me?

Their hate was tolerable because it came from fear, and fear was useful. It was, Maximus said, the same way Rome ruled the Empire.

Fear was not my only tool, however. I could also entice. I had in mind a way to capture Barak's attention with a plan to prosper him financially. Later I would capture him in other ways as well.

Freeman led us to a spot beneath the largest walnut tree. Its spreading boughs were already a canopy overhead. In response to his query I told him the location was satisfactory for my tent.

Meanwhile, I continued scanning the crowds, but the familiar faces I next discovered did not please me. Turning away as soon as he saw me was my lanky, angular, curly-haired brother, El'azar.

Tavita made a sarcastic remark about brotherly love, but I ignored it.

Beside El'azar was my squat, perennially pinch-faced, prematurely gray sister. Marta, ever conscious of public observation, returned my wave with a clenched-tooth smile.

Both of them were steeped in self-righteousness. I suspected they had conspired with Barak's father to separate us; perhaps even paying the Levite to keep quiet about me. El'azar and Marta cared more about their reputation than they ever did about me.

The separation between my siblings and me had not begun with Barak bar Halfi. It was older and deeper than that.

Bachelor brother and spinster sister lived within the confines of the walls of the Bethany estate. More to the point, they were imprisoned by religion and by a fear they shared, but never discussed.

They hated me because I had escaped their walls.

The thought cheered me. No opportunity to repay them for their coldness was allowed to pass unused and their presence at this wedding presented another such occasion.

"I'll glue myself to Marta tonight," I observed to Tavita. "During the procession. At the ceremony. At her elbow at supper."

Tavita wheezed. "She'll choke on it."

"So much the better."

Tavita could get away with scolding me, within limits of course. As she aided Freeman in the unpacking she noted, "Is that why you came to Cana? To torture your brother and sister? Or . . ."

I followed her gaze just as she concluded, ". . . or to catch a husband for yourself?"

The double meaning in her words was apparent when I saw what she saw: Barak bar Halfi, striding into view in a place of honor between the nervous-appearing groom and an elderly rabbi. Barak was the Chief Friend of the Bridegroom tonight. He was the master of the revels, greeted on every hand, and enjoying the respect of the throng.

My insides turned over at the sight of him. My breath caught in my throat and I felt my heart race. I thought I caught the scent of the bridegroom's anointing on the evening air and it called to me.

"Careful, chick," Tavita muttered, "or you'll be the one who's caught."

The warmth of the way Barak was greeted pained me, though I would never show it. Smiles were all around him just as scowls traced my progress. For an instant I thought again of the cool, still waters of the lake and pictured them closing over my head.

Then I shook away the image. Barak bar Halfi would be secretly pleased to see me here. And if his first reaction was dismay, I knew how to change it.

But first there was a barrier to pass.

My brother appeared at my elbow. He uttered my name in the same tone one might use upon lifting a rock and finding a scorpion beneath it.

In turn I displayed a generous smile. "Greetings, Brother. Isn't this pleasant?" I dismissed Tavita with a wave.

"Why are you here, Mary?" he asked bluntly.

"You don't belong here." El'azar moved sideways as if to draw me further into the orchard and away from prying eyes and ears.

I stood my ground and forced him to face me. "These are my people. My husband's family. My tenants. It would be ungracious of me not to come."

El'azar's green eyes looked everywhere but into mine, and he plucked his wiry beard. "Would have been better."

"How nice to see you also, Brother. I have gifts that should make my presence bearable for the wedding party."

"Mary." This time he spoke my name with difficulty. "You make everyone . . . uneasy."

"And how's dear Marta? And your vineyards? How was the journey from Bethany?"

"Mary." El'azar braced his thin shoulders like a man readying himself for a difficult task. "There's been talk."

"There's always talk."

"About you and a Roman."

"I have many friends among the Romans."

I was not about to make this easy for him. I could see his teeth grating when he amended, "A certain Roman centurion."

Shrugging I replied, "Cana has nothing better with which to pass the dreary days than gossip."

"Widowed only months," El'azar hissed. "Can't you even pretend to know propriety?"

I waited until I captured his gaze. "I'm not like you. I never could pretend." Involuntarily I studied Barak again and El'azar's head pivoted on his thin neck.

"He's married," he said gruffly.

"But not to me! And whose fault is that?"

El'azar's words fell to a menacing growl as his fingers dug into my arm and he dragged me behind a tree. "You can't buy these people's friendship."

"I haven't sought. . . ."

He shook his head even as he shook me. "They won't tolerate you. Not here. Not today."

"They don't have a choice!"

"Listen to me," El'azar ordered. "Everyone knows what sort of person you are. You. . . . at a wedding? Mockery! Blasphemy! Return home to your Gentile lover before you make a fool of yourself."

Bending to put his lips close to my ear he continued, "They won't accept your gifts, understand? They've been told not to. If you go through the gates to the city square they will shame you publicly. . . . perhaps even stone you. The elders have all agreed. For the last time, don't do this to yourself. Save what little reputation—"

"For your sake?" I demanded bitterly. "For Marta's?" Rage flooded me, overflowing from my eyes like the weakness I despised.

53

Reasserting control before El'azar could claim a victory I added, "So I should be grateful for your timely warning? For your brotherly intercession?"

To my surprise El'azar spoke more forthrightly than I expected. "Yes. Let your departure be the way you express your thanks. Stay in your tent until the wedding, then slip away home. In the future, if you have business here, send your steward."

My thoughts swirled. Was I being discussed in all of Cana? Was I the greatest source of amusement in the village tonight? Was I being pointed out to strangers and my fate mused about?

Knots of people stood together laughing and talking. . . . and looking toward me.

I could still sense the nearness of the bridegroom, though the wedding principals were no longer in sight.

Nor had Barak come to rescue me.

Was I the subject of every jest. . . . even his?

Only one man remained apart from the others. A tall, strongly built man with brown hair stood alone beside the stone wall across the road. He, too, looked at me, but I saw no laughter on his face . . . nothing but a glimpse of sorrow.

Unlike El'azar, who was worried about his own reputation . . . or all the rest, who desired a spectacle . . . this stranger, whoever he was, seemed to offer only a warning, as if he cared about me. *Escape, lest they crush you,* his expression cautioned.

Then a slightly built, older woman approached and captured his attention, and any connection between us was shattered.

"Mary, are you listening?" El'azar inquired.

Confusion reigned in my mind. Would the unknown man have helped me? Would he have taken my part against the mob?

Instead of strengthening me, the single offering of pity broke down my resolve. His one breath of silent kindness crushed my will to fight. How could I win with so much already decided against me? How could I even fight?

I would never let El'azar see me vanquished. Feigning boredom I tossed back at him fragments of excuse. "As it happens. . . . must go. Important news. I must . . . return to Magdala . . . at once."

"Good. Yes," El'azar intoned with evident relief. "Live however you want, but expect no warmth from your people. You've done this to yourself, but it can't be undone. Still . . . I'm sorry . . ."

"Save it!" I snapped. My eyes must have flashed danger, for he released me and backed several paces away. "In any case, none of these country clods mean anything to me. It's true. I only came to laugh at them. This isn't amusing anymore. I'm ready to leave."

• • •

As I stumbled into the tent, near blind with rage and self-pity, Tavita caught at my arms, revealing the bruises where El'azar had grasped them. "What, lamb, what?" Then, as her touch slipped to my palms she gasped as she grasped my fingers. "Your hands are freezing. You're shaking. What did he say to you? Can't he leave you alone?"

I could not bear the old woman's sympathy. I rushed to my cot and buried my face in the cushions.

Tavita was furious. "Just tell me! I'll give him what he deserves. See if I don't!"

My hand and head wavered from side-to-side as if directly attached. *No,* I soundlessly pleaded. *Don't make me say more.*

The material of the tent was too sheer; the crowd too large; the others too near. I would not give anyone in Cana the satisfaction of hearing me weep. Fear of my wealth, of my disapproval, was my weapon, and the only one I possessed. If I showed weakness the scorners would pounce like wolves on a wounded lamb.

"Go away!" I ordered Tavita. "Don't let anyone see or hear anything's wrong. You understand? No one."

Tavita instantly took my meaning and left the shelter to carry out my instructions. I heard as she and Freeman conversed with other servants in the grove. Tavita skillfully directed the chatter to the beauty of the bride and the honor of the groom and what fine children they would have. She hinted that I was occupied preparing myself for the wedding but would emerge when I was ready.

"Thank you," I whispered to the empty pavilion. I bit the pillow in my frustration. Cut off from family, from having a life among my people, my sense of isolation was near to choking me. I could fool the others, even my brother, but I could not fool myself.

Once more the lapping waves of Galilee sighed an invitation to step into their embrace.

Chapter 3

Sunset ushered in the new day, and three long, quavering calls of the shofar summoned guests to the wedding. The babble of voices around my tent receded toward Cana until only the sighing of the wind and the chirping of crickets remained.

I pictured the scene within the town: the veiled bride being escorted along a street lined with flickering oil lamps. By her side, leading her toward her husband-to-be, was the bride's mother.

I squeezed my eyes tightly shut as grief overwhelmed me again. Her mother! What would my life have been if my own mother had somehow summoned the courage to live? If she had only cared enough for me to not die?

I thought how surrounded by hate I was. My brother . . . my sister . . . Halfi . . . the scornful citizens.

And Barak? Was he too part of the plan to shame me?

I would not . . . could not . . . believe it. Barak must not know of their plan. He would never have consented to join them.

I remained wrapped in despair for an age, it seemed, until at last I was roused by the sounds of cheering and cries of "Mazel tov!"

The ceremony must be over, then, and the festivities begun. Music began and laughter.

As the melody entered my ears a new plan formed in my heart, confirmed when Tavita entered at that moment.

"Lamb?" she softly inquired. "Are you sleeping?"

"Are they all gone . . . from the orchard, I mean?"

"They've gathered for supper. Be full of wine soon enough."

"Give me your cloak and veil," I commanded, sitting up and wiping the streaks of tears from my face.

"What demon is whispering to you?" Tavita said, scowling. "You mean to go into Cana?

Pretend to be a servant? Unwelcome as you are?"

I roughly shoved aside her concern. "I won't be kept out and shunned like a common harlot. They may hate me . . . but not Barak! Not he! I'll find him. I must take this to him." Beside my cot was a tapestry bag. From within its folds I drew a box tied up together with a scrap of parchment.

"I won't help you in this madness," Tavita protested.

"You will! Or I'll turn you out. I swear it!"

"Will you never learn?" she said with narrowed eyes.

"This is business," I said, shaking the box in her face.

"Then it can wait till daylight. A public place."

"There is no public place where I can be seen with Barak bar Halfi," I returned.

Tavita looked away from my fierce reply. She knew I was right about that.

"Wicked!" she pronounced. "Headstrong! What can you possibly have for him that won't be reviled as a gift from a discarded lover?"

"A crocus bulb," I answered smugly. This was a plan I had formed long before. "Karkom . . . for growing saffron."

"Saffron? Why not just give him gold and be done with it?"

Saffron was the most expensive spice on earth. A few strands of the reddish-golden fibers equaled a day's pay. An entire field of the flowers produced only a bread-loaf's weight of the seasoning, but could be worth as much as ten years' wages. "It's the reason I came to this shabby place," I explained. "A business proposition he cannot resist."

Tavita's expression wavered between curiosity and suspicion.

"Bulbs from Persia," I went on. "Enough for the twelve-acre field that's been fallow these many years. I want Barak bar Halfi to manage the business for me."

Such an arrangement would also provide me many opportunities . . . many reasons . . . to be with him again. "It's all there in the note. A business offer. I wrote it before we left Magdala, so put away all your evil thoughts."

Tavita sniffed. "Take it to him, then," she agreed, removing her cloak to begin the clothing exchange. "But Freeman and I will begin packing, and tomorrow we're taking you home."

Outside the night air was fragrant with the grass. The aromas of the town mingled feasting and wine and perfume. I carried no light, fearing someone might see through my disguise, but I needed none. The rollicking noise of the celebration and the glow of massed lamps guided me toward the merriment.

The way toward the gathering was lined with the echo of laughter and the shouts of many toasts. *Long life! Good health! Many children!* I could not help but imagine myself as a bride again . . . only with a strong, young husband, and not bound to an ancient, passionless half-dead stick.

Forcing my thoughts back to the matter at hand, I pondered my approach. Soon enough all the guests would be too full of drink to notice me. But when? How soon would it be safe? I clutched the box of bulbs under the cloak as if it were a talisman against disaster.

What if Barak repudiated me? What if he pushed me away?

I circled outside the gleaming orb of the festivities like a cautious moth. My mouth was dry with anxiety. The town well was away from the crowd. I would quench my thirst while waiting awhile longer to approach Barak.

The water skin, half full, rested on its cord beside the rim of the well. I took a swallow, then another, regaining my composure. Idly, I flicked a pebble into the gaping dark mouth of the cistern; listened to it plunge and splash into oblivion.

The sounds of partying faded and new voices took its place. How easy it would be to lean back into the well. The cool cushion called to me. Peace. Sleep.

El'azar. Marta. Sorry at last for abandoning me, they would carry me home to rest beside Mama and Papa.

The pull of the voices was strong.

But what if I died just as I was about to possess Barak again? What if he truly loved me and we were happy together again?

What if I missed out on that one, great hope?

When I covered my ears a sharp corner of the wooden box jabbed my head, reminding me of my plan. As I shuddered away from the well to lean against a stone wall I pictured a field of purple crocus blossoms and a smiling Barak in the midst of it.

It was then I spotted a man leaving the lighted area of the feast.

He was coming toward the well. With the illumination behind Him His features were obscured . . . but the glow would be on me as He approached.

Hurriedly, I concealed myself behind a stack of stone water jars. From their shelter I held my breath and peeked out at the unknown form.

He was tall and slender, and walked with easy confidence. Still some feet away. He stopped and appeared to be examining the water casks. Had He heard me?

He seated himself beside the cistern. Had He seen me there? Had He read self-destruction in my position by the brink, or had I been recognized and was He now blocking my escape before summoning the elders?

When He came no closer I began to breathe

again. The seductive voices were gone and the joyful sounds of the revelers returned. My other senses revived as well with a renewed whiff of the aroma of the costly ointments anointing the bridegroom.

Then fear reasserted itself. A line of hand-carried lamps bobbed toward us. I crouched still lower.

Was this the strong arm of village propriety coming to seize me? Were the elders approaching to make good on their threats to expose Mary Magdalene?

I peered into the darkness.

The form heading the others was a pear-shaped female. Following her was a file of women servants. "There's my son," the leader exclaimed, pointing toward the man at the well. "There's Yeshua."

The man rose and kissed His mother on the cheek as she continued, "I've been looking all over for you."

Like a gaggle of geese, the servants babbled the reason for the quest. Something terrible had happened at the feast. The crowd was bigger than anyone expected. The wine was all gone. There was no market in Cana to buy more. What could be done?

Mother linked arms with son, drawing Him near my place of concealment, while speaking urgently: "Out of wine. Drunk every last drop, and the blessing not even yet pronounced. 'Blessed are you, Lord, King of the Universe, who created the fruit of the vine and gives us wine to drink . . .'"

I leaned forward in spite of myself. It sounded as if the woman had addressed the words to her son!

"Can such a thing happen when you are here?" the woman implored the man named Yeshua. "No wine to bless the marriage?"

I saw Him cup His mother's chin in His hand. Playfully, He chided, "Woman, what am I going to do with you? You know it's not yet my time."

What could that phrase possibly mean? "Not my time"?

Lamplight flickered on the woman's confident face and she arched one eyebrow at her child.

The music of His laughter at her expression rang on the stone water jars like the jingle of rain on a tiled roof.

Did He own a vineyard? Was there a warehouse of wine nearby after all? Would the servants be sent to fetch enough for the feast?

Her voice quietly self-assured, Yeshua's mother commanded: "Do whatever He tells you to do," then she scuttled back up the street toward the merry-making.

The double rank of attendants awaited Yeshua's instruction.

Surrounded as He was now by the gleaming

flames, Yeshua's features were perceptible to me: wideset brown eyes, dancing with golden flecks. A prominent nose above a mouth curved in a slight smile.

It was the same man I had seen earlier in the day, standing across the road from my embarrassment with El'azar.

The man whose face recorded sorrow for me.

I wriggled uncomfortably with the recollection and shrank back. Could His piercing gaze spot me now?

But Yeshua was occupied with other matters. Inclining His head toward the first rank of stone containers he said: "Fill them with water."

Burrowing back further into concealment, I heard but dared not watch as pairs of maids obeyed. They filled six jars to the brim with water from the well and paused for his next command.

What? My thoughts screamed with questions. *What sort of game is this?*

When Yeshua was satisfied the half-dozen amphorae were at capacity He said, "Now take them to the master of the feast and draw out for him."

Barak! Barak was to be the victim of this senseless prank! A ladle of water for the blessing?

A buzz of questions mirroring my own confusion circled the servants. Yeshua had already strode away from them, heading toward the village gate.

The women stared at each other. Some registered bewilderment and others anger.

"Take water to the chief of the celebration? And tell him what?" one demanded.

"Mary's son sends his compliments and these jugs of . . . water?" another scorned.

"A scandal!"

"For the blessing? It's an insult that won't be forgotten."

"Mary must be mad!"

"Well," one of them drawled. "You know her reputation."

A listener snickered and an older woman noted, "She volunteered to help. And she told us to do what He said."

"So?"

The senior servant shrugged. "So . . . we obey. He's Mary's son . . . whoever His father may be. Anyway, it's her reputation, not ours."

The rest agreed.

Perhaps I should have regarded the similarity of the gossip about Mary to my own tarnished status, but my thoughts were focused on Barak.

This was my opportunity! I could mingle with the serving girls returning to the feast. I could circulate, unrecognized. Get near enough to pass Barak the box and the note.

My heart pounded. It remained, after all,

dangerous ground. My brother might spot me. My sister might denounce me.

My legs propelled me along at the back of the returning column of women, despite my misgivings. The tempo of my pulse increased as we entered the square filled with partygoers.

Then there he was: Barak, his glossy black beard and hair oiled and sleek. His handsome features were cast in earnestness as he discussed the Roman threat to the purity of Temple worship with a semi-circle of village elders.

The trembling in my limbs returned and multiplied. Barak's listeners were the same men who vowed to shame me, punish me, expel me!

Coming here was a mistake; a huge mistake.

Now I had no strength with which to escape. My immobility forced me to watch a small drama play out before the greater one of my humiliation unfolded.

The oldest serving woman dipped a ladle into her jar and presented it with a flourish to Barak. Almost without pausing to look at her he accepted it and pronounced the traditional blessing: "Blessed art thou. . . ."

I saw the mocking smile on the face of the servant and the way she winked at her companions as Barak raised the dipper to his lips and sipped.

He tasted, closing his eyes to ponder.

I waited for an explosion that never came.

Instead, Barak exclaimed to the bridegroom, "What's this? Saved the best for last? Others always serve the good wine first and then when everyone's taste is muddled with drink, out comes cheaper wine and no one notices. But you! You turned the matter upside down. Well done!"

His face recording a befuddled grin, the newest vintage of husband thanked his friend and accepted a cup of wine for himself. He drank without complaint and smacked his lips.

Waving his hands impatiently, Barak ordered the maids: "What are you waiting for? Fill the cups! Pour the wine!"

Surreptitiously, the servants let tiny drips of wine splash on to their fingers and licked them dry.

As each tasted the miracle for herself, an expression of wonderment lit each face, brighter than the lamp flames. I read the queries erupting on every visage: *Water? Wine? Water from Cana's well? The best quality wine, too?*

Then questions about the author of the wonder: *"Where is Yeshua? Why doesn't he arrive to claim the authorship of this conjuring trick?"* Also: *"Just who is he?"*

Yeshua's mother merely smiled and nodded.

As Barak raised his glass to acknowledge the acclaim of the guests with yet another toast, I realized there could be no sweet reunion this night. As much as I longed to, I could not draw any closer to him. This occasion was too dangerous; could have no happy conclusion.

Already another wave of fear rose in my throat. Instead of wine I tasted horror in my mouth. There, across the square, was El'azar . . . and he had recognized me!

Angry, bulling his way through the press, he approached.

I fled, not pausing to look over my shoulder until I was safely back within the gloom of the orchard and at my encampment.

Out of breath I finally stopped to see how close the avenging angel was. There was no one in sight. Had El'azar taken the time to round up a mob of haters to accompany him?

I ran to Tavita. "El'azar saw me. He's coming. We must leave at once."

"I expected something like this," she said. "We're already packed. We can be away in minutes. But listen," she added, wagging a finger under my nose. "This is what your stubbornness causes: twelve miles of hiking in the dark. We may, just barely, make it home by morning!"

Chapter 4

After my return from Cana I could not sleep more than an hour at a time. Disembodied voices haunted me when I was awake, urging me to end my life.

I remembered a fragment of Scripture and tried

to fight the dark spirits of hopelessness with these words, *"My soul waits for the Lord, more than watchmen for the morning . . ."* [Ps 130:6] But the Holy Word spoke to me of my desperation, not of the coming of First Light. I could not believe that the light of hope would ever dawn in my heart.

When I lay down to sleep, familiar faces, twisted with hatred and disdain, appeared in my dreams. Old friends, family, lovers, and servants gathered rocks from the fields where I had hoped to plant saffron. Their faces changed into seven demons that encircled me, shrieking accusations as they hurled the stones.

I wished for the company of Maximus, simply because his nearness was a human touch that drew me back from the brink of madness. But he was away on some official business, dealing with wild prophets and rebels in the wilderness. Maximus was fighting battles within his own soul.

When was the last time I was happy? I wondered. Was it with Barak? After I had lost my innocence? No. The last moments of my happiness had been when I was a little girl; before my mother filled her pockets with all the pretty stones I gathered for her on the beach; before she waded into the water and sank beneath the waves.

Hopeless, I finally drank myself to sleep. Closing my eyes, I was a child again, watching my mother sleep. She was smiling in her sleep. Her teeth grinned too wide, mocking the little girl who stood in the doorway of a tomb.

Terror filled my heart. "Mama!" I cried.

Her yellow shroud was stiff with spices. Littered with dried flowers I had gathered for her. The fine bones of her hands were exposed in the dusk of the burial chamber.

"Mama, I'm sorry! Give me back the stones. I only meant them as a present. Don't put them in your pockets!"

She did not reply. Eyeless eyes, seeing nothing, stared out through rotten cloth.

Again I wondered if her drowning had truly been intentional, or had I caused it? She had filled her pockets with the stones and then waded into the water. Was it my fault?

I had learned too young about death. When I cried out, what angel heard me? And what if Mama's angel came to comfort me? Would I be burned by the fire of its beauty?

In my dream I said, "Mama, you were so beautiful."

Now the person who had once been so beautiful had become the object of my nightmares.

I questioned the corpse. . . .

Did you ever love me in my small beginnings? If you loved me, then why? Why? I remember your arms. Soft and warm. Your smile. You were patient and gentle with my endless questions. And you must have known how much I loved you. My eyes followed you when you moved across the room. I touched your hair when Father struck you and you bowed your head, weeping. Do you remember how I tried to comfort you? You raised your eyes to me. Grateful, though I was so small. You reached out and touched my cheek and then pulled me against your heart. I heard it beating. Steady and certain. Mama! Wrapped in the yellow shroud. Littered with dead flowers. Mama! Do you hear me?

Your heart. Pulse of my life. I shared your heart with you for nine months.

Your eyes. The mirror reflecting my worth.

Your love. The rudder steering my thoughts toward heaven and goodness.

In the springtime of my life I needed you! The evening star I see still waits for you to come and stand beside me and notice me and tell me to look up. Music is unheard because the waters rolled over you, and you embraced the cold waves while I watched from the shore for you to come back.

I was your purpose. Your mission. Yet you turned your back and left me as if I were no more than a pile of stones on the sand.

I was frightened when you died, wrenching yourself from all my tomorrows. But I choked back my sobs because my brother commanded I must not weep.

And then there came the star-filled night when the wind of your accusations gnawed at my face. *Mama! I'm sorry! Give the stones back to me! Don't put them in your pockets! Come back!*

But you didn't come back. And look at you. Lying beside Father. Grinning coldly. Strewn with dead flowers I once picked.

Who will I turn to in my need?

Who will hold me now?

Whose face will sleep beside mine on the pillow? *Barak! Oh, Barak! Come back! I can't do this alone anymore!*

I cowered on the ground as seven demons circled me with jagged stones raised to hurl at me. *"Guilty!"* they hissed. *"Stone her to death!"* . . .

I must have cried out in my sleep. I awakened from my nightmare with Tavita's lamp shining in my eyes.

Dear old Tavita. "Wake up, lamb! You're at it again. Dreaming. Wake up! It's long gone! Long over!"

Panting, my heart pounding, I stared into the flame of her light. "The flowers. Always the flowers you helped me pick and lay in her fingers. Remember, Tavita?"

"Yes, lamb. I remember."

"Dead flowers. Still in her fingers. Dead like her. Like me."

"No, lamb. You mustn't."

I felt as though I had forgotten how to breathe. Truth was, I wished I had not awakened. I longed for utter darkness; dreamless sleep. "But I am dead . . . inside. The stones. Always the stones. My fault."

She held a glass of water to my lips. "Never."

"I need Barak." The sense of loneliness was overwhelming.

"No, lamb. Not him. He was never good for you."

I shouted and sobbed. "Yes! Barak! I need him! I can't go on like this!"

The old woman paled. "Only a dream. Shall I stay a while?"

I leapt out of bed and shouted at her to get out and to bring me more wine. "I will not let my life go along this lonely road! I need him! Someone. Something! Just bring me more wine!"

And so my nights passed in this unbidden madness. At times I wished for the familiar comfort of Maximus, and then my obsession for Barak possessed me. I spent my days on the shore of the lake, plotting how I might bring my old love back to me.

I believe it was Tavita who contacted my brother about my nightmares. She feared for my sanity, as she had worried for my mother in the days just before her death. As I walked the same path toward self-destruction, Tavita vowed she would not let me go so easily. I was her lamb, she was fond of saying. I was a lost lamb indeed and she did not know how to bring me back from the precipice over which I had fallen. She loved me enough to risk my wrath by writing to El'azar. I did not suspect her at the time.

I was lying on my bed when I heard El'azar knock at the gate. I heard his voice speaking in low, urgent tones to Tavita as the two walked across the courtyard, but I could not make out their words.

I peered out through the lattice overlooking the courtyard as Tavita brought him water to wash his feet.

The old woman called for me to come from the foot of the stairs. I hung back, smoothing my hair and changing my rumpled clothes. Then I studied my brother from my place of concealment as he drank deeply of his wine. Sitting on the ledge of the fountain, he stared at his open hands in misery and then looked heavenward as if there might come an answer in a blaze of light.

I watched him as he pursed his lips and seemed to mentally rehearse what he would say to me.

At last I pinched my cheeks for color and left my bedchamber, emerging on the balcony above the courtyard.

El'azar glanced up in alarm at my appearance. He stood as I leaned over the balcony and gave him a look that conveyed my unhappiness at his unexpected visit.

"Shalom, Mary."

I hung back. "Well, elder brother. Why have you come to my house?"

"You are my sister. I wanted to see you." He knew he was lying and I knew as well.

"Here I am." I bowed slightly like a street performer in the souk. "That does not explain why you came."

He admitted, "The event in Cana."

"Almost a family disgrace. But you were saved embarrassment." I did not descend the stairs.

"Come down, Mary. And sit with me a while."

A wave of bitterness coursed through me. "Why should I?"

"You are my sister." His eyes displayed pity for me, which enraged me further.

"So you have said. I am your sister. But there is little evidence of our kinship. What I have become. You are a pillar in the temple. Master of Judean vineyards. Well respected . . ."

He begged me to stop. Moving to the stairs he held out his hand, imploring me to come to him.

I hesitated and then descended. He made no move to touch me, and I did not reach out to him. We were united only by blood, family obligation, and common tragedy, but not by love.

I led my brother to the dining room and closed the paneled door. The walls were decorated with Roman frescos. I indicated he should sit beside the window and I sat opposite him.

"And where is Marta, my loving sister?"

"Bethany."

"She didn't want to see her fallen sibling?" I said bitterly.

"She had to work."

"She would."

El'azar defended mildly, "Things to do with the household. Sarah is expecting a child."

"Marta's dear friend is more important than her own flesh and blood." I truly did not care to see Marta, but I feigned injury and insult. "Well, get it over with, El'azar. You have come to scold me."

"That is not why I've come."

"What is it? Come to make a business deal with your baby sister? Poor widow? Tell me what you're up to, Brother. The suspense will kill me."

He paused and drew a deep breath. "I know I have not been much of a brother to you."

I laughed. "Confession is good for the soul, they say. Sell me off to a loveless marriage to make a bond between your estates and old Yosef. Shocking. Father would be proud of you exploiting me for gain. An acceptable kind of prostitution, is it not?"

My words stung him. "Mary, what you say is true. I know that now. I did those things. But I thought it was right for you. For us. Continuing the family name."

"Of course I was the right choice. Marta was too ugly to make a bride for anyone. Who would want her? Especially with the family scandal. Madness."

"We cannot know; perhaps it was an accident."

"Stop lying to yourself. I have. So you sold me off to an old man who could not have given me a child unless he found one lying on the road. And I lived with your choice for ten lonely years. Now my life is my own. I am rich. My estates are my own. I knew enough to make certain Yosef would sign them over to me with the promise that if I ever had a child, I would name it after Yosef. This is my life. Not yours, if that is why you have come."

"No, Mary. I came because everything you say is true."

"Is this repentance? Little good it does now. Changes nothing. You're making a poor job of this, El'azar."

He looked miserable. "I always have made a poor job of trying to speak to you."

"That you have."

"You were the pretty one."

"And Marta was the hardest worker. And you were Father's one and only son. The center of his world. Only Mama thought of me. When she was gone, who was left?"

"I thought of you the other day. And I wanted to tell you something I remembered. Something about you and Mother. It was after—"

"There was no after! My life ended when she died!" I could almost not bear his words. The image of my dreams returned to my mind again. "Don't, El'azar. Don't!"

"Let me say this."

His expression was so pained. He covered his eyes with his hand for a long moment, then hoarsely continued to speak. "I heard you crying for her. No one went in to comfort you. Father said we could not. Said you had to get over it. You were so small. Everyone's little flower before Mother died. Father's favorite, I think, before . . . and then every time he looked at you, he saw her. He wondered why, all over again."

Tears stung my eyes and choked me. "I won't hear more."

"But it came to me that you might wonder why we were so . . . heartless."

"Why Father was so cold? Why he never embraced me? Never held me or comforted me?" All the ache in me spilled over. "Oh no, Brother. I never wondered. I was six years old. Little girls don't wonder. They just wish things were different."

He frowned. "I should have been kind."

"You were too busy ordering me around. I longed for Father to speak to me. I missed Mama."

"That was it. You were such a beautiful child. Like her. I think Father couldn't bear looking at you."

"Yes. Now I am like her. A disgrace."

"No."

"Is that why you came so far? So I could understand why my father rejected me? Why you and Marta gloated over my sorrow? Then you . . . separated me from the only one who ever loved me and sent me to marry an old man."

"Barak bar Halfi never loved you. He used you."

I leapt to my feet. "What would you know about love between a man and a woman? Pathetic. You never let yourself get close enough to love any woman. I want you to leave now, El'azar."

"I didn't come to talk to you about him. I came to tell you . . . I understand why you sought comfort from him. And I want to counsel you like a kinsman."

"It's too late. I don't need your counsel. I have my own life."

He was gentle as he intruded. But it was still an intrusion, and I resented it to my core. "Mary, you won't find what you seek in Barak."

"How can you know what I am looking for?

Who do you think you are? All these years and now . . ."

"He's married."

"So what?"

"Don't make a fool of yourself."

"You mean, don't make a fool of you and Marta." My fury was at high tide, washing over reason.

"I suppose. That, too."

"Too late."

He stood slowly and looked me straight in the eyes. "If you cross that line, Mary, I will have no choice."

"So this is your loving message to me? Loving brother to fallen sister. All right. You've delivered your message. Now go."

"Mary. I wish it were different."

"I wish a lot of things. I wish Mother hadn't left me. I wish I had grown up with a brother who had loved me instead of cuffing me on the ear every time I opened my mouth. I wish I had a family . . . but I don't. So I take life the way I find it. Unloved. Without hope. But I still have some small pleasures, and I am still breathing."

He reached out as if to touch me. I drew back from him. "I'm sorry it's been so hard on you."

"Save it. I'm still standing. I'll take what I want out of life. Good-bye, Brother. You can find your own way out."

And so this was my last encounter with El'azar

for many long months. I believe he meant well. Perhaps encountering Yeshua had softened him in some way. A call for repentance from some teaching I did not hear had touched my brother's heart and sent him to my gate. But for me, after so much bitterness, it was too late. I blamed him . . . and life . . . for my own heartache. I could not forgive him for the sin that was in my own soul.

Chapter 5

It was late afternoon, three days before the eve of Passover. Impatiently I stalked the corridors of my Magdala home, awaiting the arrival of Barak bar Halfi, together with his family. They were already hours later than I expected.

The approaching evening might work to my advantage, I reasoned. Perhaps I could persuade them to spend the night at my home and not resume their pilgrimage toward Jerusalem until the morning.

In my thoughts every such suggestion was accompanied by visions of Barak pulling me to him, murmuring apologies, and vowing to find a way for us to be together forever.

The images were so real that when I spotted his group among the hundreds of other travelers on the lakeshore road it was all I could do to resist running to him.

It was well I did not give in to my dream.

Barak's wife and youngest daughter perched on a scrawny donkey which he led while the other two girls trudged along behind. The road was partially obscured by dust. It pleased me the day was warm and dry; the road grit-covered; for so would be the pilgrims.

I knew the contrast would work to my advantage.

As my plan required, I alerted Tavita to their arrival and hurried upstairs to my chamber. Once there I washed and smoothed my limbs with expensive, fragrant ointment before donning a fresh linen shift.

And if my perfumed self were not enticement enough, I had yet another lure to dangle before Barak. Half a hundred sacks of Persian crocus bulbs lay in my barn, guarded by Freeman.

Every man I had ever known or even met could be governed by either wealth or passion. I already knew Barak was susceptible to passion. What would be his response when my renewed love was offered together with unimaginable wealth?

I brushed out my hair and replaited it. In my reflected image my eyes glistened with anticipation. Barak always enjoyed loosing the ribbon binding my braid. His face always hardened with desire when I shook free my hair and let it cascade over my shoulders.

I shivered with expectation.

Years had passed since the last time Barak's response had been more than a memory, yet I was confident it would be just as uncontrollable again. I had learned much in our time apart.

Now I knew how to drive him wild. I would teach him more about passion than he ever knew existed.

And his mousy little wife would never suspect.

The courtyard had long been prepared to make them welcome: basins of water and fresh towels for washing their feet, food and drink enough to stupefy the senses, cushions beside the trickling fountain, suggesting slumber.

And in the barn, beside the crocus bulbs: a secret bed as in our shared past; a renewed reality to replace the remembrance that must haunt Barak's imagination every night.

I heard Tavita reply to Barak's deep greeting. My servant played her part well, clapping her hands to summon attendants to bathe the feet of my guests and make them feel welcome and pampered.

I took several breaths to steady myself. I must not rush to greet him or appear too eager.

At last Tavita called to me from the foot of the stairs: "Mistress! Mistress Mary, Barak bar Halfi and his family have arrived."

A last look in the glass and a tug to deliberately loosen a strand of hair to hint of more unbinding to come, and I glided regally down the steps.

I addressed myself to the plump hen and her chicks first: "Welcome! You are most welcome to my home. How was the journey? Have you been offered refreshment?" Then coolly, all business, "Welcome, Barak bar Halfi."

Barak would not look me in the face. He hovered beside his wife's shoulder as if in need of her protection. "My wife, Eve," he said. "And my daughters."

He named them in order from youngest to eldest. I paid no attention, all the while nodding and smiling.

Uneasiness, and perhaps envy of the difference in our status, was easy to read in the way Barak held himself erect. His movements were stiff and awkward.

The contrast between us was heightened when I allowed my body to glide downward onto a cushion and invited my guests to join me. "Jerusalem will be more crowded than usual, I hear."

"Oh, yes. Everyone is talking about it," Eve babbled. "Our men facing off with the Roman governor over the shields they hung on the tower beside the Temple. Imagine! The Romans backed down! Barak would have gone, but I told him he must not. A married man with young daughters. What if the Romans had slaughtered everyone? Me a widow. Our girls left destitute?"

"Yes, I know what it is to be bereft," I said.

Eve colored. "Of course, of course you do. How thoughtless of me."

I waved away her apology with an airy gesture, then seized her hand and patted it. "You're a wise woman to keep your man so close."

Barak stirred uncomfortably.

"Where will you stay in Jerusalem?" I inquired.

Eve exclaimed, "Why, I thought you knew. We're staying with your brother and sister in Bethany. In fact, we wondered if you would not accompany us."

I shook my head and let my shoulders droop as if the cares of the world pressed down on them. "I have so much business to attend to. So much responsibility."

"Even during Passover?" Eve clucked.

The trio of chicks made similar sympathetic, chirping noises.

Barak interjected: "Great estates always mean important duties, my dove. Isn't that right, Lady Mary?"

How formal he sounded! How unyielding!

Sadness propped up with dignity blurred my tone when I agreed. "Almost more than one woman can manage, I fear." It was almost time to spring my trap. "That's why, Barak, I have a business proposal to suggest."

"Yes, the saffron bulbs." He spoke with evident regret. Barak seized his wife's hand. Was this his effort to resist the temptation I knew already stirred him?

Keeping my voice businesslike I suggested, "My late husband, Old Yosef, had plans for planting and growing saffron in Galilee." This was a lie. My late, unlamented husband was too old and far too conservative to take such a risk. "He always said it might succeed if—" I raised a cautioning finger—"if the right man were in charge."

Eve's dimpled cheeks glowed with pride. "I know your late husband, Lord rest his soul, always thought well of my husband. Barak is such a hard worker. How good of you to follow through on—"

"Delicate crop. May not be right for me," Barak protested. "Has to be harvested exactly right. One freeze and the entire crop is lost."

"My husband is too modest, as you already know from your revenues," Eve argued. "Barak is an excellent farmer."

I let Eve chatter away. The contest, invisible to her, was between Barak and me. He knew that to be near me again was to admit his love for me again. It would happen. And with a twelve-acre field of saffron we would also be incredibly rich.

"So it's settled then," I said, beaming. "How that relieves my mind."

"You won't be sorry," Eve continued, as if feeling a need to further convince me. "Barak is honorable, and no finer worker exists anywhere."

"My late husband would be so pleased," I murmured. "Thank you, Barak. It is such a weight off me."

Barak's forehead beaded with sweat. He was pale but had no option except to nod agreement.

I stood as if the matter was entirely resolved. "It's late. Too late to press on. You must stay with me tonight. The servants will prepare your rooms."

Barak jumped to his feet, protesting the change in plans. "No, thank you, but no. We have already made arrangements. I mean, we must push ahead."

I smiled, pretending not to care. I wanted the night hours to present the other half of my offer, but could not appear overanxious.

Eve said, "What a kind offer. Barak, don't you think you're being ungracious—"

"I said, we must leave," Barak barked.

"A pity, then," I returned, taking no notice of his rudeness. "We might have used the time to explore the planting program. Ah, well, perhaps you can stop over on your way home. But food is ready for you before you press ahead. Just through there." I indicated the doorway to the dining room. "Eve, why don't you lead your adorable girls in while I steal a moment of your husband's time to show him what has arrived from Persia . . . and the contract, of course. I have it ready for his signature."

Eve and her brood dutifully trundled away, bubbling gratitude and exclaiming over the splendor of the house. The sight of the elaborate spread of food caused renewed expressions of delight.

I knew Eve had spoken of me as a harlot, the same as the other proper little housewives did. If she only knew that for the sake of a few crocus bulbs she was throwing her husband back into my arms.

As soon as we were alone I took Barak's arm.

He jerked it away, as if I were a snapping dog.

"I won't hurt you," I teased. "Come and see the bulbs that will make both of our fortunes."

Meekly he trailed after me toward the barn.

Freeman scowled as he unlocked the door but dared not express disapproval.

The storeroom was dark. The warmth swelling around us was not only from the heat of the sun on the enclosed space but from memories of other times.

"Over here," I said, preceding him toward the sacks of bulbs in the darkest corner.

"What do you want with me?" His voice croaked. He had not followed.

I returned to his side. "I want you to harvest spice. Then you'll be rich and I'll be richer. Is that so hard to understand?"

"You were at the wedding in Cana." There was accusation in his statement.

"So?" I drew closer to him; knew he would recognize the perfume I wore.

"You know what they . . . the elders . . . would have done to you?"

"El'azar warned me," I said. "Strip me and stone me as a harlot? Is that it?" I brushed a lock of hair on his forehead, and he jumped back as if burned.

"I . . . I love my wife," he said.

Again I moved closer, sliding my arms around his waist. "You can't forget what we had any more than I can forget." My words were not as important as the silk of my breath on his cheek and the press of my body against his.

"You've made a mistake. I made a mistake. Coming here." He remained stiff; would not embrace me, yet I could feel the hammer blows of his heart.

I lifted my lips to his. "We can have it again, Barak. Everything I have is yours. Everything!"

I saw desire in his eyes. His lips crushed mine. I felt myself melting in his grasp. I had won! It would all come true!

Then a shriek resounded from the doorway. Barak's head jerked up in horror and he shoved me away, sending me sprawling to the floor.

Eve and her chicks were framed in the entry, dismay stamped on her face.

Barak towered over me, clenching and unclenching his fists as if only just forebearing to strike me. "You're a harlot! You always were. You haven't changed. I thought as much. I've been offered another orchard to tend and a house. We'll be off your property by the new moon."

"Barak!" I protested. "Don't! You don't mean it!"

Snatching up a handful of dust he flung it in my face, stinging my eyes, making me cough, cutting off my words.

"My reply to your spice," he pronounced firmly.

Through grimy, choking dust I saw him seize Eve by the arm and propel her away from the house. From the way he stormed out it was plain he wanted out of my life for good.

My Magdala estate was a gloomy place that Passover.

The holiday was meant to be a time of joyful celebration, of reuniting families.

My family was no doubt united in having me to carve up for every meal. I brooded over how the discussion would unfold when Barak arrived at Bethany at the home of my brother and sister. Eve would whisper sordid details . . . making up more than she had observed . . . in order to make herself the center of attention.

Barak, clothed in self-righteous indignation,

would denounce me to El'azar. Barak had always been weak that way: anxious to look good in the eyes of others. He had sacrificed me years before. He would sacrifice me again now to preserve his respectability.

I forgave him. If I ever got him away from the others I could replace all other thoughts in his head with visions of me. Of that I was confident.

But this year that prophecy would not be fulfilled.

Even Jewish bond-servants were allowed to make aliyah to if they wished, or to spend the week with their relatives. If the money was available each man would buy provisions . . . wine and matzo and lamb . . . and recline like a rich man. Servants would pretend to be their own masters, as if they had no need of employment.

Though he dared not speak his mind, I sensed Freeman's disapproval of me. While I had planned to make him a holiday gift of a few coins, the scowl on his face when he left for his daughter's house convinced me otherwise. What right did he have to judge me?

I did not think he would be back.

So for this celebration of freedom I was stuck within my walls with Tavita. My other companions were a trio of Syrian housemaids and their halfwit herdsmen-husbands.

Tavita wandered about the empty rooms, slamming doors, complaining about the aches and pains of old age, and finding fault with everything the other attendants did.

It was miserable. The season was made worse not only by all the abuse I was suffering but also by the memories of Passovers past.

When I was a child I loved Passover. I loved searching the house for leaven. I was the most diligent of children when it came to locating every tiny breadcrumb.

I understood that removing each fragment of leavened bread was like finding and tossing out every tiny sin: *under the cupboard door, a lie. Hidden in the back corner of the cupboard, a bit of anger. Lurking on a shelf, a bad thought.*

How simple life had been! The broken bits so easily swept together, heaped outside, and burned!

Each Passover a new beginning. A time and a method to start over every spring.

And now?

Now there were shattered pieces of my life everywhere. The bits were too many to count; too scattered to locate them all. If I could find them all to throw them away in order to start over, there would be nothing left with which to begin anew.

There was no beginning again for me. There was no use pretending. If I sacrificed a lamb and smeared the innocent blood on my doorposts the angel of death would see it and laugh.

My sins were too great to pass over.

In moments of anguish, before I drew on my well of deep anger once more, I wanted the angel of death to come to me.

I had given up expecting to start over. What my life might have been had been broken too often. In spite of all my promises and vows and determination, there was nothing left but what I had become.

Where had that little girl gone? I wondered. She wasn't me, of course. I thought of her as someone unrelated—the sweet but very naïve child of a neighbor. She knew nothing of the realities of the world. I pitied her, but knew there was no warning I could give that would make any difference.

Besides, giving up on what my life had once been, having no expectations, was a kind of freedom, wasn't it? Accepting my limits, my chains, was better than pretending.

I resisted any suggestion that I could somehow begin again . . . sweep clean my soul . . . be someone else.

Every such vision was a delusion; each voice, a mockery. I knew who I was, and how ponderous the chains I wore.

The joyous celebration of Passover mocked me. I was in bondage to loneliness, a slave to obsession, a prisoner of my own longings, and there was no one who could set me free.

· · ·

I had not left my bedchamber in two days. My head felt as if both temples were being attacked with hammers. Pains shot through my middle that ended in spasms in my back. If I attempted to move, I felt the top of my head try to separate from the rest. Orange and green flares erupted behind my tightly clamped eyelids.

When Tavita called out to me, then tapped on my door and pushed it open, her life was in serious danger. Grabbing an unlit clay lamp from my bed table, I flung it without aiming. It still only missed her by inches. "Get out! Get out! I told you to leave me alone."

"Mistress," Tavita cajoled. "There's a messenger for you. From your brother."

Groaning, I fell back on the pillow. "No one! Don't you understand?"

From the location of Tavita's voice I knew she remained close to the doorway, in case she needed a hasty exit.

"I told him so, lamb. Offered him a denarius and said I'd see you received it, soon as you were able. He said he must deliver it only to you."

"So? Then let him wait till he rots. Is he in the courtyard?"

"No, chick. He won't come inside the gate. He's planted; fixed like a tree grown up in the middle of the high road."

Because of my reputation, this was not the first

95

time the hyperpious refused to enter my property. They practiced the proverb that said, "Better to burn with thirst in the blast of the sun than find shade in the house of a harlot."

"Then he can die there for all I care. I'm dying in here!"

"People are beginning to stare."

"Get out!" I bellowed, snatching up a shoe and flinging it at her. She ducked, but my curses pursued her down the stairs.

Tavita clumped away while I went through spikes of agony in my skull and middle.

To my utter disbelief, she reappeared a few moments later.

"He still refuses to come in. A crowd is gathering, including some of those fishermen. You know the ones I mean: the ones who sell fish seasoned with gossip at every town around the lake."

The only way I would be left alone in my misery is if I dealt with this myself. Screaming another curse I seized a vase and smashed it on the floor, then flung myself out, wild-haired and wild-eyed.

Had I possessed the power, my words would have blasted Tavita, El'azar, the messenger, and all the citizens of the Galil into pillars of salt. I flung open the gate with a crash.

A startled knot of onlookers across the road stopped their whispering.

The skinny young man nearest the opening backed up from the terrifying apparition that appeared in front of him. By peeking out through eyes clenched against the glare I saw his mouth move but no sounds emerged.

"What? What's wrong with you? I'm sick! Are you deaf as well as mute?"

Finally he spoke. "You. You're Mary, sister of El'azar of Bethany?"

"Who else should I be? Idiot! Didn't my maid tell you I was sick with a blinding headache?"

At the confirmation he fumbled with the drawstrings of a leather pouch and retrieved a parchment roll. "He . . . Master El'azar . . . said to give it to you personally." He thrust it into my hands, and then his next words were flung over his shoulder as he turned and sprinted away: "And I was not to wait for a reply."

Retreating within the walls of my compound I slammed the gate shut against the world.

If only I could shut out my thoughts as easily.

I held the scroll at arms' length, as if it were a dangerous snake.

A timid serving girl and her equally rabbitty husband peered out of the laundry house door at me. "What are you staring at?" I bellowed, then I ran back inside the house, up the steps, and into my room.

Once there I bolted the door shut and flung the message onto a chair. Warily, I viewed it from across the room. Long minutes passed while I tried to control my breathing and my vision. Behind my eyes were flickering lights and jabbing needles.

At last I snatched up the roll and tore away the binding. One painful word at a time I examined what it said.

And when the substance at last penetrated my thoughts, I clutched it to my chest, sank to my knees, and wailed in an agony of grief.

The Story of Mary Magdalene,
First Century, A.D.
Translated by
Moshe Sachar, Old City, Jerusalem, 1948

My dearest Rachel,
I awakened with the painted stars of the chamber glistening above me as they must have shone over the Galil in the time of Mary. The stars that shine above us in the chamber day and night are familiar, but there are slight variations in their placement from the modern sky. However, they are still stars and that truth is unchanging.

So it is in history. I remember that beyond this cavern there are many opinions about who Mary was and the identity of her family.

As I unravel the translation of Mary's account I am reminded of the history as it is recorded in the most ancient documents of the second-century A.D. and in the writings of Eusebius and passed into the more recent writings of Legenda Sanctorum and Legenda Aurea, which are dated from about 1260.

Mary, "Bitter Sea," is also called Magdalene. *When translated, this means, "Remaining Guilty." It can also be translated "Unconquered," "Armed," and "Magnificent."*

These meanings clearly identify a progression of the sort of woman Mary was before her redemption, at the time of her redemption, and after she was redeemed. Before her encounter with Yeshua of Nazareth she remained guilty and carried the burden of eternal punishment. In her conversion, history tells us she was armed and unconquerable by the spiritual armor of repentance. For every selfish pleasure, she found a way of doing good for others. And Grace made her magnificent, because where her trespass abounded, grace was more abundant.

This cognomen, Magdalene, comes from one of her ancestral properties called Magdallum. History describes her as high-born, descended from royal stock. Conjecture says she was most likely a descendant of the Maccabees. History also records her father's name was Cyrus and her mother was called Eucharia. Her brother is called in the Hebrew, El'azar, and is more commonly known as Lazarus. Her sister Marta is also known as Martha.

She owned Magdalum, which ancient writers describe as a small-walled village along the coast of the Sea of Galilee. With her siblings, Lazarus and Martha, she also owned property in Bethany, not far from Jerusalem, and had holdings in Jerusalem as well. They had divided the properties among themselves— Martha and Lazarus remaining in Bethany and

Jerusalem, living very much aloof from their sister.

Early church historians describe Magdalene as rich. She devoted herself to the world and sensual pleasures among the wealthy rulers of the time. She abandoned her Jewish identity and turned her back on her family. She was commonly called "the sinner" by the Pharisees and was welcome in the estates of Herod Antipas and among the Roman governors.

She wandered far and was much despised by her own people as she walked the way of sorrow. Perhaps that is what makes her so beloved throughout the generations.

The dark path to Mary's redemption by grace is always lit from above by stars of Truth. She seems to descend, but at the end, she emerges into the light.

Chapter 6

When El'azar's letter arrived, I went into mourning, like a proper Jewess. I turned every looking glass to the wall. I ripped the fabric of my clothing just above my heart. I wandered shoeless about my house with ashes in my uncombed hair. I neither ate nor drank nor slept in a bed.

The one thing I could not, would not, do was recite the prayers for the dead. Grief there was, in abundance, but my mourning was incomplete.

Every time I tried to pray seven voices—shrill, taunting, scolding, nagging voices—shouted down my thoughts. *"Praying is no use for one like you,"* they shrilled. *"No one is listening when you pray. Prayers from one like you are just another sin added to the list of all the wrong you've done. Why don't you lie down and die? The world is weary of you."* I covered my ears to block out the voices even as I realized they came from within.

It was after dark when I heard Tavita and Maximus talking. I had not known until then he had returned. He had not yet come in to see me.

I could not understand all their conversation, but much was clear. Tavita explained what Maximus would find when he saw me. I heard my brother's name mentioned, and the letter.

When Tavita recited Barak's name, Maximus' voice rose in anger.

I was afraid for him to see me. He would never understand my grief. He would look at me and loathe me, or so the voices told me.

I was in mourning for myself.

My brother had written to say I was dead to them; dead in my shame. I was lost to disgrace from which there was no salvation. I must have no further contact with them. El'azar's letter accused me of tempting Barak bar Halfi to adultery and, because I was an unredeemable harlot, both my family, and Barak's, counted me as dead.

Stinking, rotten, dead. As defiling to be in the same room with as a corpse or a leper, like a leper I was now among the living dead, no matter how many more years I might exist on earth.

There was a soft tap at the door and Maximus' voice calling my name. I made no response.

He rapped louder and cried louder, "Mary!"

I heard the anger in his tone.

The chorus in my head rose up like a whirlwind: *"He'll strike you because of Barak. Can you blame him? Not even a Roman could tolerate such a harlot as you. He'll say you might as well sell yourself in the street, so low you are."*

Now he was pounding his fist on the panel, demanding entry.

If he killed me it would be a mercy. It would settle the fate I wanted for myself but was too cowardly to perform.

Something crashed against the door, making the whole house shake. His shoulder?

Another blow and then another.

I heard Tavita's squawk of protest and Maximus' snarl of defiance.

Then the jamb splintered and the door flew open as the bolt sped across the room like an arrow, nearly striking me.

Maximus was framed in the opening. He stood there, opening and closing his fists, as if stuck in a debate whether to strike or strangle me.

A moment before I thought I welcomed death.

Now I was terrified at the form in which it appeared.

I raised my eyes and lifted my hands toward him just as he said, "By all the gods, Mary! What have they done to you?"

Tavita, carrying a lamp, lurked furtively in the hallway. Maximus seized the light and strode into the chamber. His eyes were frenzied and bright with fury as he strode near.

"He'll kill you now," the voices taunted. *"One stroke of his sword, and your miserable, worthless life is over."*

I obeyed the compulsion to tug my gown away from my neck. Bowing my head I submitted to the swing of the weapon.

When the blow did not fall I dared to look up. Maximus had placed the lamp on the table where El'azar's message lay. Maximus had plucked up the parchment to read it. Quickly finished, he snorted, cursed, then dipped the edge of the sheet in the flame.

Holding it until it scorched his fingers, he dropped it to the floor and stomped it into fragments of ash.

"How long has she been like this?" he growled at Tavita.

My servant's voice quivered as she replied, "All through Passover, sir, and more."

When he caught me looking at him he moved toward me. Once more I ducked my head and waited. I sensed his nearness; felt the bulk of him towering beside me . . . and the barest touch of his hand in my tangled, matted hair.

"So he's going to throttle you," the voices crooned. *"His fingers around your throat."*

"Mary?" Maximus' tone was imploring. I sensed him kneel beside me. He lifted my chin with one finger.

My faithlessness had broken his heart. Soon he would give in to a frenzy of jealousy and crush me.

But not yet.

He brushed ash from my forehead and from my cheek.

So softly that he had to speak the command

twice, he ordered Tavita to go away and close the door.

When she had done so he asked, "Why? Why did you let them do this to you?"

Who did he mean? Barak? The elders of Israel? My brother?

The voices in my head?

His next words were thick with disgust. "Piety! Righteousness! Lunatics, all of them! I've seen enough lately to make me sick. Lie down before the governor and beg to be killed. And for what? A few Roman images staring down while they pray to their unnamed deity in the temple? Hypocrites! In that same temple the priests rob and steal from poor people coming to adore their God. Merchants, growing fat and wealthy, and always remembering to give the priests their cut? It sickens me!"

He stroked my arm. "These are the sort who cast you out."

I croaked: "I am dead to them."

To my amazement and confusion he wrapped his arms around me and pulled me close, cradling me to him. "And you're so much the better for it."

My whole frame trembled. "Cast out. . . . guilty."

He snorted. "And you think they aren't? The day before Passover I saw one Jew who seemed to understand the hypocrisy of it all. A Galilean from Nazareth. A madman, I think. Or maybe one of your prophets. He made a whip and drove the moneychangers from the Temple court. Dumped their tables. I'd like to have such a man in my cohort . . . but he won't go down well with the priests. His name is Yeshua."

Just as I thought I recognized the name the remainder of what he said was buried beneath an avalanche of screeching in my head. No words, but a long, drawn-out wail of agony and torment. I put my hands over my ears until the tempest subsided.

I knew they were still there, listening . . . watching. But for the moment my thoughts were clear and I found words again. "No one respectable will receive me. Where will I go? How will I live?"

"Little hypocrite," he teased. "You? Care about what people think? Since when?" Then, scooping me up in his arms, he threw back the curtain and carried me out onto the balcony. He did not pause there, but toted me, unresisting, down the outside stair and toward the lakeshore.

When I heard the gravel crunch under his feet I seized his neck tighter, fearing he intended to drown me after all, but he only chuckled and waded in. "Look at you! Covered in soot. Wallowing in grief. Fooling even yourself, because you never intend to change! You're built to give a man pleasure, and I'm the man you'll give it to! No, Mary, you're not alone. You're on the other side of the line. Everybody's guilty. Everybody's rotten, when you strip away the pretense. You're just sorry you got caught!"

Abruptly he shook me loose and dropped me into the water. I came up, sputtering and angry at him, but he shoved me back, ducking my head under. How dare he? Could he not see that I was grieving to death? "Why'd you do that?"

"Because you need a bath. There's a dinner tonight at the home of another Jewish outcast: Levi the Tax Collector. And we're going."

"Him? I wouldn't be caught dead in his house."

When I tried to stand he pushed me back, harder this time. "Get over it. Stop lying to yourself. You are everything they say . . . and so what? You're a harlot, and I'm glad of it."

The waves rocked me as I remained on my knees, my face in my hands. "I wish I was . . . a good woman . . . something else . . . something better. Don't you understand, Maximus?"

Now his look stiffened. "Well, you're not. I'm not. Nobody is. Nobody can be. So give up. You don't love me, you only love yourself. That's why we're perfectly suited to each other. Two of a kind, we are."

His hand resting none too gently on the top of my head he continued, "Now wash yourself. Dress so as to tantalize every man who sees you. You're mine now. Property of Rome. I claim you with a kiss." Drawing me up in his grasp he pressed himself against me and bruised my lips with his. "So, Mary Magdalene. You're now property of Maximus, centurion of Rome. I'll kill any man who trespasses on my property. If you're unfaithful to me ever again, remember what I'll do to him."

Chapter 7

Torches blazed on the marble columns framing an open courtyard. On a balcony musicians played, while reclining guests were served from silver platters.

The home of Levi Mattityahu, tax collector, was beautiful. His great wealth made it possible for his entertainment to rival the finest in Rome.

Maximus and I arrived late.

I had taken hours to prepare myself, extracting my revenge on Maximus for dunking me in the lake by making him wait. From the gleam in his eye, I gathered the delay had been worth it. I was dressed in a white linen tunic bordered in gold. The way the fabric was draped, one of my shoulders was bare, emphasizing my slender neck, while the clinging material outlined my curves.

My hair, scrubbed and perfumed, was interwoven with golden thread that twinkled in the torchlight.

Maximus, armor polished by his servant, Carta, exuded an air of authority and power.

We entered unannounced and ungreeted.

I recognized only a few at the gathering. I had met Kuza, chief steward of Herod Antipas, in commercial transactions. The man never smiled when doing the tetrarch's business, but tonight he was positively beaming. He brayed like a donkey at some joke Levi told.

Kuza's young, auburn-haired wife, Joanna, was between her husband and the tax collector. Joanna's pale face was flushed with drink, and she patted Kuza's face affectionately.

Fifty other guests were an odd mixture of overdressed customs officials, Roman civil servants, and Roman soldiers of lower rank than Maximus.

The one exception to this similarity of rank was Claudia, wife of the Governor, Pontius Pilate, who held court under an archway at the head of the chamber.

The other women in attendance matched the males in ostentatious display. None were the common harlots of the wharfs. These were the mistresses of conquerors, displayed as possessions every bit as much as their gold and silken finery.

They were alike in being the outcasts of Israel. By coming there I joined them.

I saw the same unspoken words appear on face after face as I was recognized: So the one who thinks of herself as a great lady has finally quit pretending. She's finally admitting to being what she is: one of us.

Lady Claudia was a singular anomaly. Dressed elegantly, but not extravagantly, she was reserved but not arrogant. She offered friendly greetings to all who obsequiously fawned over her, but listened more than she spoke.

"Welcome, welcome!" Levi greeted when he finally spotted and approached us. "Thought you weren't coming." His eyes swept over me appreciatively, but he was quick to look away. Waving his arm toward his sumptuous, two-story villa, he explained, "The fishermen of the Galil call my home 'Sodom,' but here're gathered the most interesting folk in the land; folk of considerable means and low reputations, eh?" He laughed, then bowed to Maximus while nodding toward me. "Most interesting, and as of tonight, the most attractive as well, eh, Centurion?"

As our host led us toward the other guests of noteworthy rank Maximus brushed his lips against my bare shoulder. "You put them all to shame, you know," he murmured. "Beautiful. Beautiful."

I knew he admired me as men admire other belongings: a fine horse, a rare, jewel-hilted sword. I also knew he would kill to keep me.

"Sorry to be late," Maximus remarked to Levi

while stroking my arm possessively. "I've been away and we had some catching up to do."

The tax collector chuckled and winked. "I'm pleased you came at all when you had such a bountiful feast already prepared."

Even while I flushed I recognized I had no right to feel shame. I was exactly what Levi imagined me to be . . . what all the others had called me before.

The introductions began then. "I believe you already know our host," Maximus inquired politely.

"Of course," I agreed. "My taxes paid for seven of his pillars and that fountain in the courtyard."

Levi laughed again at the good-natured dig. He was not embarrassed by the way he earned his fortune. Nor did those at this gathering despise him for it . . . envy him, yes, but not scorn.

"So tonight I give a little of your fortune back! Come! Eat! Kuza is filling us with tales about the latest messiah to take Jerusalem by storm. And this," Levi said, bowing, "is the Governor's lady, Lady Claudia of Rome, who graces my home with her presence."

"I thank you for your hospitality," Claudia said pleasantly, "and for the excellent wine. I fear I have other engagements so I cannot remain longer." Turning toward me she said, "I'm pleased to have met you, Mary."

After Claudia's departure Maximus and I were

placed nearest Kuza and Joanna at the head table.

"Not messiahs. Lunatics, you mean," Joanna corrected Levi, resuming the earlier conversation. She took a dainty bite of walnut-stuffed date. "Shalom, Mary. I'm angry with you. You've made me lose a bet to Kuza. He said you'd be here tonight. I claimed it would take a few more weeks. Two drachmae you cost me."

I reached for a date to cover a pang of regret for having come. So everyone knew about my brother's letter and my banishment.

Lifting my chin I replied, "Maximus has often told me that Levi served the best food and wine in Galilee."

"And in Judea," Levi corrected, saluting me with a mug of wine before draining it.

"Not even Herod Antipas' steward can compete with the banquets of Rome's most successful tax collector?" I drew renewed power from my barbed response.

Kuza responded brightly, "So where does our host get all this?" he inquired of his wife.

Grasping one of Levi's be-ringed fingers as if plucking a grape she noted, "Levi steals boldly from many estates . . . including Mary Magdalene!"

When Levi retrieved his fingers from Joanna's grip he passed me a platter of roast pheasant. His words slurred a bit. "The truth is, we've all been eating from the best of your table for years, dear lady. No conscience or remorse, I fear, but it is time for you to join in the fun."

Joanna leaned close. "You may join on one condition."

Unexpectedly I heard a note of compassion in Joanna's voice. Did she know how desperately lonely I was? "And . . . and what is that?"

The men talked over our heads as Joanna whispered, "Conscience and remorse are never allowed." She patted my hand. "My husband is Idumean, like Herod Antipas. My own father is a Levite. . . . a priest related to Aaron, the first high priest. He disowned me years ago. It hurt . . . how it hurt! But Kuza is good to me. And I have my son, Boaz. You could do worse than Maximus. You could do worse than us." She nodded at the gathering. "At least we are what we are."

I looked into her clear blue eyes. Was Joanna to be an ally in my depression? Was she to be my companion in living outside the rules?

Joanna's lips curved in a smile of acceptance and friendship.

The political discussion at the table our arrival had interrupted reasserted itself. Though reclining just on the other side of the steward, Levi bellowed, "Antipas is just like his father, eh, Kuza? Won't tolerate raging rabble, will he?"

Kuza paused to pluck a bit of sliced pheasant from his plate and wave it in Levi's face. "I say

Yochanan the Baptizer will be served up like this one of these days. Sooner if Herodias has her way in it."

"Why?" Maximus inquired in a low rumble. "What's the mistress of the tetrarch got to do with the wild man of the desert?"

I wondered if Maximus was truly friendly with this group, or if he merely used them to gain information for Roman purposes.

I realized it made no difference to me now, if it ever had.

"You don't know?" Kuza responded. "No, that's right. It happened while you were away. It seems the prophet is not satisfied to tell commoners they need to repent. Sometimes he even tells the highborn exactly what wickedness he means."

Joanna explained the topic to me. "A delicious scandal! Herodias left her husband . . . himself Antipas' half-brother . . . to be with Antipas. The one called the Baptizer denounced her! Says Antipas should throw her back." Then she added, "She'll have his head for saying that."

"What do you say, Maximus?" Kuza queried. "You survived Passover with your skin intact. Not always easy to do." He shook his head. "Are Judea and the Galil crawling with Jewish fanatics? Are they a threat to the Empire, or only to the pride of Antipas and his women?"

"Baptizer wasn't in Jerusalem so far as I know.

There I had one interesting encounter. A man . . . some sort of rabbi . . . took a whip and beat up the moneychangers and the animal sellers. Called them 'thieves' and 'sponsors of thieves.' " Parenthetically he added, "Which of course they are." Then he resumed, "Tipped over their counting tables."

"Shocking!" Levi threw his hands in the air in horror. "How could he treat money with such disrespect?"

The listeners chuckled at that, but Joanna remarked, "Driving out the moneychangers. My old father used to quote some Scripture about Messiah . . . when he comes . . . cleansing the Temple. Could this man think he's the messiah?"

"I hear you Jews have a new claimant every other month," Maximus responded drily.

"Any idea who he is?" Kuza asked.

"Only something Carta, my servant, overheard. Seems some merchants bewailing their lost coins called him *Yeshua of Nazareth*. So, perhaps you have a messiah in one of your neighbors from right here in Galilee."

My mind flashed back to the wedding at Cana. Yeshua was a fairly common name, but could this be the same man? The one I had overheard giving such surprising orders?

"There was a Yeshua . . . in Cana this was . . . performed some kind of magic trick," I offered.

"That's the one," Joanna agreed, slapping the table. "Turned water into wine!"

"Ho!" Kuza chortled. "Now that's the kind of messiah we need!"

All the listeners howled at that.

Kuza continued, "Now if he can magically produce bread to go with the wine, we can all retire."

"Oh, Levi," Joanna urged our host. "You must get him to come to your next party. See if he'll perform for us."

"Never!" Levi replied with a sour, mocking look printed on his face. "No one who knocks over counting tables will ever sit at my dinner table!"

Chapter 8

I have always loved springtime in the Galil. Wildflowers spread in a patchwork of color on the distant hills across the lake. Broad swaths of pink blooms called Farewell-to-Spring were splashed along the ridges and swales.

I was sorry when the pink blossoms began to fade. Sorry to mark the passing of spring. Maximus was packed and ready to leave. I still had not told him my secret. For almost two months I had suspected it: hoping, yet fearing, it could be true. And now I was certain I was carrying Maximus' child. I counted the weeks and figured that just after winter solstice I would deliver. The sense of a miracle grew within me with every passing day. I tried to imagine what Maximus would say. Would he be pleased?

Carta waited at the gate with the black horse. Maximus and I sipped wine on the patio. I spotted fishermen just offshore and knew they saw me there with Maximus. I no longer cared what they thought. The baby growing within me somehow stirred emotion I had never felt before. Was it possible I loved Maximus? Perhaps, I thought, this was the time to tell him.

"How long will you be away?" I stroked his wrist, wishing he would not go.

"Not long. The dispatch from Pilate says it's routine. Some Jewish matter. Immediate attention, he says. Probably some new prophet. I don't know."

I studied his face. He stared out at the russet sails. Maximus and Carta coming and going at all hours was no longer a matter of gossip. The people of my village accepted that I was a fallen woman. There was little more to discuss. But a baby would spark the fires of gossip again.

As I grew more certain of the pregnancy, I hired a Roman steward from the household of Herod Antipas. Kuza had recommended the fellow. Now I would no longer have personal contact with the common people. This shielded me from the insults and animosity of the *am ha aretz*.

My tenant farmers produced crops for me at rock bottom prices. I passed the crops along at a magnificent profit to feed the enormous household of Herod and the Roman garrison at Tiberias. Now Kuza and Joanna were often in my company at the villa.

I could see that Maximus was suspicious about my faithfulness to him. He kissed my wrist. "What will you do while I'm gone?"

"I've sold the new fig crop to Kuza. Joanna is bringing little Boaz to stay for a few days. She is good company. We two are outcasts together. I am closer to Joanna than to my own sister."

I was more content than I had been in many years. Joanna's four-year-old son adored me, as I did him. Being near him somehow prepared my heart to desperately want to mother the child I carried. My imaginings were filled with happy thoughts for the first time in many years.

Maximus seemed especially sullen this morning. I asked him what was wrong.

"I am jealous that anything or anyone but me could make you happy."

"The nights will be easier with Joanna here. We'll drink and talk. She'll keep me informed on all the court gossip. It's already almost too hot to sleep. Summer's here."

He almost smiled, but looked away. "And all this time I thought you were the reason I was burning up."

I was suddenly afraid Maximus was not coming back. I leaned forward and searched his face. "We should move to the seashore when you come back. It will be much cooler there. What do you think, Maximus? Playing in the waves by moonlight?"

"You'll miss me." He spoke without emotion.

Why did I feel so desperate? "You'll come back, won't you?"

He stood and towered over me. "If you think I could resist your invitation . . ."

I wrapped my arms around his waist. "Stay, Maximus. We have time. Stay. Carta can wait."

"But Herod Antipas can't wait. Pilate won't."

I knew he was tempted. "Stay and we'll play a while. Tell them you had to practice your swordsmanship."

He knelt in front of me. His eyes searched my face. I knew he was angry for wanting me and angry that I tempted him when there was so little time. He kissed me hard and I felt the warmth of desire surge through me. Then, instantly, he was the one in control.

I had to tell him about our child. "Maximus . . . Maximus? I'm certain I am pregnant."

He drew back from me. I clung to him, but he pushed me away.

"And who is the father?"

His accusation was a knife in my heart. "You! You are! Maximus, there has been no one but you. I swear it!"

His face was filled with cool disdain. He stared at me with contempt. "You expect me to believe your precious Barak bar Halfi turned you down? The man would have to be made of ice." Rising to his feet he saluted stiffly. "You spoke his name in your sleep last night, Mary. My sword will be sheathed until I return. And then perhaps I will run you through. Believe it. I will make you forget him."

With that he stalked away.

The joy I had felt only hours before evaporated. There were no more tears for me to cry. Maximus hated me because I had loved Barak. He suspected me, though I had not been with any man but him. I could not know that he would come back. Perhaps he would always look at the baby and wonder if it was another man's child.

I sat beside the water and hugged my knees. The sun burned my skin. Old Tavita came out to me, imploring me to return to the house.

"Grieving again? And now it is for love. But many women say farewell to their men for a time and then men come home cheerful and eager. Maximus is your good lord . . . your master. He will be back. Please, Mary!"

Her voice seemed very distant to me; as if she called from across the lake. And then I heard other voices calling me. *"Come in . . . bid your lover farewell . . . Maximus farewell . . . Come in! You will burn!"*

There was the Sea of Galilee: flat and shining in the sun like molten metal. Why not fill my pockets with stones? Wade in? Let the cool water flood my lungs and draw me down?

Maximus would come back, and I would be gone! He would be sorry. Tavita would tell him how I had vanished in the sea.

I regretted telling him about our child. Why had I told him? I should have known he would never believe the baby was his.

If I was dead, would he care? Would he regret his cruelty? I had believed he was my savior. But now I wondered if he stayed with me merely to satisfy his appetite.

Only one thought kept me moored to life. Perhaps I would miscarry the child that made him doubt my faithfulness.

If Maximus did not come back, then I would welcome death. Seven voices whispered to me throughout the day. The hours passed, and I became more certain that the child I carried had caused my unhappiness.

"Maximus will never believe me. Never," I whispered. "I will lose him forever."

It was Joanna's voice that drew me back from the brink of despair. I heard her speak to Tavita on the balcony.

"And he left her? Just like that? The swine!"

Waves lapped my ankles. Joanna's indignation

against Maximus was like a balm to soothe my soul.

I raised my head and returned from my inner thoughts to reality. I was thirsty, unaware of how many hours I had been without food or drink.

Little Boaz ran to me. I knelt and he threw his arms around my neck. "Shalom, Aunt Mary! I am so glad to see you! Mama says we will stay here for five sleeps!"

I was saved! "Shalom, Boaz!" I fingered his pale blond curls.

Joanna's shadow swept over me. "Look at you." She scolded me. "Tavita says you have been sitting here like a stone ever since he left. The swine. They're all swine. Men are. Maximus is. He's a Roman swine of the worst sort. Get up. Go get dressed."

She helped me up and I buried my face against her and wept. "Oh, Joanna! He asked me who the father was."

"You're too good to fall to pieces like this."

Boaz tugged at his mother's dress and asked what was wrong with me.

"Nothing a little common sense won't fix." She comforted me. "A little wine and common sense. It's never as bad as it seems."

The hours passed quickly as Joanna and I talked long into the night. Waves rolled in even cadence onto the shore and night birds called from the garden. The bedroom was illuminated by three candles. We had already consumed two carafes of wine. We leaned on silk cushions.

Boaz slept soundly on the window seat as Joanna and I talked in whispers.

The sweetness of the sleeping boy made me wish things could be different between Maximus and me. If only he had acted interested in the baby.

I rested my head in Joanna's lap. "I used to dream of having a little girl. Someone I could hold the way I always wished . . . after my mother . . . after she was gone."

Joanna smoothed my hair. "The only time I can hold Boaz is when he's asleep. He's moving every waking minute. Only stops bouncing when he falls asleep."

I envied her. A husband and a son to love. Though her mother and father had rejected her because of her marriage to Kuza, at least she had a family.

"You are so lucky," I said. "To be able to rock your baby to sleep and say, you know, 'This is my son. Part of me.'"

Joanna confessed. "Boaz keeps me sane. I love Kuza. Gave up everything to marry him. But he has other women. I know it. Everyone in the Court of Herod Antipas keeps mistresses. Like a stable of horses. The prophet—Yochanan the Baptizer—is preaching a lost cause if he thinks they will ever change."

"How do you stand it?"

"I tried to leave him once. We argued about something. Some little thing. A woman Antipas had grown tired of and passed along to Kuza. So I gathered my things and took Boaz home to my father's house. I was hoping. But my father would not let us enter. He called Boaz a little half-breed. Sent a servant out to tell me we were not welcome. I heard my mother crying and begging, but Father would not accept me or my son. I was told by the servant that I was never to darken the door of his home again. So here I am. Here we are. No place to go. No one to ask forgiveness for my past mistakes. My father wouldn't listen to me anyway."

I pitied her then. "I suppose we have much in common."

"I've spent my life looking for someone to really love me. See me. I believed many years ago that it was Kuza. I think he loves me in his way. But there are other women . . . and there always will be. He is a man of some power. Women find that attractive, even if a man is married. They have no shame."

Her words made me swallow hard. I thought of Barak and his little wife. I had no shame. I was like the women who threw themselves at the feet of Joanna's husband. I was no different than those who broke the heart of my friend.

"I'm sorry," I said quietly. "Sorry you have been hurt."

"Boaz is my comfort. I wouldn't trade him for anything. He is everything. I don't think I understood love until I held my son."

I stared at the guttering flame and rested my hand on my stomach where the child grew. I wanted children one day. But was this the right time for me to have a baby? Not like this. Not if it meant giving up Maximus. "Maximus will never believe this isn't Barak's child."

Joanna scoffed, "Why would you care?"

I sat up. "Because I do care. I care for him."

"You love him?" Her voice was incredulous.

"He gives me pleasure. I miss him when he's not here. I would be sorry if he left me, I think. I mean, today when he was so angry, when he accused me, I didn't want to go on living. Who do I have to go to? Joanna, I think if you hadn't come here when you did . . . you and Boaz . . ." I couldn't finish.

Joanna tried to ignore the depth of my confession. "You have a terrible sunburn."

"If I lose Maximus . . ."

"Look. Let's not sit around here and wait for him to come back. We can go to Judea for a while. The miracle worker is there, you know? The Rebbe Yeshua of Nazareth. A carpenter's son. He is a wonder. Healing cripples and giving sight to the blind, they say. A prophet. The Sadducees and their talmidim hate him almost as much as Herod Antipas hates him. My father must be foaming at the mouth. But it might be fun to go and see him ourselves."

"I'm not blind or crippled. I need to have a miscarriage. I need Maximus back. If Yeshua the miracle worker can't do that for me, then I'm not interested."

Joanna closed her eyes. She seemed very weary, as if my words had sapped her strength. "You give me a headache."

"I don't want this baby unless I can have Maximus too."

Joanna eyed me sadly. "It's not hard to get rid of a baby. Women in the court do it all the time."

I sipped my wine and asked her eagerly, "How? Tell me. You know about these things. I have heard of it. But I don't know who . . ."

Joanna looked at Boaz. "There is a priest."

"A priest? But the Law says abortion is . . ."

"Murder. Yes." She searched my face to see if the word had any effect on me. It did not. The sin of abortion seemed a small thing to keep my pleasure and my freedom.

"Tell me!"

"He is a Syrian. Keeps an altar to Molech. He lives across the lake in the Decapolis. Antipas goes to him for divination. But there are other matters. He has a medicine . . . it causes miscarriages."

I was eager to know more. "How long does it take?"

"The women I know have left Tiberias by boat and been gone a few days. They drink his potion. Made from rye grass, they say. A simple formula. It causes labor to start. But it's expensive."

"Money. What do I care? I want to be able to tell Maximus the whole thing was a mistake." I grasped her hands and held her captive to my plan. "You've got to help me, Joanna. Please. Tell me you'll help me get my life back."

Chapter 9

*T*he priest of Molech practiced the ancient religion of child sacrifice for which the evil Kings of Israel had been judged. He worshipped in the ruins of a pagan temple in the wilderness of Golan near a village called Gadara. This was only a few hours' walk from the Greek city of Hippus on the eastern shore of the Sea of Galilee. It was almost directly across the water from my estate.

The priest was an *Owb*, which in the Hebrew language means "necromancer"—a medium who consults the spirits of the dead.

The Owb's altar to Molech stood on an ancient high place cursed by the Lord in the writings of Ezekiel and named *Bamah*. The curse of the Lord upon Bamah, it was said, would remain until Messiah destroyed the place utterly, on the last day. The horror of this place seemed a light thing to me at that moment. Judgment Day was not something I believed would ever come.

The Owb of Bamah was free from the Jewish religious authority in Jerusalem. He practiced his abominations, offering the human victims of abortion to the demon god who ruled the territory governed by Philip, half-brother of Herod Antipas.

The hideous stone face of the idol scowled from the high place toward the mountains of Jerusalem.

Worshippers from Syria, Samaria, and Lebanon made frequent pilgrimage to Bamah to consult the Owb. It was here curses against any enemy could be uttered, and disaster guaranteed . . . for a price.

Wealthy Jews and tenant farmers from Judea and Galilee often visited Bamah in secret. They brought pregnant mistresses with them and unmarried daughters who had heaped disgrace upon their righteous families. The medicine of Molech's apothecary often preserved high-placed families from the scandal of unwanted children.

The Owb would not accept coins in payment. Grain, olive oil, and fine wines were carried by a donkey to the high place. This was the Owb's consultation fee. As for the appetite of Molech, the demon god, he was satisfied when a fire was stoked in his belly and the aborted infant, often still living, was placed in its red hot arms and consumed by fire.

In this way, the disgrace of immorality within the House of Israel vanished as the smoke rose over Bamah. The laws against fornication could at least appear to be obeyed. Lives could continue in secret sins without embarrassment.

Joanna spared no details as she described what she knew of the Owb of Bamah and his secret place of abomination. Perhaps she thought the light of truth would turn me back from my course. But I had spent many hours listening to the dark voices in my head that instructed me I had no choice.

I believed perhaps the Owb could speak to the spirit of my dead mother and give me some guidance.

"I must go to Bamah soon," I told Joanna.

"Please, Mary. It never turns out well. The women who go there never return happy. Or their happiness doesn't last. Come to Judea with me! Hear what this Rabbi from Nazareth has to say. His words are magical, they say, and wise."

"Could anything be wiser than the voice of my mother from beyond the grave? The Owb will speak to her for me."

"Maybe you could have the baby secretly and make an arrangement for his raising. A school in Alexandria? Half the illegitimate children in Rome are being brought up and schooled secretly."

I would not be dissuaded. The only thing that mattered to me was keeping Maximus. Yeshua of Nazareth was a holy man. I believed he would certainly denounce me as a harlot. I could not risk being publicly called out and repudiated. Instead I would make my pilgrimage to the Owb of Bamah.

And when I returned my problem would be solved.

"I will not go with you," Joanna declared. "Such a vile place is not a place I would take Boaz."

"You will not judge my choice?" I ventured.

"We are still friends. But Mary, I cannot condone such a choice."

"You won't speak of it?"

"Never. I'll die with your secret locked in my heart. But I will never cease to regret that I mentioned Bamah to you." She implored, "Please don't do this."

"My guilt is not for you to bear." I was grateful she had told me what she knew. Grateful to know that even the highest houses of the priesthood in Jerusalem had secretly paid homage to the demon god of Bamah. I was not alone in my hypocrisy.

I determined not even Tavita could know what I was about to do. The pregnancy was my problem, and I would solve it on my own.

I arranged everything. After Joanna and Boaz

left, I sent Tavita away to visit her sister in Sepphoris. Then I set to work packing clothes to give me the appearance of a wealthy Greek woman. Bronzing my skin with walnut oil, I also wore layers of heavy veils. For some days I practiced speaking Aramaic with an accent. I believed my disguise would be enough to fool the fishermen of Magdala.

The lake was calm. I passed people who should have recognized me, but no one looked twice.

Arriving at the fishing district I found two brothers of Capernaum working on their nets. They were the brawlers of the waterfront and were called Sons of Thunder. They were capable of defending themselves and me as their passenger. I told them I was traveling to Hippus to visit my mother and offered them three days' wages for the journey.

Within an hour we set sail. I sat alone in the bow of the boat. The cool spray calmed my nerves. I kept my eyes fixed on the eastern shore and the heights of Bamah above the city of Hippus. I did not allow my thoughts to turn inward to the baby. I made the child nothing. The voices assured me it was not alive, not a human. It was nothing and would pass into nothingness, and I would be rid of my problem.

Hippus was a gleaming city on the eastern shore. It had been built by Alexander the Great during the empire of the Selucids. When the city was captured by the Maccabees its pagan temples had been torn down and burned.

One hundred years later the Roman general Pompey had ordered it rebuilt. Now the population was a mix of all races and languages from all over the Empire. Among our people Hippus and Gadara still had the reputation for evil and sorcery. To step into those cities was to be defiled. I knew all this, but I had no fear; no conscience.

Perhaps the fishermen believed I spoke only Greek. They talked openly about the politics of Jerusalem, and about the Rabbi Yeshua of Nazareth. Pretending not to understand, I listened to their conversation as we scudded across the lake.

"High Priest Caiaphas is owned body and soul by Rome. He cares only that he remain in power."

"His concern is not for our souls, but for the revenue we bring when we make pilgrimage to Jerusalem."

"And these are our religious rulers."

"They are no better than Herod Antipas. And he is not even a Jew."

"We're smart to stay out of it. Our comrades have given up everything to follow Yeshua of Nazareth."

"He'll disappoint them as well. There is no one who can lead us out of the bondage of Rome."

"So many in Galilee put their faith in bar Abba, the Zealot. It is he who led the protests in Jerusalem and Caesarea against the display of Roman idols. He is a true thorn in the flesh of Rome, I think. That speaks well of him."

"Everyone's following someone. Yochanan the Baptizer. He said Messiah would come. Told us he was coming soon, but nothing ever changes."

"Now Andrew, brother of Shim'on, has left his nets to follow after Yeshua of Nazareth. And Shim'on has no one to fish with."

"Yeshua makes all the religious rulers squirm. For he speaks of the Kingdom of Heaven and loving our enemies. Who can fight against such words?"

"Just words. That's all. We've heard it all before."

"He drove out the moneychangers in the Temple. That's the profits of the high priest this Yeshua's tampering with. The religious take their cut out of every pilgrim's hide. Now Yeshua . . . one man . . . goes in and turns their tables."

"They'll hate him for that. Mark my words. No good will come of it. The politics of religion and profit must not be profaned. Yeshua will get himself flogged for such an act if he isn't careful."

"Caiaphas and the Sanhedrin hate Yeshua. But what has that to do with us poor fishermen? Have the fish multiplied since Yeshua appeared on the scene? No. The fishing is bad as always."

The two brothers paused in their conversation. "Some days we get lucky, eh? Like today? An easy way to pick up three days' wages."

I knew they were talking about me, looking at me. Beneath my walnut stain tan, I felt myself flush. They lowered their voices. Words drifted up to me, accusing and mocking.

"You think she's really going to visit her mother?"

"She smells like a garden."

"Everything else about this journey smells like fish."

"Greek? Syrian? She is very dark."

"Rich. Her hands are soft. I helped her into the boat. Never done a day's work from the feel of her hands."

They continued their speculation about me. "A courtesan. Kept by a rich man. Not the marrying kind, if you ask me."

"Why does she travel alone? No servant?"

They fell silent, and other voices whispered in my head. I knew they had guessed the reason for my journey.

I heard the voices plainly: *"You are a fool to think no one would know. Everyone will look at you and see you have made pilgrimage to the demon priest Owb of Bamah. No escape for your reputation. Fill your pockets with stones. When they turn their backs, you can slip overboard. The only way to end the pain!"*

The city of Hippus was near. I longed to be out of their little boat. I would find an inn before making the journey to Bamah in the morning.

Inns were plentiful in the teeming city of Hippus. I had heard from Joanna of an elegant establishment called the Crescent Moon, which was often used by the courtesans of Herod's Court. It was more like a palatial house than a common inn. My room was large and overlooked an elegant courtyard with a fountain. The elderly Greek proprietor was a discreet woman. I paid her in advance for five days. For this I would receive food brought up to my room. Telling her only that I wished to consult with the Owb to speak with my dead mother, she knew what I would need for the journey.

The innkeeper arranged for a servant and a pack animal to carry oil and wine as far as Gadara. The servant was an uneducated Syrian who had no tongue. It had been cut out some years before and his inability to speak made him the perfect choice for such an occupation. It was explained to me that he would guide me to Gadara but would not go on farther to Bamah. He and others feared the spiritual force that was in that place. Perhaps he had some awareness of the justice of the Almighty God, or perhaps he had seen enough to know the evil that presided over such a temple. At any rate, I must go alone to meet the Owb. Once there I would take the potion and my labor would begin.

The servant would wait for me in Gadara overnight and accompany me back down from the Bamah to the inn.

I did not sleep well. Music and laughter from a brothel across the road kept me awake. For a few moments I thought about the baby and wondered if it was a boy or a girl. In a flash of sanity, I came near to changing my mind. I thought of Joanna and her little boy. Perhaps she was right. A child would be a joy in my life. I thought of holding my baby. I could almost see his face smiling up at me . . . almost . . . so close. . . .

But then I pictured Maximus. How angry he had been! His accusation had cut deep. The voices whispered away my longing, replacing it with a burst of anger at Maximus. Why should I carry his child? I spoke aloud: "Get it over with!"

Turning my face to the wall I began to weep bitterly.

Finally I fell asleep.

Before daybreak the innkeeper knocked softly. She carried a tray of warm bread, pomegranate juice, and dried fish for breakfast.

"My dear, the donkey is loaded with gifts for the Owb," she said.

"You have made this so easy." I raised up on my elbow as she set the tray down.

"You are not the first, my dear. Nor will you be the last. You paid me well. Often women return to pray and make offerings at the Bamah more than once."

"More than once?" The thought that anyone could go through this agony more than one time seemed impossible.

"Oh yes, my dear. I have heard the second is easier than the first. . . ."

So there was no more pretence. She knew my purpose.

"I heard of your establishment from a friend."

"The Crescent Moon. A metaphor, you see." She motioned with her hands to pantomime the full round belly of a full term pregnancy. "Not a full moon, my dear. No. Just a crescent. And most of my guests desire that the moon never grows full."

"Yes. I see. The servant will not go with me to the Bamah. How will I find my way?"

"He is paid to wait for you, my dear. You will simply continue on the path. It is among the boulders above Gadara. A short walk. You will see. When you come down again he'll make certain you arrive here safely to rest and recover. My dear. My dear. It will be finished before you know it. A good choice for you." Her voice was sympathetic and warm. No doubt years in this business had taught her what desperate women needed to hear in order to follow through.

I knew as we left Hippus that this was a lucrative and well-organized business.

• • •

At sunrise I followed my mute guide through the streets of Hippus. The city displayed the prosperity of its Roman overlords in the heaps of merchandise piled on the quay. The dialects and babble of every foreign tongue filled the air as importers bargained for expensive silks and exotic perfumes brought from the east to be shipped to Tiberias, Caesarea, and even to Rome. Among my prized possessions at home were costly alabaster jars of perfume purchased from this very market.

Today I was not interested in acquiring more. My eyes were drawn from the piles of goods to the children who darted in and out among the stalls. Babies balanced on the broad hips of women bargaining with the produce sellers. A toddler, wrist tied to the apron strings of his mother, buried his face in her cloak when I smiled at him.

The servant scowled at me when he saw my heart soften. I wavered, thinking how easy it would be to turn around and leave Hippus now! I imagined holding my own baby; being refuge for a toddler; teaching my little one to walk and talk and sing!

My heart cried, *It is not too late!*

The guide jerked his thumb, and I followed him through a narrow alleyway off the main street. Behind me I heard a boatman call out for anyone who wished passage back across the lake.

And then the image of life and freedom vanished. A Roman soldier with his painted prostitute pushed past me. I saw the contempt on the faces of the respectable women. I knew I was like the prostitute, and outside the closely guarded fellowship of untainted women. This was how the world viewed me. I was the plaything of a Roman centurion. A child born to me out of wedlock would be the object of scorn.

The voices in my head whined:

"Better to be done with it."

". . . more merciful . . ."

"Get it over with."

"Any child of yours could never be happy."

I turned my heart and my eyes away from life and followed the mute guide and the donkey toward the hills of Golan.

I was weary by the time we climbed the dusty road to the outskirts of Gadara. The village was a squalid contrast to the wealth of Hippus.

Behind and below me I saw the harp-shaped lake and the distant western shore where my estate was located. I wished I had not come but was drawn forward toward what seemed, to me, inevitable.

On the high plateau swine grazed. Flies buzzed around them, and I remembered the demon god Molech was sometimes identified with

Beelzebub and called "Lord of the Flies." The stench was overpowering. I knew we were very near the Bamah.

The guide motioned, asking me if I needed to stop and rest.

I wanted to press on. He raised his filthy hand toward a rocky precipice in the east. I spotted the obelisk of the ancient high place the Lord had cursed.

"The Bamah?" I asked, feeling the oppressive energy of the place.

He nodded and secured the pack animal's lead rope. Then he showed me that I must hold to the tail of the donkey and it would pull me up to the shrine. He would go no further up the twisted path. He pointed to a gnarled tree in the center of the swine herd. He would wait for me there.

I wondered if the Owb was watching me from the rocks above us. Had he called upon the spirits of the dead to speak to me and urge me not to turn back?

I felt fear, yet like a moth drawn to flame I was drawn toward the darkness.

The path was well worn with the footsteps of many who had traveled this path before me. The emotions of my childhood returned, and I remembered when my father had pointed to the high places that ringed the valleys of Judea. He had told us about the ancient Canaanite altars where infants had been sacrificed.

I had no faith in the One True God of my ancestors. I denied his existence in my bitterness against life, and instead had begun to worship gods of nature. Still the sense of foreboding grew in me as the atmosphere of authentic evil thickened.

The voices became louder:

"Go on!"

"Too late to turn back!"

"Get it over with!"

"Harlot! Accept your life as it is!"

"Give in!"

"Nowhere else to go!"

"No one who cares for you!"

"This baby is nothing to you!"

"A gift! A gift to the Lord of the Flies!"

Sweat streaked my face as I clung to the donkey's tail and it helped me up the switchbacks. An hour passed before I reached the plateau of the Bamah that overlooked the Jordan Valley and the lake to the west.

I knew I had arrived. Enormous stone pillars surrounded the twenty-foot-high image of the demon god Molech. The broad bronze face grinned in a terrible mask. Arms of the idol were outstretched and contained the ashes and a portion of a tiny skull.

Sickened, I turned away and gasped for air. My father had taught me the demon gods were nothing. Nothing. Idols made by human hands. Grotesque faces cast by human skill. The fires of sacrifice were lit by men. The offerings were presented by men and received by something which had no life. Yet I felt evil was living here.

The pack animal lowered his head to nibble grain. I looked wildly around for the Owb. Where was this priest of darkness?

"Shalom?" I called, realizing at once the irony of calling out the greeting of peace in such a place.

The discordant piping of a pan flute sounded in the boulders above me. Mystical and plaintive, it played on.

My voice trembled as I called again. The music stopped. Silence. Leaves of an oak tree rustled. The pack animal raised its head in attention.

Suddenly I saw the Owb. He was dark-skinned, clean-shaven, tall, and lean. Camel hide was wrapped around him, secured with a belt of snakeskin. A leather pouch hung at his waist.

Flute in hand he leapt from rock to rock, observing me like a predator about to pounce. I looked for a way of escape, but the donkey blocked the path. The Owb studied me with a frank and lascivious stare. My heart pounded. *What have I been lured into?* I thought wildly. Perhaps more than child sacrifice was practiced here at the Bamah. Were the rumors true the demon god accepted the sacrifice of cripples, the mentally incompetent, and those who were a burden to their families?

The lips of the Owb drew back over even white teeth in a sneer. His words slid from his mouth like oil. "A Jew-ess. Come to offer sacrifice to Molech, son of Beelzebub. Great enemy of the God of Israel."

I could barely speak. "I . . . heard of the Owb of Bamah . . . from someone in the court of Herod Antipas." I could not look at him as he danced nearer.

His laugh was a shout. "That one! A true believer! A great customer! His seed and the seed of the Jewish priests keep the appetite of Molech sated!" He strode around me and I dared not look into his piercing black eyes. "You, too, have a weighty problem."

I managed to whisper, "Yes." Tears stung my eyes. He seemed to undress me with his gaze. I felt I could not move. All my power and will were sapped from me.

Each word he spoke was distinct. "I am the only one who can help you. I am your only hope." He leaned close and I could feel his breath on the back of my neck. "I am called the Owb, necromancer of Bamah. I am named thus because, because like this altar on the High Place, I have been cursed by the God of Israel, yet I am cherished by familiar spirits of Legion." His lips brushed my ear. "And your name is 'bitterness' and 'mourning.' You are sorrow. And the name of the thing you carry in your womb . . . I call . . . nonentity."

My legs grew weak. I pushed away from him as a surge of fear passed through me, followed by a paralyzing warmth. "I should not have come."

I heard the spirit voices growl:

"Where else will you go?"

"You have no choice!"

"Get it over with!"

Owb mocked my terror, feeding on my fear and regret.

"Yes, woman. Where else will you go? I am the only one. I am Owb! Listen to the meaning of my name! It tells you I am one who brings you hope from the spirit world. I am the only one with the cure for your sickness. Nonentity wishes to be born. Nonentity wishes to hold you captive and sap your freedom. Nonentity would destroy your life, so you must end his existence. It is your life or his. To accomplish that you yield to me, or you have no hope."

I did not know how he knew I was pregnant. Was it not true many traveled to Bamah simply to consult the dead through his powers? How did Owb know I was not simply looking for a message? I tried to ask him but could no longer speak.

Weak, I watched as his feet circled me three times. He recited some incantation I did not understand.

Then he removed a vial from the pouch on his belt. He grasped me hard and held the vial to my lips. "Drink. Drink. Your body . . . sweet . . . no room for children."

I swallowed the bitter liquid. "Help me!"

"No room for the living among the dead. Seven are waiting to take possession; to fill the place of this child. Seven waiting for your final surrender."

I sobbed as my consciousness ebbed. Darkness overwhelmed me.

I do not know how long I was unconscious. I drifted in and out, aware that I was in a cavern. Tangible darkness pressed down on me. I lay on a reed pallet on the hard stone floor. Where were my clothes? I wanted a blanket. Why was I so cold?

I heard the cry of a newborn from somewhere in the cavern. It cried and cried.

Hallucination? I strained to see but could not make out any details through the fog. After a while the wail of the newborn stopped and I heard the cackle of the Owb as he rejoiced.

Then I heard a child's whisper speak to me. I seemed to recognize it.

"Mama? Don't let them take me! Mama! Where are you?"

I tried to answer. My lips failed to form words. Then a second child replied, *"We are all going up the chimney."*

A labor pain seized me and I cried out. I panted through the agony and begged, "Bring me a lamp. Who is there?"

The antiphonal voices of many children spoke above me.

"There is no light here."

"The fire of Bamah."

"Smoke."

"Babies in the arms of Molech."

"Up the slope we walk, crying for our mothers."

"The fire of Bamah."

"We are ashes now."

"Millions."

"He burns us and still wants more."

"Beelzebub."

"Lord of the Flies."

"To destroy the promise of the God of Israel . . ."

". . . he slaughtered the babies of Egypt."

"But Moses escaped."

"In Bethlehem too he butchered us all."

"The Son of the Most High escaped."

"Beelzebub envies the innocent."

"We are the first to die."

"Our mothers give us up willingly."

"Mama, will you burn me on his altar?"

"He kills me in your womb."

"To defy the Lord, the Eternal One, you offer me up. Mama?"

"What was."

"What is."

"This slaughter is what will be in the end of days."

147

"We children."

"The innocent."

"Tiny hands."

"Velvet skin."

"Sacrificed to the god of the world."

"Hold me, Mama! Protect me! Mama!"

"Kiss my cheek and sing me to sleep."

"We babies . . ."

". . . are the true martyrs beneath the throne of the Lord."

Contractions clamped around my lower back and then my middle. Unrelenting pain held me until I could not breathe. Blood and water flowed from me and at last the baby was expelled. I felt my child move against my leg as he struggled to live . . . alive for a moment. I reached for him.

Then Owb's grinning face appeared over me. He scooped up my baby and carried him to the fires burning in the god of the Bamah.

I sobbed and called out for Maximus. My voice echoed back from the depths of the cavern. There was no one to comfort me; no mercy that could forgive what I had done; no going back.

Seven spirits claimed my body and spoke to my inmost soul. Hope for my redemption died as the smoke of my baby spiraled up from Bamah.

Chapter 10

*C*I do not know how much time passed in the cave of Bamah. Predawn light filtered through the arched opening. The sickening aroma of smoke hung on the air.

My head throbbed, as if I had spent a night drinking too much wine. My stomach was cramped, but it was not a pain worse than any monthly cycle.

I felt ill, but a pragmatic fatalism settled on me easily. It was over and done. I would forget it and get on with my life.

I closed my eyes as the dream of children's voices flashed in my mind. I tried to remember what they had told me, but the memory was confused and vague as dreams can be. I was uneasy about the message of the dream. Half expecting to see children, I opened my eyes cautiously.

My clothes lay neatly folded at my feet. There was a jug of wine mixed with water and a basket of fruit. I was hungry and grateful for the nourishment. Near my right hand was a large basin of water and a towel for washing.

Suddenly I remembered the leering face and Owb's black, lifeless eyes. Was he watching me? Waiting for me to wash and dress?

Though I got up slowly, my world was

spinning. Bracing my weight against the ledge of stone, I prepared myself for the journey back to Hippus. Groping toward the daylight I emerged from Owb's lair. I tried not to look at the grinning idol in the center of the Bamah. A pitifully thin ribbon of smoke rose from the demon god's arms.

The morning sacrifice had been made. The pagan priest who had sacrificed the offering taken from my body, was nowhere in the ring of stones.

I was alone physically, but the spiritual reality of the dark force that possessed me was all-consuming. At the smell of smoke, nausea washed over me. As I clung to a boulder and retched, I remembered the first part of the dream. Children. Yes. Perhaps my own child had cried out to me, accusing me.

There was more, but I could not remember it.

My voice was slurred as I spoke. "I want to go home."

The donkey, minus the gifts I had brought to the Bamah, was already tethered to the tree and saddled for me. All was well-ordered—each step designed to make the murder of a child in the womb as carefree as possible.

Staggering to the waiting animal, I leaned all my weight against it. I managed to mount it and ride down the crooked path to the place where the mute guide waited patiently.

He nodded up toward the Bamah as if to ask if I was well.

"Yes. Well enough."

Glancing back over my shoulder just once, I thought I saw Owb watching us from the shadow of a large boulder. I felt . . . I was certain . . . that I was carrying away something horrid from that place. It was, I sensed, within me—watching, waiting coldly for the right time to reveal itself and speak to me again.

I uttered these words as we traveled down from the high place: "I have sold my soul. Sold my soul. What have I gained? What will it cost me?"

The sights and sound of Hippus were a welcome diversion to me when we reached the city. The veil covered my face completely. Exhausted, I swayed, dangerously close to unconsciousness, as the mute led me back to the Inn of the Crescent Moon.

"I'll take her to her room." The innkeeper helped me from the animal and supported me across the courtyard to the elegant serenity of my bedchamber.

Managing a tentative thanks, I collapsed onto the clean linens of the bed.

"There, there." The woman was so sympathetic, patronizing. "It wasn't so bad, now was it?"

Inexplicably, as she tended to my needs, I began to weep. "Not so bad," I choked. "Never again. Never."

A sly smile played on the old woman's lips. "I have heard that before. Aye. The second time is easier than the first. And the third time is nothing. These babies. Nonentity." She used the exact formula as did Owb. "Nothing." She snapped her fingers. "You will grow hardened to it as time passes. You will tell others about the Bamah and the Owb as they have need of his services. You courtesans. It will happen again. Remember, to keep your figure, you must come to Bamah as soon as you suspect."

I was too weary to argue with her. Too exhausted to care what she said. Closing my eyes, I only hoped I would not dream.

It was five days before I left the inn at Hippus. The mute guide located some Jewish fishermen willing to rent me the use of their boat. They had been forced to spend a day on the east shore of the lake by the Sabbath prohibition against travel. They were pleased to have the extra income for transporting me, and eager to sail as soon as sunset brought the day of rest to an end.

For my part I would be glad to go home under the cover of darkness. There would be less chance of curious neighbors gossiping where Mary had been if no one saw me returning from the eastern shore.

Tavita would continue to believe I had been visiting with Joanna in Capernaum.

Only Joanna and I would know the truth.

So pleased was I with this arrangement I was struck with consternation to discover my sailors were the same men as had brought me across. A third man also joined John and Ya'acov on this voyage.

"You," John cried. Then, perhaps noting my lack of mourning garb, he inquired, "Did your mother recover?"

There was a taunting smile on the face of the mute guide. I paid him, wishing he had urgent business elsewhere. The less he and I were connected the better I would like it.

"Yes," I said abruptly. "Shall we go?"

"Glad to hear it," Ya'acov remarked. "Summer fever's going 'round. Half Capernaum's down with it."

"I'm not going to Capernaum. Magdala. The home of a friend: Mary."

The trio of fishermen exchanged glances.

The newest member of the crew, named to me as Shim'on, was stripped to the waist and brawny as a young bear. He eyed me doubtfully. "What do you want with the company of that one?" Raising his arms he made a face, shook his fists, and shouted at the guide to be off, the same as if he were chasing away a stray dog.

When my mute companion took the hint and ran, the trio laughed. John jerked his thumb at Shim'on. "Our partner is a madman. Enjoys scaring helpless creatures, but never mind."

Shim'on's chest puffed up as he defended himself. "That so-called *helpless creature* is a demon. Known to be from Gadara. He's a pickpocket too. And hires himself out to take women to . . ."

He had no need to finish the list of crimes. I saw by Ya'acov's rapidly blinking eyes he had already deciphered the identity of the Guide of Bamah.

Speculation flickered between the three men as they considered what errand besides an ill relative might call for a woman's visit to the east shore of the lake.

My anger rose at the curiosity of this ignorant, ill-mannered lot. Who gave them the right to stare? What business of theirs was it where I had been?

I left them to finish launching the boat while I picked my way forward over nets and rigging to sit in the bow.

Shim'on's bass voice, given to forceful declarations, was ill-suited to whispering. It did not serve now to conceal his words about me: "My wife will kill me if she learns what our cargo is this night. What sort of woman returns to the home of the wicked woman of Magdala after a visit to the Owb of Bamah?"

Ya'acov made the sign against the evil eye. "You know what kind: somebody's mistress. Maybe she belongs to Antipas himself."

By their clasped hands they agreed it was better for them if they told no one else about this night's work.

That decision suited me as well.

"Shove off," Shim'on shouted.

Once underway the trio ignored me, but I still heard their conversation. Two Zealots of bar Abba's band had been crucified. Other arrests had been made.

"I hear the Baptizer's been arrested," John noted.

Shim'on nodded. "Likely that fellow Yeshua and his band are in danger too. Wonder if my brother Andrew's got sense enough to stop following after Yeshua before they all get trapped?"

"Rome and Antipas clamping down on anything that smells like rebellion. Can't sneeze without someone hollering 'Treason,'" Ya'acov said.

"Andrew's smart, but foolish," Shim'on offered, raising the issue of how both statements could be true of the same man. "Smart enough to get away from breaking his back fishing," Shim'on chortled, "only to land in a frying pan like a fish himself!"

All around the lake winked the night-fishing fire lures of other boats. Even in the dark my three sailors recognized and named each craft and crew from the arrangement of the lamps and the outline of the rigging lit by the glow.

Then I heard Shim'on hiss: "What if them others see what we got aboard?"

I could not see the gesture but I imagined this time a big thumb jerked toward me.

With that I covered myself with my cloak and tried to sleep; pretended to sleep, anyway.

"So, ho!" I heard Shim'on chuckle. "To the villa of Mary Magdalene, is it? Wonder if our passenger expects her friend, the Roman centurion, to be there when she gets home?"

All my efforts at disguise and concealment had fooled no one.

Chapter 11

Though the moon set early there was still no difficulty steering toward Magdala. The stars provided guidance for more than half the distance. A bright orange beacon, whose name I did not know, hung above us in the west when we sailed. It continued to beckon as it sank toward the horizon, but it appeared distant and aloof.

Nor were the stars the only means of navigating by night. By law all the cities around the lake kept lamps burning for just such crossings as mine.

So another orange glow replaced the setting star. This light came from an oil flame in the window of my stone shed near the shore. Its friendly beam called me across the waves. I was ready for . . . I needed . . . familiar, comfortable surroundings.

As we neared the end of the journey the scent of jasmine blooming in my garden wafted to me. I saw the white crescent of sand marking my beach and then the keel grated, and my voyage was complete.

I paid John and Ya'acov the agreed-upon passage money. Shim'on jumped out; a human donkey dragging the little ship higher up on the shoal. John helped me into knee-deep water and passed my bundle of belongings.

Shim'on shoved off as I waded ashore. I turned to say good-bye, but the boat had already vanished into the night. Perhaps the three fishermen believed their reputations would be better preserved if any dealings with me were kept as secret as possible.

I was home.

Much had changed in the last week. I told myself things would return to the way they had been before. I would belong to Maximus. We would not have love, but we would have pleasure and companionship.

And if my thoughts were on another lover, he did not need to know, did he?

Before trudging up to my room I once more studied the stars. The constellation known in other lands as The Archer was dipping westward.

My people knew it as The Lamp, because the outline suggested an oil-burning clay lamp.

Just now its spout seemed to pour out stars upon the hill country where Barak lived. I heard he worked a shabby farm near Nazareth. Was he happy there? I wondered. Or did he view his shabby life and think about what he might have had?

Aloud I whispered to the stars, "Barak, I haven't forgotten."

As I ascended the stairs to my balcony I was surprised to see a light gleaming in my bedchamber. The outside door stood open. Was someone in my room?

Wary, I reached the landing without either making or hearing a sound. I peered in.

Inside sat Maximus with a scowl on his face. His arms were folded across his chest.

Anger radiated from his frown and the stiffness of his pose. Apprehensive of startling him, I cleared my throat to alert him to my arrival.

He looked up and his lips tightened over his teeth in a grimace. "Where were you?" he demanded.

"What are you doing here?" I responded. It was, after all, my house.

"Where were you?" he said again, tersely.

Lifting a fold of my robe I displayed the dampness of the hem. "Swimming."

"For three hours?" he challenged. "I've been waiting here three hours."

"I wasn't aware. Why didn't you let someone know?" Casually I tossed my bundle onto the bed beside him.

Eyeing it suspiciously, he repeated yet again, "Where were you?"

"This is growing tiresome," I said lightly, but his hostility looked dangerous. "You mean, for the last three days? I was with Joanna."

"Liar!" he spouted, leaping up and lunging at me like a guard dog charging to the end of a restraining rope . . . only there was no cord to hold him back. "Liar!"

My gaze darted everywhere, seeking an answer I could not locate. I pivoted away as if he did not frighten me. I would turn the tables on him. "You're drunk," I said.

Now he seized me, grabbing both my arms and spinning me to face him. "And if I am? Drunk? Drunk enough to kill you? I say you're a liar. And a harlot!"

Terrified of his rage, I kicked and struggled in his grip. "You're hurting me!" When I momentarily freed one hand I scored his cheek with my nails. "Let go of me!"

When he pinned my hands again I bent and bit him, hard. As hard as I could. It drew blood. He roared and jerked his forearm free from my teeth.

Grasping my hair, he yanked my head

backward as I cried out in pain and terror. "I should break your neck," he threatened. He was already near to doing it. Had he brought his knee up into my back and yanked downward with both hands I would have snapped like a twig. "I should. It would liberate all the men you keep dangling."

"Maximus!" I cried, knowing my next breath might be my last.

He laced his fingers in my hair. "Or I could crush this pretty head between my hands. Jews would thank me. Rome wouldn't care." He began to squeeze.

My breath came in little shuddering gulps. My head felt like an eggshell an instant away from being shattered. His grip tightened still further.

"Maximus! I wasn't at Joanna's! Wait! Let me tell you," I begged.

Breath reeking of wine he demanded, "Who were you with?"

"I went . . . I went to . . ."

"Who? Who were you with?"

"Gadara! I went to Gadara. To get rid of . . ."

Drawing a parchment scroll from his belt he slapped my face with it. "Was he there? Was he? Tell me!"

He had found a half-written love letter from me to Barak!

I was sobbing. "No! I'm trying to . . . I went to . . ."

Again and again he beat me across the cheek with the scroll, preventing me from speaking. "Where did you stay with him? I told you what I'd do. I told you I'd kill any man you were unfaithful with. I'll lay both of you in the grave together!"

Another slash beside my ear.

Despite all my struggles I could not free myself. My strength was failing. "No! Please, listen. Gadara." My words were hoarse. "Went to . . . to get rid of . . . the baby!"

My words were like a solid punch landed against his chest. Maximus shoved me, sending me sprawling. The back of my legs hit the bed frame and I stumbled and tumbled in a heap.

He towered over me, brandishing the parchment scroll as if he would stab me with it.

I recognized it: the scroll in which I professed my love for Barak.

How I hated Maximus in that moment! If a knife had been to hand I would have cut his throat or blinded him. Rubbing my bruised cheek I at last made it clear to him: "I've been to the Bamah! I got rid of the child."

"It's not . . ." His hands hung limply at his sides, all the fury drained from him. "It's not what I wanted." Shaking his head from side-to-side he winced and said again, "Not what I wanted."

Now it was my rage that could not be

contained. Cursing as I leapt upright, I beat his chest with my fists; clawed for his eyes. Despite my fury he controlled me easily, keeping me at bay by twisting my wrist until I shrieked.

Finally I fell again, slumped at his feet in exhaustion.

Raw, undiluted hatred poured from me.

And from him? Cold disdain. "I pity you," he said. "Almost. Beautiful, unnatural creature that you are. Almost . . . pity." Spreading his hands he looked toward heaven and inquired, "Is this all there is?"

I panted. "What? What are you saying?"

In barely audible, hollow-sounding words he said, "To my life?"

He mopped his face with his hand like a man awakening from a troubled sleep, then turned and left my chamber without another word. By the time I had struggled to my feet he had vanished.

Chapter 12

The day after my brawl with Maximus I kept to my room. My face was bruised, my lips battered, my eyes swollen and I ached all over. I admitted no one but Tavita, but this did nothing to prevent my other servants from gossiping.

Apparently they had heard my altercation with Maximus.

Their voices drifted up from my courtyard. There was no longer any deference in their tone. "The Roman despises her," one said.

"She's a brawler," returned another.

"Like the lake. Too unpredictable . . . and too dangerous."

I made up my mind to dismiss the lot of them the following day.

Then Tavita returned with the news they were all quitting. They were ashamed to work for me, they reported.

Quite apart from the battle with Maximus, everyone knew of my journey and the reason behind it. My three fishermen had been seen and recognized when they picked me up at the quay in Hippus, and so was the mute guide.

No part of my life was secret anymore, it seemed. All of Galilee knew . . . or would soon know . . . that I had been to the Owb of Bamah. I had sacrificed a child to Molech.

Only Tavita and the overseer of my crops remained. The only replacement staff willing to work for a person of my reputation were slovenly, lazy complainers, without manners or respect.

As the days passed my wounds healed, but inside I sank lower and lower into depression. I did not leave the house, preferring to remain isolated, blaming Maximus for my loneliness.

Each day I dozed and paced.

Each night I was tormented by the voices urging me to end it all.

The only pleasure remaining was planning my funeral. I dispatched the farm steward to purchase a plot of land on a hill overlooking the lake for my tomb. I wrote out elaborate instructions for the service: how I was to be dressed, what music should be played, even who should be invited.

I kept a costly alabaster bottle of spikenard with me at all times. It was to be used to anoint my body for burial.

The bottle became my touchstone with life on the edge of death. Seldom relinquishing the jug, even to sleep, I wanted it with me all the time. I knew that whenever I chose I would be dead and then the contents of sweet ointment would be used. The jar was like a last kindness I would perform for myself, when no one else would even have a kind word.

There was one exception to this despair; one person who might actually mourn my loss.

It was for her sake I delayed ending it all.

Joanna, with Boaz playing in the waves, sat beside me on the lakeshore. "You've got to pull yourself together," she urged. "So what if you're hated? The common people hate us for no reason. They wish evil on anyone who has more than they do. They rejoice to see you brought low . . . so fight back."

Hugging my knees I stared at the water lapping the shore. "Am I worse than everyone else?"

Joanna snorted. "Of course not. Half the women at court have had affairs. More than half, probably. Men . . . supposedly Kuza's friends . . . proposition me all the time. That's why I'd rather stay in Capernaum. Practical. Affairs always end badly. One person hates the other. People treat it as part of the entertainment. Greek plays are nothing compared to passion and pain in real life. And if it's someone you know? The gossip makes a delicious feast. But listen: soon they'll tire of you and move on to someone else."

"When?" I said, flicking sand on a beetle and watching him struggle to extract himself.

Joanna shrugged. "When you take another lover. Or when Maximus does."

"I don't want just . . . another. I want Barak bar Halfi. That's what started all this."

"Why? What do you see in him? He's poor, he sounds weak-willed, and he's mired in his religion."

"He's a good man," I argued, defending him.

Laughing scornfully Joanna commented, "No such thing. Not if he's married and still comes to your bed."

"I know he loves me," I asserted.

"Do you still believe in love? Even after that one has spurned you twice? You're a hopeless case. Love!"

The finality and hopelessness of her words wounded me. "But I want to be loved. I've never . . . it's never been within reach. Are you truly such a cynic?"

Her eyes darted toward Boaz and the lines in her face softened. "My son," she admitted. "My son is my life. Kuza may have other women. I don't care. Less bother for me. As long as I have Boaz what else do I need? Bo is everything."

I felt a flash of sorrow and envy mingled together. Unable to mask it completely I struck back with, "Barak is not like Kuza. Barak would be faithful to me."

"You believe that? Ha! Remove his righteous exterior and see what remains: lascivious as Herod Antipas, most likely. Listen, Mary: right now your Barak is really concerned about what people think. He's a thorough hypocrite, yes? What would happen to him if you won him back to your bed because he managed to stop caring about his reputation? If he lost that prop to his self-image?"

When I did not respond Joanna answered for me. "Here's what: he'd leap from female to female like a he-goat. Only his precious image restrains him now!"

Bristling I retorted, "I won't hear it. I don't believe it. He's not like other men. I saw it in his eyes. He still cares for me. If it weren't for these ultra-religious preachers all over the country . . ."

Pressing her lips together, Joanna stared at a boat making for land. "You have a point there. Who cares who Antipas has in his bed? Denouncing him's a game. The job of fanatics is to keep everyone stirred up. But Yochanan the Baptizer is a doomed man. Herodias won't be satisfied unless he's silenced. His own fault, too. Why doesn't he keep his mouth shut? All this stirring things up will hurt a lot of people."

Laying my cheek on my knee I closed my eyes. "It's all gone wrong for me," I said.

"Just feels like it."

"But when will I ever be able to show my face again?"

"When you quit caring what people think. In all friendship, you're as great a hypocrite as your man Barak."

I was not ready to take responsibility so I changed the subject. "I dread seeing Maximus again."

"Ah. Well, here's comfort for you: he's out of favor."

I was pleased at the news. Maybe it was his turn to be hurt. "How so?"

"I don't know politics . . . boring! But somehow he got at odds with a Praetorian commander. And," she added, "they say he's accused of being too sympathetic to Jews." She wagged her head. "Not a good reputation for a Roman officer to have. Sympathetic to Jews."

"Not to me he wasn't!" I smiled finally.

"You're a Jew only by birth. Kuza thinks Maximus will be transferred, unless this Praetorian Vara finds a way to make a charge of treason stick. Then they'd crucify him."

Pantomiming swinging a hammer and driving a nail I said, "Either is all right by me. I'd volunteer to plant the first spike."

Joanna frowned at me. "He must have really hurt you."

"No," I denied forcefully. "Only my pride."

The Story of Mary Magdalene,
First Century, A.D.
Translated by
Moshe Sachar, Old City, Jerusalem, 1948

Dearest Rachel,
   I knew you'd be wondering what else is known about Mary after her part in the Gospels ends.
   It was Saint Ambrose, in about 370 A.D., who recorded the history of Mary Magdalene. He remarked that Yeshua conferred great grace upon her. He cast seven devils out of her, counted her among his closest friends. He defended her when Pharisees called her "unclean" and when her sister Martha called her lazy. For love of her it is written that Yeshua raised her brother from death after he had been in the tomb four days. He rebuked Judas when he called her act of kindness to the Lord "wasteful."
   Ambrose wrote, "She (called Mary Magdalene) it was, I say, who washed the Lord's feet with her tears, dried them with her hair and anointed them with ointment, who in time of grace did solemn penance, who chose the best part, who sat at the Lord's feet and listened to his word, who anointed his head, who stood beside his cross at the Passion, who prepared the sweet

spices with which to anoint his body, who, when the disciples left the tomb, did not go away, to whom the risen Christ first appeared, making her apostle to the apostles."

Scorned by her own brother and sister before her repentance and redemption, she later entreated the Lord for Lazarus, who received back his life.

Chapter 13

hree months had passed after Barak left the orchard. A new tenant took his place, and the revenue from the groves in Cana was down by half. The midsummer harvest of figs was a financial disappointment.

I sold the saffron bulbs to make up the shortfall. It was like selling my dream.

As I labored over the accounts with my steward, I could only blame the new tenant. My steward, it was plain, blamed something else.

"He says your grove is cursed."

I studied the hills across the lake where the pagan altar of Bamah was hidden in the afternoon haze. "The trees are healthy. The groves of my neighbors bear fruit. Cursed. What does he mean by this?"

"Your grove is barren."

Rage engulfed me. I threw my cup down and shouted, "It is barren because it is mine?"

Shocked by my outburst, the steward closed his tablet and sat back. "No offense meant to you . . . he is reporting fact."

"That the fig groves of Mary Magdalene are barren. And my wheat fields. And my vineyard in Capernaum. All barren. As I am barren. Is that what they are saying?"

I did not tell him that this accusation came

171

daily into my own mind. Accusations from voices none could hear but me.

He stammered. "Wheat sown on rocky soil. Difficult."

"My enemies planted weeds in my fields to ruin me."

"The *khamseen* wind often carries bad seed from the wilderness to our fields."

"Superstition! The demons of the Bamah."

"Wind from the east. A fact every farmer knows."

"Winds from the Bamah! Winds from the high places of Gadara!"

"You're not the first to lose a crop of wheat to weeds."

"Or the lambs of my flocks miscarried? And maybe you think I am cursed? My lands cursed because of me?"

"No, my lady."

"If you can't get a profit from these ignorant peasants, maybe I have misplaced all trust in you."

The religious rulers believed such misfortune was a judgment upon the unrighteous. I believed that Yeshua of Nazareth, as he preached around the Galil, had perhaps placed a curse upon my trees and flocks and fields. If not Yeshua, then perhaps my enemies had done these things to me.

I railed against him, "You will show me improvement, or I will find another steward!"

Tavita came out at the sound of my shouts. The steward gave her a pleading look and lapsed into silence.

Tavita stepped between us. "You're tired, lamb."

I screamed at him around her. "Get out of my sight."

He slunk from the garden.

My head roared with a headache. "Who can I trust, Tavita? Who?"

Tavita gave me a message brought by courier from Capernaum. "From Joanna. Perhaps her news is cheerful."

I opened the letter and read:

Come to me quickly in Capernaum, dear friend. Our sweet son, our only son, is dying. The court physicians of Herod Antipas have kindly come to examine him. Likewise the personal physician of Governor Pilate's wife, Claudia, was sent to us. Yet they say it is hopeless. Our Boaz sleeps near the sleep of death. Kuza is frantic with grief.

I prepared quickly for the journey to Capernaum. Tavita gathered my clothing and the steward was sent to procure a boat for me to sail north, which was the quickest way to reach the town.

Tavita with me, we set sail just after noon, in the fishing boat of an older fisherman named

Jonas and his youngest son. These two were relatives of the young men who had left their boats and nets to follow Yeshua of Nazareth.

We sat in the bow but could not escape the conversation of these fellows.

Jonas seemed angry. "What's the good of it, I ask you? Leave their profession to tramp around the Galil?"

"They seem intent on it, Father. They say he is the one who will break the yoke of Rome."

"They'll break our yoke? How will we plow without a yoke, I ask you? Were we better off with the Hasmonean princes? Before Rome the yoke of Greece was upon us. And the yoke of Herod."

"If this fellow Yeshua is the Messiah . . ."

"Messiah? You're too young to know how many Messiahs have come and gone in Israel. All these years we have been waiting for one like Mosheh, the Lawgiver. He never comes, though we shed our blood and die for the cause of freedom about once a generation. I could not imagine your brothers would be so foolish."

"But the miracles Yeshua performs . . ."

"Miracles," Jonas scoffed. "Illusions more like. Don't know how he does it, but I won't believe it till I see for myself."

"As my brothers have sent to you often, Father, may we not go join them and see these things with our own eyes?"

"I tell you this: I've lost two sons and two is enough. These Messiah quests never end well. Crucifixions and torture. Imprisonment and the galley ships. I won't attend his gatherings, nor will I give you permission to follow after your brothers."

And so their argument continued unabated the whole while. I felt justified by their doubt about Yeshua. The conversation of the father and son reinforced my opinion that Yeshua was dangerous . . . all religious fanatics were a danger.

The wind was at our backs, so we reached the shore of Capernaum by late-afternoon.

The father and son were still arguing about Yeshua when Tavita and I paid our passage and the fishermen at the beach.

Chapter 14

We came to the gate of the estate within minutes. I recognized Maximus' black horse and his servant Carta, outside, waiting as his master paid his respects.

The sight of the youthful servant of my former lover renewed in me a sense of rage. I knew that I must see Maximus in the house, but I determined I would not speak to him.

As I raised my chin in determination, Carta smiled and bowed slightly in respect of my presence. I did not respond to him.

Tavita knocked upon the gate. A frail, grim doorman ushered us into the courtyard. The paved area around the fountain was empty except for a few servants who muttered together about the tragedy taking place within.

Tavita said, "My Lady Mary was sent for by your mistress."

The house steward led me into the house and to the dark bedchamber of the precious child.

Maximus and Kuza were across the room, near the window. Beyond them the twilight purpled the skies of the east.

Kuza wept openly. Maximus glared down fiercely at the dying child. Joanna, her eyes red from weeping, sat upon the floor and mourned the certain death of her beloved. Boaz's frail body seemed so tiny in the bed. His blond curls were damp with the sweat of agony. His belly was swollen; his lips colorless as he struggled to breathe.

Joanna held his hand.

I was certain Boaz was past all hope.

Joanna raised her eyes to me, imploring. "Mary?"

I knew the questions raging in her mind. *How could this happen? Why? God must be very cruel to allow such a thing.*

I ignored Maximus' pained expression and rushed to kneel beside Joanna. I felt his sad, sad gaze upon me as I held her in my arms.

Joanna sobbed for a time, then tried to speak. "They say some organ has ruptured. The poison of his bile has spread everywhere. Poor baby. Poor baby. He screamed and screamed from the pain. For me to help him, but there is nothing for me to do. The physician of Claudia, wife of Pontius, has given him the juice of poppies to kill the pain. The light of my life is setting! Oh, Mary!"

I felt her body almost convulse with sorrow. So deep was her anguish, I thought perhaps Joanna would die with her son.

Kuza fell to his knees and cried, "We are being punished by the Eternal for our sins."

Maximus scowled. "What kind of god would this Hebrew god be if he murders children in judgment of the fathers?"

And I said, "A god without pity."

Kuza replied with a sigh, "It is His will."

Maximus cursed and crossed his arms. "You're all crazy. Crazy Jews. If you believe this . . ."

It came to me that perhaps he was speaking to me. I stared at him angrily, and he shut up.

As Maximus strode to take Boaz's hand and caressed it, I saw this proud centurion had a tender heart for the child. He spoke. "But never mind. Perhaps there is something yet to be done. Someone who can help."

Joanna did not look up. "Nothing. My life ends when he breathes his last."

Maximus would not be silent. The light of hope

beamed from his face. "In Judea I saw the rabbi from Nazareth work some sort of spell. Yeshua healed a child. A cripple. I saw it with my own eyes. And now I heard that Yeshua of Nazareth has returned to Galilee."

At these words, Kuza raised his head and took Maximus by the arm. "Where is this Yeshua now? How can we find him? I will crawl to him on my knees and beg."

Maximus' face became set with determination. "He's in Cana, last I heard. We can ride all night. Fetch him back here and make him work his magic on Boaz."

And so Maximus and Kuza left in a cloud of dust and galloping hooves.

I was angry at Maximus for bringing false hope to the hopeless. I was angry at Kuza for leaving poor Joanna to face the death of their only son on her own.

Boaz's struggle to survive became more difficult as the hours passed. Joanna, my dearest friend, was broken before my eyes. Hands clasped and eyes upraised, she pleaded for mercy from a deity whom I believed was too far away and too uncaring to hear her desperate prayers.

At the bottom of my anger was bitterness against God; rejection of the thought that prayer could alter what was the certain ending of this tragedy.

I knew that by morning Boaz would be supper for worms. The weight of that truth was too heavy for me to bear. Again and again I asked myself how such a thing could happen . . . and why?

I deeply loved Boaz. I had looked forward to seeing him. His affection, untainted by judgment of my sins, cheered me. Now even this reflected light was about to be extinguished.

I was anxious for it to end. I thought that Joanna would be so much better off when this ordeal of his suffering was over.

At midnight when he began to stir he cried out, "Mama! Hold me! I hurt!"

Joanna dripped the poppy juice into his mouth and held him, singing his favorite lullaby.

I sat in the shadows watching all this. Boaz slept again and Joanna cried, "Oh Lord! Take my life instead of his! I am the one who should not live! Lord! Hear my prayer! Spare my child and take my life instead of his!"

I knew this was an impossible prayer. No person could ever take the hurts of another. How many times in every day was such a prayer offered? And when was it ever answered by God? No one could die in another's place.

Joanna was so pitiful and agonizing I turned away. My gaze fell upon the vial of poppy juice. I heard a voice in my thoughts, then, *Why not give him a few more drops of the medicine to speed him on his way?*

I contemplated this. Wouldn't such action be mercy? Wouldn't it be the same as preventing the birth of an unwanted child, as I had done at Bamah?

Joanna prayed again, "O Most High! God of my fathers! Of Abraham, Isaac and Jacob! Only true God of Israel, help Kuza and Maximus to find the Rabbi, Yeshua of Nazareth, and bring him here to give me back the life of my son!"

Of all things that angered me that night, this hopeless prayer brought a silent fury into my soul. I was certain no charlatan from Nazareth could bring the life of Boaz back.

Joanna said, "I have nothing in the house to anoint his body for burial."

I answered, "I'll send Carta to my house to fetch some. I have an alabaster bottle of perfume. Pure spikenard from Alexandria. I've kept it. Saving it for something. I don't know why. Fit to anoint a King of Israel. So if you let me, it will be my offering for this innocent life."

Joanna touched his brow. "I was angry at him four days ago. He broke a vase. If I had known . . . I forgot to notice him. Oh God, let me die with him."

I could not bear any more. I stalked from the room, grateful that I had no child. I had no one I cared about in life. The future was too uncertain. I had learned as a child when my mother died that love was too dangerous to let in my heart.

Throughout the agonizing night Maximus and Kuza rode in search of Yeshua. I believed that even if they completed their fool's errand they would return too late. Boaz would be dead before sunrise.

I closed my eyes, certain there was no hope for the child to be found in Yeshua of Nazareth.

Chapter 15

I stared into the dappled leaves of the grape arbor, certain little Boaz would not last another hour. Once, many months before, Maximus had kissed me in this quiet retreat after a banquet. We had discussed Joanna and Kuza and their child with such envy then.

In an instant I thought again how lucky I was. Yes: lucky not to love; happy I did not have a child to worry about or grieve over. The demon voices of Bamah had been right, I thought. Love for a child makes a woman's heart a prisoner.

Peacocks strutted through the garden in search of Boaz. The child took great pleasure in the birds. Every morning he fed them breadcrumbs. Kuza had raised peacocks, thinking of the extravagant dinner table of Herod Antipas. But when the butcher showed up, Boaz had squealed and declared the slaughter-man would not pass. The boy had made the birds pets. He had won the battle. Now, I wondered, who would protect the elegant creatures?

The great wealth that had come with Kuza's position as Steward to Herod seemed worth nothing. I knew Kuza and Joanna would be happy in a tiny house in the hills if only Boaz could be near, traipsing after his peacocks.

The villa already seemed desolate to me. Without Boaz as the center of the world, what would Joanna do with herself?

A heaviness filled the air: the presence of death. The Dark Angel had come to gather the soul of Boaz and carry him away.

A peacock near the water's edge stretched his neck and gave a loud, eerie wail. From all around the gardens, peahens and peacocks joined in the keening. Great proud birds spread their tails, flapping and crying as they hurried toward the house.

I stood and followed the deafening clamor.

How could they know their young master had died?

At that instant I heard a shriek from inside the house. Joanna cried, "Boaz! Oh, Boaz! My son! My son!"

So it had come to this. All her love wasted. Her life worse now than if she had never given birth. The emotional burden of this was almost more than I could carry. My knees grew weak and threatened to buckle beneath me. Sorrow squeezed my heart as I made my way to the steps, where a score of peahens clustered.

Then I saw what they were looking at! My breath drew in with amazement. I gasped and reeled back at the sight of little Bo standing in his white linen robe at the top of the steps.

Was I seeing a ghost, I wondered? Had he died and his spirit come to say farewell?

Behind the boy, Joanna clung to the doorframe for support. She sobbed and stared at him.

How could this be?

Boaz was well and whole. Fully healed.

Or he was dead and about to fly away?

I could not tell.

Then Boaz grinned down at his hungry audience. "Shalom, birds! Sorry I was not here for your breakfast. I was sleeping a lot. Dreaming of heaven. Be patient, birds. I'll go fetch your bread for you."

Joanna sent Carta galloping off to carry the news of Boaz's healing to Maximus and Kuza. Before they ever returned to the house they believed Yeshua had performed a long-distance miracle, and saved Boaz's life.

What a reunion there was that day! Dusty and exhausted from their frantic quest, the men came shouting and rejoicing into the house.

Maximus and Carta and I stood awkwardly watching as Kuza and Joanna embraced Boaz and praised the Most High God together. I imagined that the lights of the torches blazed a little brighter as Kuza, the wayward husband and father, realized what really mattered in life. His tears were unrestrained. He said again and again, "I am so grateful . . . another chance . . . another chance. I will do better."

Maximus was breathless with wonder and excitement. "Yeshua told us His Father had heard his prayer! He told Kuza to go home and rejoice! That Boaz was healed!"

Sorrow overwhelmed me. I would never have another chance. My baby was gone. Gone. I was forever damned and would never have a chance to make it right or change the outcome now.

Maximus touched my arm . . . too tenderly. His eyes searched my face with such pity. I turned away from him, left the house, and went outside.

The wind stirred, whipping my hair as I approached the lakeshore. The stones beneath my feet seemed to beg me to pick them up, put them in my pockets, and wade into the lake. There were no lights on the water tonight. Perhaps the wind prevented boats from sailing.

I heard the voices behind me . . . joyful . . . praising the God I did not know; the God who could only despise me.

I told myself I did not believe in miracles—not really. Yes, Boaz stood before us, rosy cheeked and well, but I found myself certain he would have recovered somehow, even if Maximus and Kuza had not ridden to find Yeshua. Miracles did not happen, I reasoned. Rather, whatever was meant to be would simply unfold without prayer or divine intervention.

I was pleased and surprised by Boaz's recovery but resented the obvious gratitude that Joanna and Boaz had for Yeshua. How could I believe Yeshua could have brought the boy back from over the brink of death?

Maximus had followed me. He told me, "Mary! I want you to come with me. Something has happened. Surely you see it. This . . . with Boaz."

Defensive, a rage boiled up in me. "Why should I go anywhere with you?"

"The power of Yeshua. I want you to see Him. Hear Him."

"Then what?"

"I want you to meet Him for yourself." He sounded astonished by his encounter with the Nazarean preacher. "If you could only speak with Him. Then perhaps . . ."

"Perhaps what?" I was defiant.

"Maybe He can help."

Fury consumed me. Who was Maximus to say I needed help? "Go see this healer yourself. I don't need help! You do. You're the one, not me."

Maximus fell silent. When he spoke again, his voice was quiet. "Yes. You're right. I wasn't saying . . . I didn't mean it was only you. Maybe it's everyone. The whole world needs Him. The truth is, Mary, I am a Roman. Not of His people. Not worthy to ask Him."

"And what am I? Shunned by my own people. Your harlot. And now . . . Bamah."

"He is so kind."

"A righteous man. A prophet. This Yeshua would pick me out of the crowd from afar. He would call my name and gather the stones Himself for my stoning. And He would be right to do it . . ." How could I explain to Maximus that what I had done had separated me from my people and the God of my fathers forever?

Maximus pleaded, "If only you could hear Him. He healed Boaz."

"Bo is an innocent child. Why would Yeshua refuse to help a child? If He had the power. And . . . but we don't know if He did it. And I am content with my life the way it is." I knew the gulf between my guilt and forgiveness was so wide I could never cross over.

Maximus said sadly, "I have been a fool," then he turned on his heel and left me.

I had no more tears. The man I had been so desperate to hold onto was gone.

Chapter 16

Boaz approached as I sat on the edge of my courtyard fountain. The spray took the edge off the autumn afternoon heat. Despite the heavy roof tiles the interior of my home was an oven, but here on the terrace it was pleasant in the shade.

The boy was shining clean and dressed in his best suit of clothing. One hand clutched a handful of peacock feathers. The other carefully cradled my alabaster jar of spikenard. Gravely, with great care, he placed the costly ointment next to me on the fountain's rim. "You forgot this."

The child had no clear knowledge of having been the focus of an extraordinary event. He did not know the perfume had been intended for his burial.

"And these are for you," he added, thrusting the feathers toward me like a bouquet of flowers.

"Lovely. Did you find them all yourself?"

Boaz nodded. "Long ones and short ones. On the garden path."

"Thank you," I said, matching his serious air. "Are your peacocks well?"

"Not happy," he replied.

Joanna, arriving after her son, explained, "Well, but cranky. Molting. Losing their feathers and their pride all over the grounds. But Bo gathered these especially for you."

"Then thank you again," I said. "And I'm glad you're well."

Boaz rubbed one sandaled foot against the back of the other leg as if not clear what was the issue causing all the attention. "I was sick. Then I got better. It was a nice dream. A pretty dream. There was singing. Then the voice told me to get up and go feed my birds. So I did."

"And . . . did the voice say anything else to you?"

Boaz ducked his chin. "Said I was loved."

"Boaz," Joanna said, "why don't you sort the feathers from longest to shortest? When you've done that, let's see if we can pick the prettiest three of them."

The boy obligingly plopped down on a clean square stone and set to work.

His mother leaned closer to me and urged, "Mary, I want you to come to Nazareth with us."

I studied her. She was dressed in a plain, homespun robe and wore no jewelry. Her hair was pulled back severely and hidden beneath a scarf. "Why?"

"The teacher's mother lives there."

I knew without names which teacher she meant.

"I want to see Him. . . . see if what they say is true. And I want to thank Him."

"And is that the reason for this . . . disguise?"

Joanna attached a veil across her features. "So I won't be recognized and get Kuza in trouble. He told me Herod Antipas has spies keeping an eye on Yeshua."

"Nazareth?" I said doubtfully, trying to think how to gracefully avoid the trip and also avoid offending Joanna. I had decided there was no miracle connected with the boy's recovery. He had passed some sort of crisis and survived a dreadful illness. Everyone was pleasantly surprised. But there had been no magic, just a happy turn of fate. "There's no decent place to stay in that hilltop village. We'd have to sleep under the stars."

Proving that he was still listening, Boaz clapped his hands and jumped up with excitement. "I'd love to sleep under the stars."

Joanna tugged the veil down again. A tender smile was displayed on her face and a drop of moisture at the corner of each eyelid. Everything about her expression radiated light and joy.

She looks like a woman in love, I thought.

"I have a donkey loaded with gifts," Joanna added, gesturing toward my gate. "I want to meet Him. Show Him Boaz. Tell Him. . . . tell Him what it means to have my son back."

There was iron in the timbre of her words. She would be going to Nazareth whether I accompanied them or not.

I tried one last time to save us all an unnecessary journey and possible harassment from Herod. "What if the good rabbi had nothing to do with—" I gestured toward Boaz.

"You can't mean it," Joanna challenged with an arched eyebrow.

"But I do. What if?"

"Bo was dying," Joanna retorted softly but with intensity.

"Kuza hears all the news," I shot back. "What do Herod's spies say?"

"That Yeshua has . . . power."

Just then a howling storm of protest rose in my head: voices hurling protests, accusations, mockery. "And maybe His power's not a good thing."

Joanna placed a protective arm around her son. "How can saving my son's life be not good? How!"

"Maybe He uses sorcery. What if He used a spell to make Boaz sick and another to make him well again?"

"Why would He do such a thing?"

I was relentless. "Herod arrested the Baptizer. Kuza is Herod's steward. Boaz is Kuza's son. What if this sorceror was making a point?"

"He saved my son's life," Joanna repeated. "He gave me back my son!"

"Perhaps."

Joanna dismissed my skepticism with an angry

wave of her fist. "No matter what you say . . . I saw with my own eyes."

For that instant I saw on her face the image of the terror of watching Boaz die, then shook it away. "Well, it doesn't matter anyway. I can't come. Business to tend to."

My friend studied me. "Mary? Why not? Why not hear him for yourself?"

Shrugging, I concluded, "I admit I'm curious, but I can't."

"You mean, *won't.*"

"If you like," I said agreeably.

"What are you fearful of?"

Despite my effort to control it, my voice trembled with resentment when I replied, "Afraid? Why are you pushing me?"

Joanna did not back off. "Why are you afraid to go to Nazareth?"

"Come with us, Aunt Mary," Boaz piped. "It'll be fun. Sleep under the stars."

Nazareth. Barak lived there. What if I bumped into him? More to the point: What if I met his wife? Then what would happen? They'd never believe I had not come to see Barak.

The possibilities were unbearable.

"I'm sorry," I said, addressing the boy. "I can't. I have a tenant in Cana who is just ruining my figs and . . . I just can't, that's all."

Disappointment clouded Boaz's countenance, but he said nothing further.

Joanna guessed at last what troubled me. "It's that man you told me about, isn't it? The one who betrayed you . . . or his wife caught you. That's it. He lives near there. I remember you said so."

Putting my hand over my mouth I bobbed my head in assent. My fingers shook and muffled my words. "If his wife saw me . . . You know, she already poisoned my brother and sister against me. Barak never betrayed me; I know he wouldn't."

I still wanted this conclusion to be true. I needed to believe he still wanted me but was too weak to force past his prized reputation. When Eve came into the barn, of course Barak was forced to deny her . . . but it wasn't his fault. There'd be another chance; another time.

"Joanna," I said, "if I was recognized . . ."

Relief accompanied Joanna's response. "Why didn't you just tell me? You can wear a veil too. Dress plain. Wear a disguise. No one will know it's you. If you see this fellow or his shrewish wife, you go the other way. No one will be the wiser."

Barak's wife was a convenient half-truth. I could not admit that I was even more afraid of what I had heard of Yeshua and His power. What would a true prophet reveal about me? If He was truly a righteous man, wouldn't He strip away my last shred of pride and reveal me to the world for what I truly was? Didn't the prophets of old always denounce women like me in sternest terms? What if He presented me to the crowd as the perfect example of wickedness?

But the combined willpower of Boaz and Joanna overcame my objections with a final promise: "We'll stay at the back. You can get away if you have to . . . whenever you have to," Joanna argued.

With a heavy sigh I conceded. "All right, I'll come with you. You two go help yourselves to some food while I pack a few things."

Chapter 17

My feet hurt as we neared the end of the journey from Magdala to Nazareth. Joanna had insisted that common folk such as we were pretending to be never traveled any other way than walking.

Seventeen miles never felt so far before.

Nor did we have any servants. Just Joanna, Boaz, and me. Boaz, full of boundless energy, ran ahead of us. He investigated blackbird nests in the thornbushes and trailed rabbits to their warrens.

No onlooker would ever have believed the five-year-old had ever been ill—much less recently near death.

We spent a night on the trip at the town of

Gath-hepher. As far as the quality of the inn was concerned I had seen cleaner stables, but we had no option. No matter of pretense this time; there were no other accommodations.

When I rolled up in a blanket to sleep I stopped complaining about the dirt on the hard floor. The bedbugs kept me occupied instead.

Early next morning we were off. We trudged southward in the shadow of Mount Tabor, the place where my beloved's namesake, the Jewish general Barak, defeated Sisera in battle. The connection made me think of seeing my Barak again soon, despite my misgivings.

We reached Nazareth well before sundown ended Jewish travel as the Sabbath began. Here we found an inn much cleaner than the first. It was crowded, but we managed to secure the last available room just as the shofar's blasts announced the arrival of the day of rest.

The second morning of our journey I awoke to find the humble hamlet crowded with people. They all hurried past the inn as if heading toward a common goal.

"Good Shabbat," Joanna called to a passerby. "What is it? What's happening?"

"Rebbe Yeshua will speak at the synagogue service," was the hasty reply. "Everyone wants to see Him."

"Quickly, Mary," Joanna prodded with barely

controlled agitation. "We can hear Him speak and I can take Boaz to see Him after!"

From a distance Nazareth appeared to be an appropriate location for an enigmatic rabbi to call home. It was perched on a hillside above lush pastures and fertile fields. Though sheltered from the wintry storms blowing in from the sea, it still had impressive vistas to the south, across the Vale of Jezreel.

Apart from its location, it was unpretentious. The presence of people had not improved Nazareth's appeal. Less than a mile across, the whole of the village proper was smaller than my most modest walnut grove. A single, dusty street was lined with single-story homes and one-room shops. The synagogue, though easily the only building of substance, was a squat, brown structure dwarfed by the limestone ridge that was the backbone of the town. A sheer cliff at one end of Nazareth limited its ability to grow any further, dooming it to insignificance. I thought how nothing of importance could possible happen in, or come from, Nazareth.

Never having seen a place less likely to produce an important man, I said as much to Joanna. Predictably, she was undeterred by my lack of enthusiasm. "I want to meet Yeshua," she reiterated.

I also had someone I was longing to see, but it was not an itinerant teacher. My gaze was in constant motion, scanning the throngs for any glimpse of Barak bar Halfi.

Studying the synagogue-goers slowed my steps until Boaz tugged impatiently at my elbow. "Come on, Aunt Mir," he chided. "There won't be any room left."

Along the street I overheard many comments about Nazareth's newly famous citizen. "There's his shop," one resident indicated to a visiting friend.

Searching the one-time carpenter's business for clues to his wisdom or mystic powers was a disappointment. There was no grandeur or mystery to it. Formed of a single room, with a single door barely protected from heat or rain by a cloth awning, it looked like many of the other struggling shops.

Casting a critical eye over his wares I inspected a pair of chairs with sycamore frames and woven-cane seats and backs. The products displayed pride of craftsmanship, I mentally allowed. So too did a shelf of amber-hued, olivewood boxes. As we swooped past I noted inlay work of oak and walnut, and a few in crimson almond wood, all with perfectly fitted joints.

Almost grudgingly I said to Joanna, "He's a fine workman, I'll give Him that. Nothing sloppy about His craft."

Chapter 18

The entry to the women's gallery was at the side of the synagogue. The doorway was already jammed with people who could not be squeezed inside. "Are you certain about this?" I queried. "Wouldn't it be easier to wait and see Him after? Not fight through the crowd?"

Joanna was adamant: "We've come all this way."

There was no arguing with Joanna when she was acting the part of mother hen.

Shrugging, I remarked, "Then at least let me handle this." Loudly I called out, "Excuse me! Please excuse me. Watch out for my nephew here. Look out for the boy as we come by. Careful!"

Each time a woman turned sideways to see what was causing the disturbance I pressed through the momentary opening and dragged Boaz and Joanna behind me.

By this means we managed to arrive in the gallery. This was a cramped passage that stood along one wall of the sanctuary, separated from the rest of the room by a latticework screen.

It had been a long time since I had last been in a synagogue, and I felt a momentary qualm again. I told myself that even if Yeshua could truly read minds and see into hearts, He could scarcely single me out from the mob.

Even so I herded Joanna and Boaz ahead of me so their faces pressed against the partition. I told myself this was simple courtesy since they had wanted to see the rabbi, not me.

In the eager air displayed by the spectators I recognized that although I was in the building I was still an outsider. This was such a colossal waste of time. Here I was, packed among none-too-fragrant country laborers for the doubtful joy of listening to a rustic preacher.

I had such a sense of superiority as I looked around me, all the time being nagged by a persistent notion of being completely unworthy to be present at all.

The shrill voices in my head reminded me over and over that I did not belong there.

I recognized how crazy the whole inner debate would have sounded to anyone else, but I could not make it stop.

All around me women hefted babies and small children so they could see over the heads of the others. Beside Joanna I noticed a triangular opening in the lattice about the size of my hand. Through it I saw the males of the congregation bobbing and bowing in prayer.

Then I spotted Yeshua, clearly recognizable as the same man I had seen in Cana. He stood at the end of a row on the far side of the chamber. He faced me and I saw Him plainly: a wisp of brown hair straggled across His forehead from under the hood formed by His prayer shawl. His jaw was strong, matched in temperament by His thick brows and dark eyes. His large, calloused hands hung quietly at His sides, showing that He was relaxed and felt at home.

The elders of the body greeted Him as an old acquaintance.

Beside Yeshua fidgeted a boy of perhaps thirteen. From the nervous looks the lad shot around him I guessed he was just bar mitzvah age and being called to the bema to read for the first time. He wiped his forehead with the back of his hand, and his shoulders rose and fell noticeably with his anxious breathing.

Yeshua nudged him gently and when the boy turned expectantly, Yeshua nodded and smiled. The gesture was enough to remind the teenager that every man of the Jews had gone through this experience. Yeshua's confident glance told the apprehensive youngster he would do well.

The boy smiled back.

Then the vibrant noise of the packed multitude subsided and the service began. Almost immediately an expectant hum rose again.

The man leading the prayers was elderly. I could barely hear his quavering words above the murmuring. Impatiently I turned my gaze away from the lectern and scanned the men crammed into the space on either side of the front row.

It was while performing this neck-craning

exercise that I spotted Barak bar Halfi. My heart leapt! He was almost close enough to touch, or so it seemed. Then an unavoidable companion issue struck me: If Barak was present, then wouldn't his dumpy wife be there also? Eve must be in the same gallery with me.

Hastily I plucked at my headscarf and adjusted my veil. Unreasonable fear, yes, but I felt trapped.

The seven whining voices confirmed this dilemma. *"You shouldn't have come!"* they hissed. *"Run! Or else you'll be discovered,"* they sneered. *"You'll be humiliated . . . or worse. Flee back to Magdala while there's still time! We told you that you didn't belong here."*

The Shema began: "Hear, O Israel: The Lord our God, the Lord is one." The affirmation burst from every throat inside the synagogue, then was picked up by those standing in the doorways, then passed to the first rank outside. It swelled and grew in volume as every increasing numbers repeated it. It echoed back and forth between the hills as though the rocks themselves uttered it.

For me there was no joy in belonging.

At the very moment the Shema began, the voices in my head erupted into one continuous, discordant shriek. I could keep no coherent thoughts, neither could I escape, though I buried my face in my hands. I swayed, and would have fallen, had the press of the crowd not buoyed me up.

At last all the voices—human and other—subsided. I clung to the lattice, gasping for breath.

Joanna whispered to me, "Are you unwell?"

"Too hot," I croaked. "Too close." Of course it was much, much more than that. I wanted to escape this place to run back to the safety of my home. The voices were driving me.

But I had no strength to fight past the throng.

Dizzily, my eyes half shut, I stared dully as the shammash, the synagogue attendant, approached the dais. Despite his thick chest and brawny arms, there was tenderness in the way he embraced an oaken container, as if cradling a baby.

I could not tear my eyes away.

With obvious reverence he opened the box and removed a linen-wrapped cylinder: a Torah scroll.

Even then it seemed to me to be an infant swaddled in blankets.

The image appeared edged with fire! It would not go away, no matter how tightly I squeezed my eyes or how rapidly I blinked.

The shammash held the roll aloft and pivoted with great deliberation so that all might see. As he turned, heads bowed reverently, acknowledging the word of the Lord.

What nonsense, I silently protested.

Had I thought those words . . . or was it another?

When I was a child the display of the Word sent thrills of excitement up my spine. How long had it been since I had believed?

With effort I tore my gaze away and focused on Barak instead. There was no internal protest against this selection of a substitute object for my worship. The voices were silent.

I would have him again, I reminded myself. He would occupy every vacant place in my life, every abandoned childhood joy, every lost bit of contentment.

The service dragged interminably: more blessings, more prayers, more participation in which I played no part and to which I felt no connection.

But it did not matter as long as the god of my idolatry remained central to my adoration.

Then my enjoyment increased further as Barak was called to the lectern to read. I was thrilled, not because of the Scripture but because I now had an unobstructed view of him.

The scroll was opened and an attendant indicated the place from B'resheet . . . the Book of Beginnings. Reading the story of Father Abraham being ordered to sacrifice his son Barak intoned:

"When they came to the place of which God had told him, Abraham built the altar there and laid the wood in order and bound Isaac

his son and laid him on the altar, on top of the wood. Then Abraham reached out his hand and took the knife to slaughter his son."
[Gen. 22:9-10]

At this, the most dramatic part of the message, I happened to glance at Yeshua. I don't know what made me pull my gaze away from Barak, but I did. The teacher remained with His prayer shawl pulled close about His face. His head was bowed, as if in deep reflection, and His features lost in shadow.

Barak continued:

"But the Angel of the Lord called to him out of heaven. And said, 'Abraham, Abraham!' And he said, 'Here I am.' He said, 'Do not lay your hand on the boy or do anything to him, for now I know that you fear God, seeing you have not withheld your son, your only son, from me.'

And Abraham lifted up his eyes and looked, and behold, behind him was a ram, caught in a thicket by his horns. And Abraham went and took the ram and offered it up as a burnt offering instead of his son. So Abraham called the name of that place 'The Lord Will Provide'; as it is said to this day, 'On the mount of the Lord it shall be provided.' " [Gen. 22:11-14]

"The word of the Lord," Barak murmured, kissing the scroll.

Clasping my arms as if Barak were enfolded in them, I swelled with pride. He was so much more than a farmer, and soon again he would be mine.

Through what followed . . . commentary and exposition . . . I was lost in my pleasant daydreams.

The teenager was also called up to read. Visibly shaking, his voice swapping every other sentence from manly to piping, he recited from the Eightieth Psalm:

"Give ear, O Shepherd of Israel,
You who lead Joseph like a flock!
You who are enthroned upon the cherubim,
*   shine forth!*
Before Ephraim and Benjamin and Manasseh,
*   stir up Your might;*
And come to save us!
Restore us, O God;
let Your face shine, that we may be saved!"
[Ps. 80:1-3]

These words seemed to rouse Yeshua at last. He lifted His chin and beamed His approval at the reader, and evident pleasure suffused his face.

There was another blessing before the quavering tones of the presider summoned

Yeshua to read the *Haftarah*, a portion of the prophets. Then the room grew silent. This was the moment the packed crowd had been awaiting.

Gravely He accepted the wooden-handled pointer with the silver tip as the scroll was opened to the Prophet Isaiah.

It was the same clear, confident voice I had heard in Cana, yet indistinct for me because of the incessant humming in my head. For once it seemed my constant companions were speechless, though still attempting to divert my attention.

When Yeshua began to read it seemed to me as if He were not reading at all, but speaking from memory. This was unexpected and unapproved since articulating the phrases without a single mistake called for careful scrutiny of each and every phrase before pronouncing it.

Yet Yeshua did not hesitate.

With His gaze embracing everyone around Him He proclaimed:

"The Spirit of the Lord is upon me, because He has anointed Me to proclaim Good News to the poor. He has sent Me to proclaim liberty to the captives and recovering of sight to the blind, to set at liberty those who are oppressed, to proclaim the year of the Lord's favor."
[Isa. 61:1-2; Luke 4:18-19]

He stopped there. This was not the end of the passage. Had He lost His place? Had overconfidence caused Him to fumble? But Yeshua's gaze remained eager, secure.

Everyone expected Him to resume reading, but He did not. In fact, without warning, He rerolled the scroll, handed it to the attendant, and sat down.

Was He making a point with this suspenseful silence? A thoughtful hush descended as the congregation considered what they had just heard.

When Yeshua spoke again, it was not from Isaiah. Gently, as if trying to tutor a child, He commented, "Today, this passage of Scripture is fulfilled in your hearing."

Every eye, including mine, was fixed on Yeshua as He stepped away from the platform.

What did He mean? What would happen now?

Quizzical looks all around told me the entire audience was reviewing the Scripture passage and trying to make sense of "Fulfilled . . . today . . . in your hearing."

Yeshua's turn of phrase meant He called upon all of us as witnesses.

But witnesses to what?

The "anointing" mentioned by the prophet referred to the Anointed One . . . the Messiah. The signs recorded in the passage were all wonders and miracles Messiah would perform when He was revealed.

Surely Yeshua was not claiming . . .

The large woman whose body and breath crowded me from behind queried, "What's He mean? What's this fulfilled? I didn't see nothing fulfilled."

Her companion shrugged and replied, "*Meshugge*! Him and his mother. Always have been."

A counter-argument was raised. "He's a good boy. A fine son. And isn't He a graceful speaker?"

"Hush!" Joanna scolded. "He's speaking again."

"No doubt you will quote to me this proverb: 'Physician, heal yourself!' Do here in your hometown what we heard you've done in Capernaum." [Luke 4:23]

I shivered. In Capernaum? Boaz was healed in Capernaum. Yeshua had not even been there . . . but the miracle was.

As if to underscore that same connection Yeshua faced the women's gallery. He stared directly toward Boaz and Joanna as if the partition did not exist; as if He saw them plainly.

I saw Joanna clutch her son with tears running down her face. Her reaction said plainly she believed Yeshua meant her boy.

Yeshua resumed, "Next you'll say, 'Now do the same miracles here.' I tell you the truth, a prophet is not without honor except in his own country. When Elijah was in Israel, and the sky was sealed off for three and a half years, so that the land suffered a severe famine, there were many widows; but Elijah was sent to none of them, only to a widow in Zarephath in the land of Sidon." [Luke 4:24-26]

The stout woman behind me muttered, "What's He saying? We're not good enough to see miracles here in Nazareth? We don't measure up to Capernaum? We aren't as good as them?"

Even the woman who had spoken kindly of Yeshua was cowed into submission.

For my part, I studied Barak. How would he respond to the controversy? He was silent, but his face provided the answer: it was irate and hate-filled.

Another member of the women's gallery suggested, "It's not as if He's anybody! What's this about 'anointed'? Isn't He the carpenter? Haven't I known His family forever? Scraping by, just like the rest of us! Where does He get off, putting on airs?"

The seven unseen voices shrilled; triumphant echoes of what I heard around me: *"See? Joanna was wrong! Yeshua is nothing. He's arrogant. He's full of himself. What right does he have?"*

The buzz of resentment increased to a hum of challenge. The air was filled with a confused clamor to match that inside my head. Hands waved over agitated faces; then fists.

Barak bar Halfi drew every eye to himself when

he rose before the congregation. In a dramatic gesture he deliberately tore the lapel of his robe. "Blasphemy!" he cried. "We *are* witnesses, but not in the way He—" here he leveled an accusatory finger at Yeshua—"not as He would have it. Blasphemy, I say, and I denounce it!"

Other men leapt to their feet and imitated Barak.

Over the rising tumult I could barely hear Yeshua: "There were many people with leprosy in Israel during the time of the prophet Elisha; but not one of them was healed. Only Naaman the Syrian was healed." [Luke 4:27]

My portly neighbor loudly commented, "So He's saying we have leprosy? We're the living dead?"

"We're not as good as some pagan Syrian?" yelped another woman.

A clamorous rank of men, led by Barak, surged forward, urged on by their screaming, gesticulating women. Barak and others seized Yeshua by the arms. The husky shammash grabbed Him from behind.

Were they going to throw Him out? Or were they angry enough to do something far worse?

The penalty for blasphemy was stoning! Death by a mob pelting you with stones is not a pleasant way to die. . . . battered and crushed.

I had endured nightmares about being stoned.

Adultery was punished in the same way.

The refrain in my head became a chanted exaltation of celebration.

Rattling the lattice screen and shouting "Please, stop!" Joanna was alternately weeping and begging. "Wait! Here's proof of His words. Here's my son. He healed my son in Capernaum. Won't you listen? In Capernaum!"

But they would not listen. The mob had passed a point of being reasonable.

Small body racked with sobs Boaz pleaded, "What are they doing, Mama? Make them stop."

It was no longer possible to see what was happening in the main body of the synagogue. The last glimpse I had of Yeshua before He was obscured by the mob was of Him being pulled in two directions as if they would split Him asunder.

Then someone yelled, "Stone Him," and there was a general stampede toward the exits.

Had that scream of rage really happened or did it exist only in my mind? Or did all the other red-faced, furious participants hear the voices?

It was almost impossible to move and the bottleneck at the doorway was frightening, yet I found myself swept along like a bit of bark on a raging torrent through a constricted canyon. After being caught in the crush of women trying to escape the confines of the gallery, I had an even harder time pushing through the exterior crowd. The closely packed semi-circle of onlookers outside the building had no comprehension of what was happening and were trying to get in, even as we fought to emerge.

I heard Yeshua's mother calling out to Him and for Him and against the fury of the horde of haters. "Stop!" she cried, trying to break through to her son. "Please, dear friends, don't do this! Oh, please stop!"

Again and again she begged her neighbors to spare the life of her boy, but they ignored, or were deaf to, her every plea.

Even when I finally emerged from the press into breathing space it was impossible to separate the howling of the mob from the screeching in my head. "Stone Him!" I shouted, my voice lost amid the uproar. "Stone Him! Stone Him!" I was laughing with hysterical delight. This great healer, this miracle worker; couldn't even save Himself! Being righteous is no better than being wicked. Either way people would despise you and hunt for ways to destroy you.

"Stone Him!" I chanted, my invisible companions urging me on.

By now I realized there would be no stoning. The mob was too ready for the kill to pause even long enough for an execution. Instead they were going to hurl Yeshua over the cliff at the edge of town.

Barak bar Halfi on one side and the shammash on the other hurried the soon-to-be extinct holy man to the precipice.

At the very brink the crowd halted and the volume of the verbal assault diminished, though not the chorus inside me: *"Kill Him! Push Him over! He's no one! Arrogant! Prideful! Does He think He's the messiah? Away with Him! Do it now!"*

I saw Yeshua face the shammash—a man He had known perhaps all His life. There was no fear on Yeshua's face. I could not read what was written there, but it was not fear.

Even on the edge of death Yeshua looked in each irate countenance. They all knew Him well; had watched Him grow up among them.

And He knew them.

Even across the distance still separating me from the scene I watched the synagogue attendant release his hold and withdraw. He looked down at his hands and at the cliff edge as if he could not fathom what he was doing there; as if his body had been operating without his direction. Then he covered his face and backed away in evident confusion.

Under Yeshua's steady, bold examination Barak also released Yeshua. Barak's arms hung limply at his sides, and his expression registered bewilderment.

Then I watched as Yeshua stepped between the two men. The crowd likewise parted for Him. No one moved to stop Him. No one tried to intercept Him. No one threw a stone.

The chanted hatred died away.

On all sides the attackers fell back as if struck by invisible hands. They reeled away from Him as crowds withdraw from a leper.

Yeshua studied each face, registering acquaintances and marking neighbors. There was no anger, no bitterness, but I read there . . . what?

Yeshua's mother called out to Him in tones stricken with grief, but He did not acknowledge her. He strode away into a silence as complete as a tomb's.

His back toward His hometown, I watched Yeshua's form diminish as He walked away from Nazareth and from the mob.

Chapter 19

Even though Yeshua walked through the crowd and disappeared, the tumult in Nazareth did not immediately subside. Groups of outraged, pride-damaged men, egged on by some of their women, scoured the neighborhood looking for him.

Fights broke out between the most irate and a handful of Yeshua's neighbors who dared speak well of Him. Any who suggested waiting for tempers to cool were threatened or called blasphemers. Homes were broken into as some of the less belligerent were accused of "harboring a blasphemer."

He was not located, of course.

Apart from the most vigilant of the haters, the rest of the community and its visitors attempted to make sense of what they had seen and heard. In small groups they recounted, discussed, dissected, and deliberated.

No conclusion was offered without being challenged. Long-time friends eyed each other with suspicion.

Instead of shrieking, my inner voices bubbled over with ecstatic, unrepressed laughter at the scene. Occasionally the interior merriment erupted as an outburst from my own lips.

It was during one of these fits of hilarity I located Joanna and Boaz. She was seated on a boulder, on the hillside overlooking the village, as Boaz dabbled in a shallow stream, launching twig boats into the current.

Joanna's eyes were red-rimmed from crying, but when I approached they narrowed in anger.

Trying to make light of the whole farce I suggested, "So much for your holy man. Worthy of a circus in Rome, I'd say." As I seated myself beside her she twitched aside the hem of her robe. "Except . . . He did get away with his life," I added. "Never would have ended like that in Rome."

Joanna neither laughed at my joke nor spoke. Instead her gaze was fixed on her son.

"Well, what did you expect?" I asked.

Scooting still further away, Joanna said through clenched teeth, "You're mad! You must be mad."

Surprised by the violent rebuff I tried again to lighten the mood. Shrugging, I agreed: "We've known that for some time, haven't we?"

"You were screaming. Screaming!" Joanna said in accusation. "And laughing."

When she put it that way it sounded crazy, so I lied. "I don't recall."

"Yelling he should be stoned. 'Stone Him! Kill Him!'"

Uneasily, defensively, I protested, "So was everyone else."

Stretching out her palm toward her son she turned a withering stare on me. "I took Boaz away. Didn't want him to see or hear you like that. Didn't want him to witness it if you killed the man who saved his life!"

"Me? I killed no one."

"But you cheered for His death! It's the same as if you hurled the first stone."

Desperately wanting to shift the subject away from myself, I said, "You don't know He healed Bo. It could be coincidence. Bo might have gotten well anyway. I've always thought so."

"Shut up. Shut up!" Joanna rebuked, bristling and shaking as if barely restrained from striking me. "I know what Yeshua did. Kuza knows. Maximus knows. Yeshua is . . ."

Plucking a handful of grass I tossed it at her. "A what? A charlatan? He's arrogant, that's certain. The messiah? Come now, Joanna! You don't believe that. These people know Him better than anyone. They all know what He is and what He is not. A maker of tables and chairs, not a prophet! Chests for bar mitzvah gifts and cupboards for weddings and . . . and hoe handles for farmers." I loaded my words with as much disdain as I could muster, trying to break through to her; make her see reason. "His mother pregnant before she was married. A lot of speculation—" I let the word hang in the air— "about who His father really is. Maybe even . . . a Roman soldier."

I rejoiced to recite the list of sins alleged against Yeshua's mother. Somehow accusing a so-called prophet of having a tainted past vindicated me.

Joanna replied stiffly, "That's rich, that is! Condemnation of Him . . . coming from you? Even the devil laughs at that."

"Well, at most He's a clever magician."

Icily, Joanna challenged, "And . . . at worst?"

Was she listening? Admitting she might have been duped? "A self-deluded . . ."

Joanna's hand slashed downward like the killing stroke of a Roman sword. "That's enough! No more. I won't hear it." Like a snake striking at me her other palm snapped up and pressed across my lips. "I don't want you around Bo anymore. Not at all. Don't try. I thought . . . I hoped Yeshua could help you, but you're crazy."

"Me?" I was stunned. Recovering my defenses I flung sarcasm in her teeth: "You think this country bumpkin is the messiah, and I'm the crazy one?"

Joanna wasn't listening; seemed unaffected by my jab, except she sounded weary. "And me. Hoped he could help me. Maybe He still can."

"So that's it," I taunted. "Needing a challenge? Thought you could seduce the famous rabbi? Fill up your miserable life. Get back at Kuza by. . . ." I was angry now, willing to say anything to hurt, to wound, to defeat her.

Joanna stared back in stony silence. "What if you're beyond hope, Mary?" she said dully.

Flustered by the way she had bolted an emotional lock I replied, "I've been saying that for years."

"As a joke. What if it's true? But listen: I reject you. I turn my back on you. I renounce you, and all your lies, and all your works."

The hair on the back of my neck bristled, and a whining, as of a mosquito, buzzed inside my head. Joanna had recited the formula for the rite of exorcism—for casting out a demon.

"Joanna? Joanna! My friend!" I protested.

"Don't call me friend!" she responded

menacingly. "You're not welcome in my home, Mary. If you see me in the street, I'll turn away. Save yourself the bother and the shame . . . if you're still capable of feeling any. Don't speak to my child or try to contact us in any way. Pity is wasted in you. Your brother and sister are right to reject you."

Covering my ears with my hands I cried, "Don't! Please stop!"

Joanna, once roused, was relentless. "You are. . . . a bottomless pit. A well of selfishness that cannot be filled. You say you only want to be loved? You don't even know the meaning of the word!"

"Please, don't!"

"And when love finally, for once, gets close enough for you to touch . . . near enough for you to grasp, what do you do? You imagine it must be something else . . . something filthy, something trivial . . . like you, Mary. Just like you. Hear me," she pronounced with finality. "You are dead to me."

"Don't!" I pleaded.

Putting both palms to her forehead in frustration Joanna concluded: "I don't need this."

Calling Boaz sharply to her side, Joanna seized his wrist and stormed out away from me.

I was dazed, confused and exhausted. For the moment there were no voices in my head.

Even they had left me.

By the time I dragged myself upright and wandered back to the inn Joanna had departed.

I trudged back to Magdala alone, brooding all the while about what I considered Joanna's mistreatment of me. When I entered the gates of my house, she was inside, sitting beside the fountain.

Her expression was one of sorrow and regret.

"What are you doing here?" I asked.

"Mary," she began to speak, paused, then spread her hands. "I am concerned for you."

Once again anger boiled up inside me. "Concerned for me? I'm fine. What are you saying? What do you mean?"

"I am your friend. And I . . ."

"Oh, so now we're friends again? Just like that? No, I don't think so. You shout at me, you accuse me. You think something is wrong with me because I can't fawn over your new prophet? What's happened to you?"

Joanna sighed. "A lot has happened to me. I almost lost my son. If it hadn't been for Yeshua . . ."

I held my hands up in a gesture that told her I did not want to hear more. "I've had enough. Heard enough. Seen enough. Just leave me alone!"

"You don't want that."

"I do! Leave me alone! Let me choose my own way of life."

"Mary, I know . . . in spite of everything. Even

after what happened today . . . I know Yeshua can help you."

At those words I turned my back and left her. I do not know how long she stayed. I told myself that I was in control of my own life. I was the one who no longer wanted her friendship.

But as the weeks passed, my loneliness increased.

Chapter 20

I heard from Tavita that though the chasm between Maximus and me could not be crossed, still I had one friend who defended me. I had turned my back on Joanna, but she did not turn her heart away from me. She knew I was desperate and lost and still she loved me. I believe she prayed for me.

Tavita was my lifeline. The old woman heard all the gossip from Joanna's servants in the marketplace. I made her repeat every detail. The reports that came back were surprising. Maximus and Kuza had become fast friends, changed by their desperate journey to find Yeshua on the night Boaz lay dying. Now the two men worked together on a plan to rebuild the synagogue in Capernaum.

Once Joanna spoke to Maximus quietly, asking him if he heard what happened in Nazareth.

Maximus admitted he knew the presence of

Yeshua had provoked a riot. He admitted, "I believe Mary's friend, Barak bar Halfi, had something to do with stirring up the opposition. And Mary followed the mob with a stone in her hand. I hope Yeshua will do a better job staying out of trouble. He's no business of mine . . . or Rome's."

She asked, "Even after what you have witnessed? Is this what you will tell Pilate? No business of Rome's?"

"Believe me, it is better for Yeshua if many of us Romans tell other Romans to look the other way and stay away from him."

Joanna seemed to understand that reasoning. There was safety for Yeshua in obscurity. "But Mary is your concern."

Maximus snapped, "Not any longer."

"Maximus, something happened to her. Something inside her soul."

He shrugged, "What's that to me?"

"She's not herself."

"Insane, you mean. Mary Magdalene is no concern of mine, no matter what you may say."

Joanna would not draw back in her defense of me, though Kuza tried to silence her.

"She was cheering when Barak took the lead in trying to kill Yeshua. And this after seeing Boaz healed. I lost my temper with her. But what I saw in her eyes then . . . something terrible has taken hold of her, and I'm worried."

Maximus seemed cold to Joanna's concerns. "She and Barak were lovers. You can't be surprised she would follow after him. You can't think she wanted to meet Yeshua. She went there because she knew Barak would be there. It was his baby she got rid of."

At this accusation, Joanna exploded. "It was your child. Mary had never been with any man but you since you met!"

Kuza tried to intervene, but the battle was joined. "Joanna. Don't be rude to our guest . . . our Roman guest."

Joanna did not back down. "The only reason she went to Bamah for an abortion was to keep you coming 'round! She thought getting rid of the baby was what you wanted!"

Maximus grew thoughtful. "It never was. I did not wish that."

Joanna persisted to uncover the truth. "I was with her the night you left her so cruelly. It was your child, Maximus. And you're the reason she traveled to Bamah. She was desperate to keep you. The incantations of Owb have driven her quite mad. I don't know if she will let me speak to her, but I am afraid she will harm herself unless someone intervenes."

"And you think I could?"

"I think you are the only one who can."

Tavita repeated this gossip to me over supper. "So, my lamb, perhaps they both still love you.

Perhaps time will heal this wound as time heals all wounds."

"Not all." I pretended to be cool and unconcerned.

I was secretly delighted that Joanna had defended me to Maximus. Regret stirred in me that Maximus had not wished for me to end the life of our baby. If only I had known, how different my life might have been. At the same time I was insulted that they spoke of me with such pity and contempt.

The confusion of my thoughts and feelings brought tears of rage.

As for myself, I hated Yeshua, blaming Him for my breach with Joanna. But in the swirling thoughts of the *others* who possessed my mind, I hoped losing Joanna might still help me bring back Barak.

I had one plan. I believed I had one chance.

I decided I would make myself an ally in the official war against Yeshua. Barak would love me for my loyalty, I reasoned.

I sat down to scratch out a letter to Barak. Here is a true copy of that letter. I let my venom spill out lie upon lie.

Dear Barak,

I know how in Nazareth you bravely led the people to drive out the arrogant false prophet Yeshua from the synagogue. I have seen that wherever He goes people become divided. Families and friendships are broken. Yeshua has come to reside in Capernaum, and fools flock to Him like lost sheep needing a shepherd. Just as you question Him, so do wise teachers. He has been examined by the great men and declared to be a servant of Beelzebub. I myself have given up a good friend who believes Yeshua performs miracles and proclaims truth. She will not speak to me because I do not agree. Now word comes that you have severed your friendship with my brother El'azar over this. Yeshua is a danger to us all. If ever you are in Magdala please call on me. I would like to make amends for my stupidity.

Mary

I hoped for a reply from Barak, but I did not expect it to come so soon. Tavita awakened me near midnight and told me I must get up.

I was groggy from wine. "Has something happened?"

The old woman was not happy to give me the news. "Barak bar Halfi is here."

I gasped and spoke with joy. "Barak here? Alone?" It had only been one week since I sent my message to him.

Tavita was disgusted and did not attempt to conceal her disapproval of my actions. "Alone.

He says he just arrived in Magdala and that you two have unfinished business. Something about the bulbs and saffron."

The bulbs were still stored in a cool cellar. Dormant, like I imagined my life to be, waiting for the sunlight of Barak to shine upon them. My confidence bloomed and with it a coy arrogance. I would make him wait.

"Tell him I have to dress. Tell him I'll be down. Show him to my private garden. Let him sit beside the fountain. Two goblets of wine. A single candle."

Of course Tavita knew my plan to seduce him. She scowled at me and closed the door. No point arguing with me. I had long ago set my plan in motion. Adultery was no longer a fleeting temptation. I had planted the seed and cultivated it until tonight it would yield a harvest from my hours of longing.

Looking at my own image in the bronze mirror I liked what I saw, and I knew Barak would be unable to resist me. My skin glowed through the thin fabric of my shift. I wrapped myself in a shawl and imagined his reaction when I let it slip accidentally. I was an actress in a play, rehearsing my part.

I brushed my hair and daubed perfume on my throat, wrists and behind my knees, getting ready for my scene. Descending the stairs, I let the wrap slide off one shoulder. I entered the garden silently and hung back for a moment, allowing my scent to fill the air. From the shadows I observed as he raised his head and inhaled deeply the aroma of my perfume, then stared intently at the flame. I knew the look on his face. He was thinking about me, wanting me. But propriety and hypocrisy demanded that he not show me his desire.

He was also acting in a play.

The breeze ruffled my gown as I moved, carrying my perfume to him; alerting him that I was near. He turned, searching the shadows for me.

It was my cue. Clutching the shawl and feigning innocence, I stepped from the shadows and let him drink in my image. He swallowed hard and looked away. Blinking as though he had been blinded by lightning, he looked back and this time did not turn away.

"I don't know why I came," he lied, spreading his hands in a gesture of helplessness.

I smiled and took a hesitant step toward him. Letting go of the wrap, I pretended to attempt to retrieve it as it slipped to the ground at my feet.

This dance of forbidden passion was superbly planned. Resistance. Yielding. Protest. Urging. We managed to maintain some illusion of our own helplessness, though we both knew better.

Did he consider his wife and children? Perhaps, but they paled compared to what I gave him.

Afterwards, we pledged our love and determined we must keep this night, and those that were ahead, a secret.

In all this, we lied to one another and to ourselves. We played our parts in the unholy game of adultery.

I did not remember that any man who would betray the wife of his sacred vows could not be trusted in anything. He was false to his core and so was I.

Barak was destined to betray his lover as well.

Chapter 21

My waking hours revolved around the moment when I would see Barak again. Tavita heard the news that his wife was pregnant, and this, my servant told me, was the reason he was so eager to be with me. I confronted him with the information and he did not deny it.

"Pregnant? Yes. She is my wife, after all, even though I have never loved anyone but you."

I believed him, telling myself such details did not matter, as long as we were together.

Barak was a skilled deceiver, creating fictional reasons why he needed to be away from his family. Every lie he told her was meant to conceal that he was in my bed.

My pleasure was tempered by fear. After all, adultery was an offense punishable by stoning.

Barak could not divorce his pregnant wife. I believed the time would come when he would divorce her, and then he would be mine without deception.

However, things began to change. His visits became less frequent. Our conversation had an irritated edge, and he looked at me with disdain.

As time neared for his wife to deliver the child, he put off a visit to me for the third time in a month. I was not patient, sending him notes that pleaded and messages that scolded.

When I slept, I dreamed of him, reaching into the darkness for him.

When he came to me at last I could not bear for him to be out of my sight for a second. He looked at me with such revulsion and boredom that I knew he had grown weary of acting in the play.

When it was time for him to return to Nazareth, I begged him not to leave; to stay an hour longer. He called me childish and dangerous. I shouted he did not love me any longer. To this charge, he did not reply.

When I threatened to kill myself, he turned his back on me with stony indifference and stalked out of the house.

I commanded Tavita to follow him; certain that he must have some other mistress in the village. When she returned to me hours later, I could not believe her report.

"He went to the caravansary," Tavita declared.

"It is another woman, then?"

"It is his wife he swears he loves."

"How can you say this? You're lying," I shouted.

"Suit yourself!" The old woman was adamant. She did not say the words, "I told you so," but she could have said them.

"Tell me what you know."

"The brother of his wife was there to confront him. There was a great deal of shouting. Barak says you are nothing but a common trollop. He says you have filled his need because his woman turned him away. He says you have many lovers and make no distinction if a man is married if only he will pay you a good price."

I felt as though she had taken a knife and shoved it into my heart. I could not breathe. Could not weep. The blood drained from my head and I had to sit down before I fell.

"He couldn't."

"There's more. He offered to give his time in your bed to a Roman soldier in the caravansary. He said it would not matter to you as long as you were paid well."

I shouted at her, disbelieving her warning. "He didn't! He wouldn't! I don't believe you! My brother has paid you to slander him! Get out! Get out!" I threw a vase at her as she escaped from the bedchamber.

I remained in the dark room, curtains closed,

for many days. Tavita brought me my food and cajoled me to take bits of nourishment.

The voices in my head urged me to go to the water; to swim toward the light; to meet my mother somewhere beneath the depths. Only the belief that Tavita had lied kept me living.

Days of misery passed, and then weeks. Word came that Barak's wife had delivered a healthy baby girl, but that the woman was desperately ill on her childbed. I rejoiced that she might die, leaving Barak a widower, and clearing the way for me to marry him without scandal. Slowly she recovered, yet I did not give up hope that he would leave her.

The voices whispered to me as I walked on the shore:

"Make him jealous."

"The play is not over."

"Don't let him know you love him."

"Hurt him with jealousy as he has hurt you by returning to his family."

I knew he was too proud to think of me enjoying the constant love of another man. Late one night I wrote him a note. It was sane and reasoned, congratulating him on the birth of his daughter. I wished him well and told him how happy I was with new company. I did not tell him I was driven to madness since his betrayal, but I invited him to stop by with his family if ever they were in Magdala.

• • •

Only days passed before I received a reply to my message. It was scrawled in Barak's familiar, untrained handwriting. I rolled the papyrus into a scarf and carried it above my heart. To the wonder of Tavita and the servants I seemed myself again. My heart was light and happy. I gathered flowers in the gardens and placed them in vases around the house.

Though old Tavita suspected something, I did not speak a word to reveal my secret. The message from Barak was meant for my eyes alone.

I am coming to Magdala. I will be alone at the midnight watch. Third day after the new moon, be at the orchard gate.

Chapter 22

The quarter moon smiled down from the midst of countless stars. The servants had gone to bed, and I alone was awake.

On the lake the lanterns of night fishermen bobbed and gleamed from their boats as they worked for their catch.

Feeling exhilarated, I bathed in the dark waters, then dressed and perfumed myself, preparing for my clandestine meeting. I arranged every sensory delight. My bed was made up with fresh, crisp linens covered in rose petals. I filled the oil lamps, wanting my image to burn in his mind long after he was gone.

Before the hour of our reunion I left the house and walked through the olive orchard to wait for him beside the gate. Constellations drifted above me. The air was scented with the aromas of sage and jasmine.

Some time passed. He was nearly a half hour late. After an hour, when he did not come, I began to fret. I was filled with anger that he could keep me waiting when I only wanted him.

Then I was worried that something had happened to him.

I knew bar Abba's bandits were at work between my home and Nazareth. I imagined dreadful things. I pictured him on the road—injured, with no one to help him.

Just when I thought I could stand the waiting no longer I heard a muffled voice call to me playfully from the other side of the gate, "Mary!"

With a cry of joy I threw back the bolt and fell into the arms of his shadowed figure. "Where were you?" I demanded as he kissed me eagerly.

He did not answer, but held me tightly as he entered the garden and kicked the gate closed.

He was rough and demanding. I protested, gently at first, and then tried to free myself from his grasp. "Barak! Please! Not here!"

Laughing, he enjoyed the struggle. And then I knew the terrible truth: It was not Barak who held me.

"Who are you? Let me go!" I cried.

"Barak bar Halfi seemed to think you were woman enough to satisfy Rome! We'll see."

The accent was Roman. His hands were rough and cruel. Was he a bandit? A deserter from the army? Had he killed Barak?

"What have you done? Have you hurt him?"

I bit his wrist and tore free, attempting to escape. He roared and chased me through the darkness and caught me, throwing me down and pinning my shoulders to the ground.

He sneered. "I always wondered why Maximus thought so highly of you. But I see there's plenty of fight in you!"

Still I struggled, fighting to escape, but he was as strong as an animal. "Where is Barak?"

His face inches from mine, his rancid breath smelled of wine. "Home with his wife. I told him I would personally bring you the message he couldn't come. So . . . I have come in his place." He held me fast in the dirt and clamped his hand over my mouth. "Harlot of Magdala, I pay better than Barak or Maximus."

Madness claimed me after that terrible night. I knew what I was; how others perceived me.

Barak had betrayed me to the Roman Vara.

There was no longer a question of loving or being loved.

As I walked through the souk of my village, I was aware that Jewish men turned their faces from me, shielding their eyes as I approached.

Jewish mothers held their children back lest my shadow touch them.

Only the Roman soldiers looked at me unashamedly. They whispered and grinned as they discussed me openly.

"It's that woman. Hey! Come here."

"I only entertain officers. Or very rich and handsome fellows. You are neither," I remarked as I strolled past. No pretense was left to me.

Word of the pleasures I offered spread even as my spirit collapsed within me.

I no longer had to search for companionship. I dined only with wealthy, strong men who brought me gifts and entertained me over sumptuous meals with stories of faraway lands.

It is true that I rewarded those who pleased me. Those whom I judged unworthy, foolish, or boring I turned out on the street after supper. I was very selective about who I allowed to stay the night.

It was said that the Courtesan of Magdala became a legend discussed in taverns from Jerusalem to Rome. The fantasy far overreached the reality I gave my guests.

I was mad, after all, and my madness erupted

234

violently in the quiet moments of the night. None among my suitors dared mention to others the violence and fury I displayed. Perhaps each man believed he was the only one to disappoint me. Better to explain claw marks on a face as passion.

The reality was that every man was a disappointment. I loved no one; hated them all. I despised myself for what I had become.

There was no way of escape or redemption for me.

I could no longer bargain with Hebrew merchants. They ignored me and tossed whatever I touched into the charity basket as hopelessly defiled.

Though no one called "unclean" as I walked through the souk, being on the same street with me was something to be avoided.

Chapter 23

I became arrogant; defiant in my way of life; believing everyone else was a hypocrite. I was hated by the *am ha aretz*, the common folk who had families and who lived according to the Torah.

But what did it matter?

I held my head up when I heard the whispers as I passed a group of women in the market square.

Still it surprised me when the piping voice of Boaz called out to me in public, "Aunt Mary!"

Turning, I saw the child darting through the crowd. He ran right to me, his face full of joy as he wrapped his arms around my waist. I stood rooted and rigid, stripped of my brazen air. I felt unclean; unworthy to be touched by a child.

He grinned up at me. "Aunt Mary! Where have you been? Mama and I went to your house. You weren't there. Tavita said you went to market looking for something. We couldn't find you!"

I drew myself erect as I caught sight of Simon the Pharisee glaring at me. Then I sank to my knees and wrapped my arms around Boaz. "I am glad to see you, Bo. You've grown."

He made a muscle to show me. "Yes. Feel this. I am so strong, Uncle Maximus says I am strong enough to fight a lion."

As I tested the little arm, I was aware the gossips were buzzing. "Very well done."

"And Uncle Maximus says . . ."

Abruptly the image of Maximus swept over me. Could it be that he remained close to Joanna and Kuza after everything? Had brought him into the circle of their lives while I had been cut out? Emotion constricted my throat. A wave of loneliness washed over me. I missed the old days, the fun times, but I would not let the jackals of Magdala see I cared.

Through the crowded market, beyond a heap of

limes, I spotted Joanna. Her beautiful red hair glistened in the sunlight. More than that, her face shone with joy. Everything about her demeanor had changed. She was happy and radiant.

She raised her hand to me in greeting as though nothing had ever happened. Did she not know I had gained a reputation as a notorious harlot in the Galil?

"Mary! Shalom! Oh, my friend! We've been looking for you everywhere!"

I withdrew my arms from Boaz and stood, expecting Joanna to scold me or pick up the quarrel where we had left it, but she said nothing. Her gaze locked on my eyes and I saw a flash of sorrow and compassion.

Why was Joanna so excited? Why had she come to find me? We could not speak in public.

Joanna grasped my arm and propelled me from the crowds. "I hope you were finished shopping."

I did not tell her I had come to the market in hopes of meeting some man to keep me company tonight. I did not admit that my life had come to that low point.

Joanna headed toward a copse of trees beyond the synagogue. Boaz raced ahead. Like a puppy he bounded around us, to and fro. When he leapt onto the trunk of a fallen tree he instructed us we must talk together in the shade.

"So sit, Mary." Joanna was smiling, gentle in her excitement.

I resisted. Bitterness tinged my happiness at seeing a friendly face. "Why are you here? I am anathema. To speak to me is a sin. You must know that! Are you taunting me?"

Joanna waved my self-pity away. "Forget all that."

"I'd like to, but it's impossible. So?"

"I've been thinking . . ."

"A dangerous thing for a woman these days."

Joanna laughed, "You're right. But nonetheless . . ."

Boaz let the secret out. "The rebbe is coming to our house tomorrow to teach! To our very own house! I told Mama and Papa that I wanted Aunt Mary to come too! You must come!"

Looking down at my hands, I realized Joanna had come to find me at the request of her little boy. I could not help taking offense. They wanted me to hear Yeshua, the rabbi. I did not raise my eyes lest Boaz see my disdain for the suggestion. How dare they come here to drag me off to hear the one who had caused our rift in the first place?

Boaz sat down beside me. "I want you to meet Yeshua, the one who made me well."

Joanna agreed. "Bo thought of you first. When we talked about who we should invite, he said all he wanted was for Aunt Mary to come. After all, you were there when he was healed."

I was cool. "Yes I was. And I was also there

when Yeshua's neighbors decided He was a false prophet."

Joanna remained calm in the face of my resentment. "Mary, please come." Then she told Boaz to go play at the water's edge while we talked.

Every heartache I had spilled over.

"I've been without a friend for nine months, since that day in Nazareth. And my best friend told me she never wanted to see me again. And never wanted her child to come near me. You know what I have become. Oh well, I always was what I am now, only now I have no hypocrisy. Not worse than when I knew you, only more open. You have good reason for wanting to keep Boaz away from me."

Joanna took my hand. "No. I was wrong."

I shook my head. "You weren't wrong. I can't come to your house. Your Rebbe Yeshua will be the first to throw a stone at me."

"He's not like that."

"I've never seen a rabbi who isn't."

Joanna tried to lift my chin, but I could not look into her eyes. She said, "Mary, if only you could hear Him, you would know. Mary, He's not like anyone else. Not anyone in the world! He can somehow see into the hearts of people who meet Him."

"So. That lets me out. Oh, what He would see if He looked into the blackness of my heart! I am . .

. the madness that is there. Do you suppose it's my mother's madness? At least she put an end to her insanity. I'm still alive . . . barely. The only way I can forget my unhappiness is to be with a man. So much darkness there is no room for myself anymore. Lies and anger and . . . I don't know where I've gone! I am lost, Joanna! Lost!"

"Come home with me, Mary. Yeshua can help you sort it out. Find yourself again under all that."

Without emotion I said, "Nothing left of me to save."

Still she urged me, "Come home with us. And if you don't like what He says you can leave. But you won't find what you are searching for in the souk. You won't find happiness in a man."

"I don't know what I am searching for."

"What we're all searching for. Love. Mercy. Some way to start over. To be born again with a soul bright and clean. Perfect. Like a newborn baby."

"No power on earth can give me that."

"Only come. Just as you are. Hear what He has to say." Joanna was compelling. "See for yourself, or you'll never know if you have missed your chance."

Chapter 24

Despite my misgivings and my doubts, I let Joanna entice me to her home to hear Yeshua speak once again. I was so grateful to have Joanna back in my life, to have any company in my crippling loneliness that I wanted to please her. While I had no expectations for myself I was willing to take a risk for the sake of her friendship.

Kuza's home was jammed with onlookers. A hundred invitations had gone out; perhaps seven hundred curious souls crowded into every available space in hallways and doors and hanging in at windows. The steward himself was not present. Joanna openly supported Yeshua and welcomed Him, but Kuza hoped by his absence to placate Herod Antipas if Yeshua's visit became known.

How could it not become known? Every village around the northern end of Sea of Galilee was represented, and many eager listeners had traveled much further than that.

The decorative pool in the center of the terrace glowed pleasantly with torchlight and much of the chamber was illuminated as well. While the flickering flames focused attention on the center of the space as if it were a stage, they also left the corners in deep shadow.

It was into one of these gloomy recesses I tucked myself, out of the way of attention and, I hoped, away from recognition and malicious comment.

In grimmer moments I imagined myself being driven from Kuza's home. Would "the Famous Harlot of Magdala" be discovered and flogged through the streets?

Why had I come? What a fearful, stupid risk to take.

Fear of such an outcome make me shiver and drove me to think of escape. It was already too late. Flight from the packed space would practically mean climbing over people. Such a clamor would draw to me the very attention I sought to avoid.

I shrank back even further into my corner and willed myself to become anonymous.

Others were not concerned with being recognized, or indeed, they expected and encouraged it. Pompous religious figures, like the wealthy Simon the Pharisee, were easily identified by their rich robes and broad phylacteries. Simon radiated piety and dripped scorn like an oil lamp in a high wind. His glare alone was enough to keep a space around him clear of other spectators, even if his oversize girth could not.

"Love your enemies," Yeshua preached that day. "And pray for those who persecute you, so that you may be sons of your Father who is in heaven." [Matt. 5:44-45] The Teacher stood in the center of the room. He exhibited quiet confidence despite the scowls evident on the faces of many skeptics.

His was unlike any other message I had ever heard. Others were astonished and challenged as well.

"If you love those who love you, what reward do you have? Do not even the tax collectors do the same?" [Matt. 5:46]

Across the room from Simon the Pharisee was Levi Mattityahu the Tax Collector. From my vantage point I saw their eyes meet and instantly dart away. It was clear to me neither man could imagine loving the other. Hyper-religious Pharisees regarded Roman appointed publicans as unclean apostates, and not Jews at all.

Tax collectors returned the scorn with interest, justified so Levi would have said, by the fact Simon was a pious fraud and a hypocrite.

The hostile warmth of their mutual glares would have lit the room even without the torches, but Yeshua continued speaking as if He had not noticed the effect of His words. "If you forgive others their trespasses, your heavenly Father will also forgive you, but if you do not forgive others their trespasses, neither will your Father forgive your trespasses." [Matt. 6:14-15]

Simon redirected his glower toward Yeshua.

Pharisees rarely felt the need of forgiveness for themselves. Instead they occupied their lives in pointing out others' faults.

In any case, this message seemed futile. Bitter rivals such as tax collectors and Pharisees were more likely to pray for their opponents to be utterly crushed.

Bribing the gods to be on your side in a conflict had universal appeal. Hadn't Maximus told me of a sacred spring in Rome dedicated to Jove that stopped flowing? When the priests investigated, they found it clogged with prayers inscribed on clay tablets, tossed in by worshippers asking for Jove's aid.

As they examined the votive offerings they found fully half the prayers were curses leveled against enemies; as many as all the other requests combined.

Forgiveness and tolerance did not seem to be a natural part of people. Perhaps the standard Yeshua required was impossible to keep.

The moment after I remembered Maximus' words I saw him standing not far from Levi. I ducked back again, hoping he had not seen me. Claudia, Governor Pilate's wife, stood nearby, so perhaps Maximus was part of her bodyguard detail.

He did not seem to have noticed me.

Now Yeshua embarked on a story: "There was a man who had two sons. And the younger of them said to his father, 'Father, give me the share of property that is coming to me.' " [Matt. 15:11-12]

All around me I heard indignant noises. Such a request was unbelievably rude. It was the same as wishing for the father's death!

Yeshua certainly had the crowd's attention, including mine.

"And he divided his property between them," the rabbi continued. [Matt. 15:12]

"That father's a fool," I overheard someone mutter.

"Not many days later, the younger son gathered all he had and took a journey into a far country, and there he squandered his property in reckless living. And when he had spent everything, a severe famine arose in that country, and he began to be in need." [Matt.15:13-14]

"Serves him right," a listener commented.

"Shhh," three others replied.

"So he went and hired himself out to one of the citizens of that country, who sent him into his fields to feed pigs. And he was longing to be fed with the pods the pigs ate, and no one gave him anything." [Matt.15:15-16]

I marveled at what impressive speaking ability was demonstrated by this country preacher from rustic Nazareth. As quickly as He had made us resent the greedy son He also made us feel a twinge of pity for him.

The *am ha aretz* understood what it was to be

hungry and in want and forced into unpleasant labor.

The well-to-do politicians hated the notion of a freeborn heir having to do menial labor.

The pious religious folk objected most to the daily contact with the most unclean of all unclean animals.

Yeshua had all these diverse folk in rapt attention.

"But when he came to himself, he said, 'How many of my father's hired servants have more than enough bread, but I perish here with hunger! I will arise and go to my father, and I will say to him, "Father, I have sinned against heaven and before you. I am no longer worthy to be called your son. Treat me like one of your hired servants."'" [Matt. 15:17-19]

Many of the Pharisees present looked satisfied with this comment. The rude, irresponsible, immoral son had gotten what he deserved, including a permanent reduction in his social standing—all very neat and proper.

Simon the Pharisee's eyebrows drew together. I think he suspected Yeshua was laying a trap.

"And he arose and came to his father." [Matt.15:20]

This part of the story made me wince. I could not imagine returning to my brother and sister. What sort of welcome home would I receive? Being pelted with stones and having the dogs set on me might be the best treatment I could expect. My inner pangs made me want to cry out, "Don't do it!" to the imaginary boy in the tale.

Yeshua resumed, "But while he was still a long way off, his father saw him and felt compassion, and ran and embraced him and kissed him." [Matt. 15:20]

I heard gasps of astonishment from some and saw nods of approval from others.

"And the son said to him, 'Father, I have sinned against heaven and before you. I am no longer worthy to be called your son.' But the father said to his servants, 'Bring quickly the best robe, and put it on him, and put a ring on his hand, and shoes on feet. And bring the fattened calf and kill it, and let us eat and celebrate. For this my son was dead, and is alive again; he was lost, and is found.' And they began to celebrate." [Matt.15:21-24]

That is how the Almighty looked at us, His wayward children? All He demanded was that we recognize our separation from Him and return to Him and He would forgive us?

But how to return? What did that mean? Especially what did it mean for one as distant as me?

The voices in my head were curiously subdued, almost as if something repressed their ability to speak. But when I reached the conclusion that any such forgiveness and restoration would never work for me there was a hum of agreement inside.

Right after that instant this refrain about my family was silently chanted: *"Not your fault. They drove you out. Not your fault. They drove you away. They'd never want you back, anyway. And your brother claims God's on his side. You don't want to go back to anyone that cruel."*

Distracted by this mental discourse I missed the first moments of an interruption. I suddenly caught sight of everyone staring up toward the ceiling. Was it an angel?

A portion of the roof slates had been removed, revealing a hole through which the sky was visible. But only briefly, for an instant later a rectangular object was lowered into the room by ropes attached to its four corners.

What could this mean? Was it a robbery? An attack by rebels?

From outside on the rooftop a voice shouted: "Take the stretcher! Guide it down!"

Four men stepped forward and grasped the handles of what I could now see was a stretcher bearing a sick man. [Luke 5:18-19]

By standing on tiptoe I made out his withered and twisted legs—a cripple, despite the fact he was no more than twenty and strongly muscled through his neck and shoulders.

"Rabbi!" the voice from the roof called, "we couldn't get in by the door! Too crowded! We had to get him in this way. We're his friends, you see."

I had the sense that everyone around me was leaning forward with anticipation. Many had come just for the chance to witness a miracle.

Of course some, like Simon the Pharisee, were equally excited to see Yeshua fail.

Moving to the side of the pallet Yeshua extended His hand.

The paralytic grasped it eagerly.

"Friend," Yeshua said.

There was utter silence in the chamber. There was no chance of fakery here. This man's limbs were misshapen and shrunken. The room was jammed with witnesses.

Even my chattering unseen companions were hushed.

"Friend, your sins are forgiven you." [Luke 5:20]

Involuntarily I jerked my head back as if I'd been slapped in the face.

There was a single heartbeat during which the absolute stillness remained unbroken, then a muttered uproar broke loose.

The crimson on the countenance of Simon the Pharisee suggested a man whose head was about to pop.

Muttered hostilities circled the space. *"Who but God can forgive sin? Who does this man think he is? What sort of blasphemy is this?"* [Luke 5:21]

Or was I hearing the echoes of other people's thoughts?

Yeshua exhibited no concern over the enmity in the throng. In fact, when He spoke again, He said, "Why do you question in your hearts? Which is easier? To say 'your sins are forgiven you,' or to say, 'Rise and walk?'" [Luke 5:22-23]

The buzzing and humming inside me was renewed. It had almost a desperate quality I had not sensed before. Trying to ignore the distraction, I pondered Yeshua's question. No one but the sinner himself could recognize how sinful he was. No one but the sinner himself . . . or herself . . . would know whether forgiveness had been offered and accepted.

How paralyzed and twisted was my soul? I had betrayed everyone and everything I'd ever known. I betrayed my God, my family, myself. *"There's no forgiveness for you,"* my voices sneered. *"Don't even look for it. Your soul is more crippled than that man's legs."*

Could Yeshua really grant release to one whose whole world was a space of canvas little bigger than his contorted body? If He could create a way of escape for one trapped in a rectangle of helplessness, then might He not also be able to . . .

Yeshua words rang out with an air of command: "But that you may know that the Son of Man has authority on earth to forgive sins . . ." Here He leaned down and held the young man by both hands. ". . . I say to you, rise, pick up your bed and go home." [Luke 5:24]

If an earthquake had struck Kuza's home it could not have caused a greater tumult than Yeshua's words and the result.

The cripple leapt to his feet!

Blinking, I rubbed my eyes. Had Yeshua pulled the cripple upright? Would he fall again, a pitiful wretch, at his first step? Was this all a cruel hoax?

But no! I saw with my own eyes the same feet that had been gnarled and useless stood squarely on the paving tiles. The knotted, emaciated calves were muscled and sturdy; the protruding knobs that had been the paralytic's knees were smooth.

No trace of his deformity remained . . . and he was leaping about the room.

Yeshua had to quietly remind the man to retrieve the pallet!

And Yeshua said the healing was the proof the sins were already forgiven.

"But not for you," my companions reminded me. *"Never for you."*

I could no longer bear to remain. While all stared and praised God, or stared with their mouths hanging open, or shouted their own needs to Yeshua, I fled.

Forcing my way through the crowd of amazed

onlookers was like swimming in a sea of mud.

I saw Claudia standing with her eyes wide and her mouth open in astonishment.

I saw a Pharisee fall to his knees and raise his arms toward heaven reciting the blessing: "Blessed art thou, O Lord, King of the Universe, who has permitted us to see this day!"

I saw Levi Mattityahu clutch Maximus' hand while repeating over and over in an awed voice, "Forgiven! Forgiven!"

But not for me. Never for me.

Turning my back to the scene, I ran away, sobbing.

Chapter 25

orgiven?
The word drove me into the darkness like a lash.

Cheers of wonder erupting from Joanna's home pursued me, hounded me. Sounds of joy I could never experience tore at my heels like a pack of wild dogs.

Forgiveness?

For someone, yes, but not for me. Never for me!

Yeshua could straighten the legs of a cripple, but no one could make my twisted soul whole again. Forgiving my sins required too great a miracle, even for someone who turned water into wine.

My life was poison; deadly to me; deadly to anyone I touched. No one could take it and remove just the taint. If the core of my life were removed, there would be nothing else left.

Healing me of what paralyzed me required the restoration of something not merely injured or broken but completely, irrevocably shattered.

I had told so many lies, lived so many lies, I could not even recognize truth if I met it.

Whatever existence I had once possessed now shimmered in pieces like an alabaster bottle shattered against a stone. Flash and color, to no purpose, the original form of my existence was unrecognizable.

And like fragments of glass on the floor of a darkened room, I was a danger to anyone who approached me unwarily.

More shouts of wonder and praise from behind me.

But not for me.

There was no going back . . . not to Joanna; not to El'azar and Marta; not to myself.

The voices applauded my flight: *"Forgiven? Not you. Never you."*

In Yeshua's parable the prodigal's family had left open a door of return. Such an option did not exist for me. No one waited on a hill for me, unless it was to throw a stone and drive me away. No one searched the horizon for me, unless it was to sound the warning of my approach.

No one prayed for me; for my return. If they prayed about me at all it was for me to go away and stay away . . . forever.

I was starving to death for lack of forgiveness, but there was no one to offer it to me. For me there was no happy ending.

It was too late.

I ran on, blindly, stumbling and lurching and sobbing.

The vision of unattainable forgiveness haunted me. If I slowed for even an instant despair would overtake me and devour me.

If only my legs were paralyzed! If only my misshapenness of soul could be repaired when someone carried me into the presence of the Man from Nazareth and placed me at His feet.

Four friends to carry me to Yeshua. . . . companions who would brave the laughter and the scorn for the chance. . . . the merest moment of hope . . . that I might be healed.

I knew the truth. There was no one able to take me to Him, not without my consent. I could never force myself to go to Him, because His light would reveal the blackness of my heart. The truth about me was a glare too blinding for me to endure.

Bumbling on, I blundered away in the night until the lights of Capernaum had disappeared.

And still I ran, gasping for breath, terrified of stopping.

The clop of a horse's hooves pursued me. A moving black shape overtook me. I looked for a place to hide; a deeper pool of obscurity in which to immerse myself.

Unerringly, inescapably, horse and rider halted near me. My heart pounded; blood rushed in my ears.

"Mary? I know you're there." It was Maximus. "I saw you at Joanna's. Why did you run? Come back with me."

Drawing my cloak over my head I pressed my face against a boulder as if I could melt into the stone. Crickets chirping in the grass were not as loud as my throbbing heart.

"I won't hurt you," Maximus coaxed, as if calling a wounded creature.

I did not believe him, for he had already hurt me horribly. I knew it was Maximus who completed my destruction. Barak would never betray me. For Vara to attack me could only have been caused by Maximus taking revenge. It was him. It had to be him.

Like an animal at bay I snarled at him, "Why not just kill me? Why turn that Roman dog loose on me? Why?"

"Mary?" Maximus spoke with astonishment. "What are you saying? Come back with me. Speak to the Rabbi. He can help you. He healed Boaz. You know He did. He helped that man tonight."

"Help what? I'm not a cripple." Prancing nervously, his horse shied from the fierceness of my reply. "I don't need help. I don't want your kind of help. Never!"

When I heard the sound of Maximus dismounting and coming nearer I flinched and backed up.

"Mary," he coaxed again. "I think . . . I think He is someone you can talk to; someone you can tell anything. Everything."

Now I was shouting: "And what difference would it make? Go away, Maximus! Keep away from me."

"What have you got to lose?" he asked patiently.

"It's . . . too . . . late! Don't you understand? Too late for me. Too late to try."

Firmly he said, "I'm not asking you to try. Just speak with Him. Listen to Him."

"I heard Him already. He has nothing for me."

He took another pace closer.

"Keep away, Maximus," I warned. My fists were clenched. "Or draw your sword. This time, kill me, like you said before, instead of sending Vara to take your vengeance for you. Be merciful. Just kill me!"

"You can't think I had anything . . ."

Now I was shrieking: "Don't pretend. Don't lie to me, Maximus. I know all about lies. I can see through your lies even without seeing you."

"It wasn't my doing!"

I was not listening. Some part of my brain registered his words, but I kept screaming as if he were not even talking. "Jealous! You were jealous of Barak. You knew I'd open the gate for Barak. You knew . . ." I gathered my strength and continued, "You knew what Vara would do to me. You thought I'd blame Barak, but I figured it out, Maximus. Not right away, but I know the truth. It's the only thing that makes sense. Jealous hatred. Why didn't you just kill me?"

With those words I sank to the ground, fully expecting a quick thrust of his sword to silence me forever.

And welcoming it.

Instead he fell silent. I knew then my accusation had hit home. His failure to deny any further convinced me I was right about his guilt.

No blow from his sword followed.

The horse snorted and pranced again as Maximus sprang into the saddle. "Go on, then," he said. "Believe what you want. You say you're not crippled, but you are blind, you know. So mired in your own lies you don't even notice when the waters close over your head. Lies and half-truths of your own creation are sucking you down. You're not even trying to cling to the truth that would keep you afloat."

"What is truth?" I retorted with sarcasm.

He did not reply in anger. "Good question. I

don't know yet. Not for certain. Not completely."
Then he laughed. Laughed! "Here's an even
better question: if I did know, would you care?
Or are you too content to wallow in self-pity and
misery and blame to want to climb out again?"

Seizing a handful of dust and gravel I flung it
at him. I was pleased when some pebbles rattled
off his armor. "Go away! Kill me or go away!
You understand? I hate you!"

The horse cried out sharply as Maximus jerked
savagely on the reins, whirling the animal
around. Then he galloped toward Capernaum,
leaving me alone in the dark to pick my way
home.

Chapter 26

Outside my window the vineyard leaves
tinted the hillsides red and orange with fall
colors. Inside, my heart was the sallow shade of
withered grass.

Tavita bustled in several times a day, loaded
with food and criticism and complaint. "You've
hardly touched your food," she said, clucking
like a disapproving hen. "You're fading to
nothing. What will happen to me if you grow
sick and die? Answer me that? At my age where
can I go?"

"Anywhere you like," I said without malice, or
even interest.

"Humph! I'm old and childless and without any family. Where should I go? Lamb, why don't you eat? Just a bite."

She bullied me into a mouthful of broth or a morsel of bread. I had no care about eating, and only obliged so she would leave me alone.

Apart from crumbs of conversation with Tavita I had hardly spoken at all since my return from Joanna's. Over and over I examined the prison that was my life. I knew I was too hopelessly trapped in my sins to find escape. I was too unworthy to beg the Rabbi of Nazareth for aid.

Even if I did, what would He say to me? Stop sinning? What good would that advice do me now?

I no longer gave in to fits of sobbing, much to Tavita's relief. My grief, too deep even for tears, was replaced with calm determination. I gave strict orders no one was to disturb me. Even Joanna was turned away at the gate.

My hours—days and nights both, since I seldom slept—no longer pondered a life without love. Instead I invested every coherent thought in remembering my mother. I finally understood why she did what she did. I recognized how she had been driven; how she had found it harder to go on existing than to accept becoming . . . nothing.

If life no longer meant anything, what did it matter if I continued breathing or not?

Had Mama had all these same thoughts before the end? And what had been the final signal? What had given her the courage to say, "Enough!"

My recollections of Mama were clear: her silence. Her furrowed brow. The sad looks she often bestowed on her three children and the hasty turning away when I caught her. Even as a young child I carried my mother's unexplained grief, though my brother and sister never seemed to notice.

There was the clearest picture in my mind of the sunlit morning at the lakeshore when I went about gathering stones. With great care and much deliberation I selected only the prettiest, most precious rocks to carry to Mama. I presented them to her as if they were jewels. Round. Flat. Smooth.

Holding each one aloft Mama praised its quality, its sheen, its uniqueness. She thanked me for each.

But her voice was laden with sorrow.

I did not understand the reason for her sadness. I was proud. I was happy. My gift had been accepted.

And in the bright sunlight of my memory I saw her gravely receive each of my offerings and place them in her pockets as if she would treasure them forever.

Then she stood and waded into the water.

There was nothing dramatic in her departure, except that she did not look back when I called to her. "Mama? Mama! Where are you going? Come back, Mama!"

She waded straight across the placid surface, straight past the drop-off at the edge of the shoreline. She let the weight of the stones . . . my precious stones . . . my gift . . . carry her down.

The water was not even very deep.

Just deep enough.

The stones held her under, even though she might have wanted to breathe. What if she was only going in to cool herself? What if it had all been a mistake? A tragedy my stones caused . . . that *I* caused?

When she did not emerge, did not reappear, I screamed. First, I screamed for help.

Later, I just screamed.

Long black tresses floated above her. Uncoiling in the slight swell, her curls looked living. It was as if the lake breathed on her, and she stirred, shaking her hair.

I was rooted to the sand. Gulping for air as if I were the one who was drowning, I called for her to "Come back! Mama! Come back!"

By the time the servants heard me, and the men waded in to drag her out of the water's embrace, she was dead. Her skin was blue, like the lake on a cloudy day. Her eyes were open and her lips parted in a strange smile.

The men stood around awkwardly. No one touched me or held me. No one spoke. My own voice was the only sound I heard.

No matter how much I begged, she stared through me, beyond me. When I seized her hand to plead with her not to leave me, she was already cool to the touch.

When they picked her up to carry her into the house, stones dribbled out of her pockets.

Death became real to me in that moment and yet not real at all. Mama was cold and unresponsive. Where had she gone?

Standing before Mama's tomb El'azar told me of the scribes who said there was no heaven and no hell. "Don't worry about her being punished," he said. "But don't picture her with Father Abraham either. She's not waiting for you under a tree somewhere."

"Then where is she?" I begged.

Shrugging he said, "Sleeping. A long sleep with no awakening."

Perhaps he thought he was comforting me. Perhaps he spoke the only words he knew to speak about a departure he could not comprehend.

All I knew is that I wanted it to be different. I wanted Mama to come back and hold me. I wanted to shout at her to never, ever, ever go near the lake again. I wished I could ask her: "Did I do something wrong? Did I make you want to leave?" I wanted to take back the stones and throw them away.

When I emerged from the cold, gray memories into the pallid present, I was grateful for just one thing: that I had no children to leave, grieving, behind me. I would never do to a child what my mother had done to me.

Being abandoned was being betrayed. Was there any crime so cruel as betrayal?

Everyone I had ever loved had betrayed me. Everyone I had ever loved had abandoned me. Was it my fault?

If Mama had loved me enough to go on living, to fight against her demons for my sake, would my life have turned out differently?

What if my childhood memories were of building castles on the sand, instead of nightmares about the stones tumbling from my dead mother's pockets? Would things have been changed for me?

I had no answer.

Barak had reminded me the punishment for adultery was stoning. Stoning to death.

Then so be it. But I would select the stones of my execution myself. No one would have that triumph over me. I alone would choose the moment of my ending.

Day after day, while Tavita hovered nearby, pretending not to watch me, I strolled the narrow ribbon of sand between my home and the lake.

Carefully, thoughtfully, I gathered the stones of my punishment: round, smooth, flat, fist-sized. I cherished each one.

I knew it would be over quickly. Fill my pockets. Walk in until the cool touch closed over my head. Surrender myself to the caress of the water, grateful for the aid of my precious stones.

The knowledge, the careful preparation, gave me pleasure, or satisfaction, or at least a sense that relief from my prison was near.

But I did not yet have the courage to begin my last walk. Not yet. Soon, but not yet.

Here's what held me back: what if Barak came to my door an hour after I drowned? What if a chance for happiness came to my home and the stones weighed me down and I could not turn and find it?

It would be a fair punishment. It would be just.

Some part of me—a very small, mostly unassertive part—resisted loading my pockets with the stones, though they were hidden from Tavita in a drawer in my room.

Somehow I knew I would recognize the right time when it came: when there was nothing but despair left. Then I would take the only avenue that would free me from yearning for what I could never have.

Chapter 27

Early morning in the Galil. A mist hung above the water as I crouched on the sand. Beside me was a heap of stones. The mountains beyond the eastern shore loomed large but indistinct. Across there, somewhere shrouded in the mist and purple light, was Gadara.

What would my baby have looked like? Might he have resembled me, or would he have had Maximus' crooked smile? Would his hands be square and strong, or his fingers lithe and tapered?

How soon would he have turned his head to the sound of my voice?

I had destroyed the only human being who might have loved me.

The gray mist might have been smoke above the hills. Whose child was being sacrificed to Molech today? What little life was to be snuffed out like a candle flame by the Owb of Bamah?

Where was there even a glimmer of hope for one like me?

I nudged the pile of rocks with my toe. Almost time. Almost hopeless enough.

Yeshua's face came unbidden to my mind. Squeezing my eyes shut I tried to force the picture from me. I saw again the compassion in His eyes as the Rabbi spoke to the crippled man at Joanna's home.

What had He said? *Your sins are forgiven. . . .*

Cruelty! Agony to be in the presence of such forgiveness and find none for myself. Who gave Him the right to say such a thing? No one could forgive sins but the Lord alone.

And yet. And yet . . . if only it were true.

If only Yeshua would look at me and say such words to me and reach out to me and somehow make them true.

I paused on the edge of the water—on the brink between life and death. Was there one last hope? Was there one more chance?

My choice was simple: speak to Him and perhaps live, or remain here alone . . . and die.

I had only enough resolve for one attempt— one last, probably futile effort.

It did not matter much. My faithful lovers would not desert me: The lake would be waiting for me. The stones would be waiting for me.

When I reached the souk of Magdala it was almost deserted, and today was a market day. Where had everyone gone? The stalls were empty, the shoreline littered with the discarded nets of absent fishermen.

Locating a grizzled Nabatean wool merchant whose dirty gray cap was the same hue as his beard and his hair, I asked what was happening.

"Run off," he said. "Gone to see the miracle worker. Bad for business, I tell you. Wool trade is bust. If I was a baker it'd be different. Take my trays right into the crowd. Captive market, then, eh? Not good for wool." He shook his head.

"But where?"

"Eh?"

"Where have they gone?" I repeated.

"Carrying their sick kinfolk to see Him. Or hear Him teach. Or hoping to see a miracle. I dunno. They'll straggle back and I'll be here waiting when they does."

Impatiently I persisted, "But where is He teaching? Do you know?"

"As to that," he answered with a shrug. "Along the highway. North." He jerked his chin. "Capernaum. A mile beyond, mebbe a bit more. But He'll be finished soon. They'll all be back, you'll see."

Two hours of steady walking took me to the fringe of a crowd spread across a broad, bare field, like a living blanket thrown on the soil. The stubble left after the harvest had been plowed under, leaving the earth soft and cool. Children played beside the road.

Cloaking the field and spilling across the natural bowl of the nearby hillside was a crowd beyond my counting. Thousands, surely. Jerusalem, Judea, the coastlands: All were represented by their differing dress.

Twenty Roman soldiers stood near the back of the gathering. There to intimidate, to dampen any enthusiasm for rebellion, they also appeared to be listening. I inspected the troop carefully to see if Maximus was with them. They took no notice of me.

On top of a boulder at the edge of the field was Yeshua. He was teaching. I wanted to get closer, to be near enough to speak to Him.

Then I spotted the fishermen: Shim'on, Ya'acov, and John. The same trio who had sailed with me from Gadara stood in a knot together near the healer. They would recognize me. They had guessed where I had been on the east shore of the lake; they knew why I had been there.

"Go home," an inner voice urged.

"This is hopeless."

"You don't belong here."

I sank to the moist ground to watch and listen. Could I get closer, or was my mission already a failure?

"Fool's errand," I was scolded.

"Why should He forgive you?"

"And who's He to forgive someone anyway?"

"What do you think you'll find here, anyway, Harlot of Magdala?"

The only way I could resist the clamor was to speak aloud my protest: "Something. Hope. Something to believe again."

Nearby heads swiveled curiously toward me. I fell silent under the disapproving stares.

Inside my head the accusers shrieked all the

louder, so that I fought to hear Yeshua over their chatter.

Then I had a vision that spoke of possibility.

Seated at Yeshua's feet was Levi Mattityahu, the tax collector. I had been to supper at his house. He was Maximus' friend and Joanna's. He would not reject me at once, as others might . . . would he?

The publican had seen the same healing I had witnessed. If he were now one of Yeshua's followers he would understand my need; recognize my struggle. If I could reach Levi, wouldn't he introduce me to Yeshua?

Still I hesitated, fearful.

Yeshua's words were clear, resounding like a trumpet from the encircling hills. The echoes formed a chorus that warred against my inner voices.

The battle went on inside my head.

Digging my fingers into the soil, I tried to root myself to a furrow to keep from running away.

Yeshua seemed to be speaking directly to me. In the midst of my struggle His words pierced my heart like a shaft of light penetrates the deepest darkness.

"But how can I live again?" I whispered through clenched teeth.

"I say to you who hear," Yeshua said, "love your enemies, do good to those who hate you, bless those who curse you, pray for those who abuse you. To one who strikes you on the cheek, offer the other also, and from one who takes away your cloak do not withhold your tunic either. Give to everyone who begs from you, and from one who takes away your goods do not demand them back. And as you wish that others would do to you, do so to them." [Luke 6:27-31]

This was the world's normal response turned upside down. But how could these ideals apply to me?

The inner debate began afresh: *Don't I deserve the scorn of my family? Of my neighbors? Do something kind to someone who hates me? What can I offer anyone that would not be spat on? Give? Bless? Pray?*

How?

Yeshua's words spun away like fallen, withered leaves before an autumn tempest. I strained to hear, but they were lost to me. Suddenly I was seized with a scorching headache. Digging my fists into my ears made no difference to the reverberating clangor.

Now I caught only scraps of the Teacher's phrases: "Don't judge and you will not be . . . Don't condemn and you will not be . . . Forgive and you will be . . ."

How much longer could I hold on? How much more could I take? The sun was fierce—too bright. When it dipped behind Yeshua I was almost blinded; could no longer distinguish Him against the glare.

"The good person out of the good treasure of his heart produces good, and the evil person out of his evil treasure produces evil, for out of the abundance of the heart his mouth speaks." [Luke 6:45]

Was there any good to be found in my heart? How could I hope to practice what Yeshua preached? It was hopeless! I could barely manage to whisper, "Help me, Lord!"

I heard His next melancholy words clearly: "Why do you call me Lord, and don't do what I tell you? Everyone who comes to me and hears my words and does them, I will show you what he is like: he is like a man building a house, who dug deep and laid the foundation on the rock. And when a flood arose, the stream broke against that house and could not shake it, because it had been well built. But the one who hears and does not do them is like a man who built a house on the ground without a foundation. When the stream broke against it, immediately it fell, and the ruin of that house was great." [Luke 6:46-49]

He was describing my life! No foundation and a great crash! Destruction! The floods found me without underpinning or the strength to resist. I was drowning . . . drowning on dry land. I was gasping for breath even before I filled my pockets with stones.

And now all was over.

Yeshua was finished teaching. I had barely

heard anything of what He said. But that was not why I came, was it? I had not just come to hear Him; I had come to meet Him. Was it remotely possible?

My face remained buried in my hands while all around me families gathered blankets and children. Knots of onlookers, discussing what they had heard, drifted apart into their routine lives and mundane problems.

Several minutes passed before I looked up.

There were still at least a thousand clustered around Yeshua. A handful of petitioners crowded around Him; some carried forward; others respectfully waiting.

Couldn't I join the group next to Him? If I stood nearby, might I not be able to talk to Him; ask Him how I could live again. Tell Him . . . everything?

Picking my way through the throng and across the furrows I heard Him speaking with His closest disciples. The three fishermen were like a wall around Yeshua, but so far their backs were to me.

Where was Levi? Where had he gone? Why had I lost sight of him?

One word from Yeshua! That's what I craved: a single word.

Forgiven!

If I could hear Him address that word to me, how would my life be transformed?

I was near enough to see Him well. Loops of dark curls plastered by perspiration on His forehead, He listened attentively to a pair of men inquiring, "Are you the one who is to come? Yochanan the Baptizer sent us to ask. Are you he, or should we wait for another?" [Luke 7:20, paraphrased]

I edged still closer. I could almost touch Him!

Yeshua smiled at the questioners. "Go and tell Yochanan what you have seen and heard: the blind receive their sight, the lame walk, lepers are cleansed, and the deaf hear, the dead are raised up, the poor have good news preached to them." [Luke 7:22]

This answer was also for me! I had been blind. I was crippled. I was an outcast, like a leper. . . . and dead. Wasn't I almost dead? I wanted to wave my arms and shout for Him to see me, but still I hung back.

Yeshua spoke again to Yochanan's messengers. "Walk with me. We will speak further."

Now! Now was the time. I could move up alongside him; get His attention. Ask Him . . . what?

But He would even know the questions, wouldn't He?

As I moved forward, eagerness in my steps for the first time in long ages, a rough hand grasped my elbow. "So it's you," Shim'on's gruff voice declared. "Didn't think you'd have the nerve.

What're you doing here? What do you want?" His tone was harsh, his gaze suspicious.

Yeshua moved away. Follower and supplicants coalesced around Him, hiding Him from my sight.

How could I explain? "Just . . . just to speak with Him. Please!"

"Go away," Shim'on menaced. "Get away from here. The rabbi doesn't need your kind following after Him."

I stopped in my tracks as if he had struck me. Of course he was right. What had I even been thinking? How could a righteous man like the Teacher speak to a woman like me and not be ruined, hopelessly defiled?

Shim'on continued to glare at me over his shoulder as he left me standing there. His contempt kept me from taking one more step to follow after.

Chapter 28

The Feast of Tabernacles, the most joyous time of the year, was near. Autumn's tang was in the air. The harvests of grapes, olives, and late-ripening wheat were in. My steward reported I had achieved the most profitable year ever. All across the Promised Land, it felt that way: full of promise.

Yet it was not so for me. I was so far sunken

into despair I could barely raise my head or emerge from my room. I could not make the effort to go to the lakeshore. It was solely this lack of energy that prevented me from taking my own life, yet it was only a matter of time.

There was no reprieve for me—neither human nor divine.

So I had no expectations when a Roman post rider appeared at my gates with a message for me from Jerusalem. He banged his fist against the panel until Tavita received him.

Over the dull roar that was all that remained to me of conscious thought I barely heard the old woman exclaim, "Praise be to the Eternal." Next I heard the clumping of her feet at she ascended the stairs toward my room.

Into my hands she thrust a sealed scroll, then hovered nearby.

Her unusual behavior was explained when I recognized Barak's writing on the roll. Tavita knew his script as well as I.

"Well?" she urged. "Break the seal! Open it!"

I ordered her from the chamber. "Get out," I said in a barely audible voice. "Not your business."

The light in her eye dimming, Tavita bowed and backed away, shutting the door behind her.

Only then did I break the seal. My fingers trembled as I did so. What if it was more bad news? Could I bear another attack, or did anything even matter anymore?

Three tries were required to unroll the message. It kept snapping from my nerveless grasp as if unwilling to reveal its contents.

At last I succeeded, scanned it quickly, then reread it again, more slowly.

When the communication sank in at last, I cried out with joy! It read:

My dearest love,

I am in Jerusalem alone. Feast of Tabernacles. I crave your company. I am in hell without you these past weeks. Have been helpless to contact you. Trust me. I will explain everything. Have rented a room for us above the shop of the cobbler two doors on the right just inside Damascus Gate. He has been told to expect you. Wait for me there. Come at once.

Barak

Chapter 29

I joined a band of pilgrims from Chorazin making aliyah to Jerusalem for the festival. They did not recognize me. I introduced myself as "Mary of Bethany" in case Mary Magdalene was notorious in Chorazin as well.

They were a cheerful bunch, a blend of two families and their servants—twelve of them in all. As a woman traveling alone I was accepted as a member of their group without question. Though I contributed little to either supplies or conversation, they were not nosey and the journey was pleasant enough.

The discussions on the trail and in camp were all about the glory of the Temple. They also chattered about the relatives they would visit, and the other sights they would take in while sojourning in the Holy City. They were content to ascribe their own motives to me, even without asking.

Of course I told them no different.

When we had climbed the trail to the last summit before arriving at Jerusalem, and the entire Holy City lay displayed before us, the air was full of exclamations of wonder and praise.

"Doesn't it make your heart beat faster to see it and know we're so near?" one of the women observed.

I agreed with her response but refrained from adding any more personal explanation.

A psalm of thanksgiving, in which I did not join, erupted from their throats:

"Come, bless the Lord, all you servants of the Lord,
who stand by night in the house of the Lord!
Lift up your hands to the Holy Place and bless the Lord!
May the Lord bless you from Zion, He who made heaven and earth." [Ps. 134]

Though I felt cut off from the family and from my people and from my God, I still experienced a stirring of my emotions at the sight. There was a lump in my throat as I considered how Jerusalem, played on by sunlight and shadow, was truly the picture of a holy place favored by a powerful deity.

The Mount of Olives hung over the eastern approach to the city. Like a giant, lumbering, multi-colored beast, the hill was festooned with multitudes of pilgrims who had chosen its flanks for their encampments.

The city itself was surrounded by walls thirty feet high, punctuated by high towers, and pierced at intervals by guarded gates. But from any angle the chief attraction, and indeed a wonder of the world, was the Sanctuary itself. Gleaming in white and gold, the Temple loomed a hundred feet higher than all the rest. It dazzled the eye with its magnificence—a snow-capped peak, dripping with precious metals.

Haze softened the autumn air. The smoke of ten thousand campfires testified to the number of pilgrims who had already arrived. While the others fretted about finding a proper camping spot, I was silently grateful for Barak's foresight in engaging a room. I might be one of the few travelers who actually slept in a bed.

When we arrived at Damascus Gate I parted from my companions and made my way inside the city alone. Glancing up at the signs hanging over the stalls and shops I quickly located the shoemaker's location, exactly as Barak promised.

Would Barak be waiting for me in the room?

When that thought came to me, I fully expected my pulse to flutter, but it did not. In fact, I was strangely without excitement. Analyzing this surprising lack, I thought it was only because I was tired from the journey. Dead inside from all that had gone before, I would revive when I was reunited with him, wouldn't I?

That's what I told myself.

When I entered the shop the proprietor was busy with customers. I pretended to examine his wares, picking up sandals to study and then replacing them. As I waited for the shopkeeper to be free I was struck with such a sense of futility that it made me reel.

Why had I bothered to come? Why had I traveled all the way to Jerusalem? For what? A few days with Barak?

As the holidays ended and he returned to Eve, his wife, as surely he would, my problems would not be solved; my unhappiness would remain.

Twice I made the decision to leave the store and to abandon the plan to meet Barak. Twice I could not make my feet move. The counter-argument was: I had been dying of loneliness. Grief at not seeing him again would send me to my death.

There was no beginning anew, it seemed. Starting over was not possible for me. The big fisherman had made it clear I was not welcome around the Rabbi of Nazareth. Such a holy man had no answers for the likes of me.

While I pondered my hopelessness the family paid for three pair of shoes for their boys and left.

"Sandals?" the shop owner queried, grinning. Business was good, it seemed, and he was cheerful.

"No. My brother, you see. He rented a room."

"Yes, yes! So you're the one. Upstairs, just there. Second floor. Your brother says to tell you he'll return after dark. Wait for him here, he says; he'll bring food. Rest now. You need rest after your trip and before the lamplighting celebration and the dancing tonight, eh?" There was a pause while the shoemaker stared at the ceiling while counting off bits of the message on his calloused fingertips. "Wait, food, rest . . . yes, that's all."

I thanked him, grateful he showed no suspicion that my "brother" was not who he claimed to be.

The lodgings were cramped but comfortable. A low table and an oil lamp were beside the bed. There was a pottery jug of wine, from which I drank freely. Barak's things were piled in a corner.

A small window looked out at the Western Wall of the Temple. Another even smaller opening faced the street, letting in the hum and clatter of the continuous stream of pilgrims.

Throwing open the shutter on the street side I sat on the ledge and leaned out to watch the latest arrivals.

As the human tide ebbed and flowed below me I spotted people I recognized: Shim'on, the big fisherman, Levi, and a swarm of other talmidim followed Yeshua up the lane.

The sight of the Healer did nothing to improve my despair. He might restore cripples, open the eyes of the blind, and even raise the dead to life again, but He could do nothing for me. He could not repair what was wrong with my soul.

Shim'on had warned me to keep away from Yeshua.

And so I would.

Chapter 30

Hour by hour, though the light changed, the ever-trudging mass of humans always seemed the same. The Jerusalem street was like a canyon enclosing a river. The pilgrims were the water—one drop indistinguishable from the next. My position at the window over the lane, looking up toward Damascus Gate, afforded me a god-like view.

The sun slipped lower in the sky, a ball of liquid flame barely prevented from crashing to earth by the haze in the air. As it dripped toward the horizon it ignited countless campfires as though birthing children to represent it through the night.

At dusk a company of Roman soldiers, prodding and shoving and barking orders, cleared a path for Governor Pilate and Claudia.

Riding beside Pilate's litter was Praetorian Vara. Could Claudia possibly know what an evil man he was? I could not believe it. Instantly I withdrew, shuddering, and shuttered the window until long after the sound of their progress died away in the distance.

An hour later and a fanfare of trumpets announced another important arrival. Surrounded by two hundred courtiers and slaves, Herod Antipas and his mistress reached Jerusalem. Amid the tribe of fawning sycophants was Kuza, dusty, disheveled, and harried as he hurried along. I did not see Joanna. Perhaps she kept Boaz at home in the Galil.

I would have been glad for her company.

That was an unexpected thought. I had not pictured being around her in months.

Lamplighting time came. Shop windows up and down the lane glowed yellow and orange. Music drifted down from the Temple Mount.

The crowds on the road finally thinned as night descended. Pilgrims and locals alike were at their destinations as the festivities began. Only the food stalls—bread, dates, and the like—remained busy, as late arrivals hurried to purchase their supplies.

The scene was so pleasant, so cheerful, I was moved to go out and join the holiday-makers. But fear of being recognized kept me bound in the dim confines of the room. What if Vara recognized me? What a horror that would be.

What if my brother turned up? Home in Bethany was but a few miles away. What if I turned a corner and bumped into El'azar and Marta?

I left the lamp on the table unlit, preferring the semi-darkness and the anonymity within the shadows of the room. More hours passed and still Barak did not come. Evening meals for thousands perfumed the night air with roasted lamb and fresh-baked bread.

My mouth watered. I could so easily go out and return quickly with a skewer of meat. Just as I mustered my courage and checked the street once again, a pair of legionaries on patrol tramped past. What if Vara found me?

What if Vara stopped me and Barak saw us together?

My mind played out a dozen scenes, none of them pleasant. I trembled all over at the memory of Vara in the orchard that night. How had Vara known I would be there? What had he done to Barak to gain that information?

There was still so much unexplained. I knew I had been summoned to Jerusalem. Somehow I had found the will to make the journey. Now, I was certain, I would find the answers I sought.

When I saw Vara in the lane I locked the door to my chamber. Each time he came to mind again I rechecked the bolt. I would not open it until I was absolutely sure it was Barak.

Everything would be resolved when he came, I told myself. We would share a meal and talk. Our passion would reignite as if we had never been apart. We would be together, and no one would tear us apart.

Only . . . where was he? What kept him from me?

To keep my thoughts from running to anxiety I made up reasons for his tardiness: could not escape from family responsibility . . . had business to attend . . . was making special plans for me to prove his devotion.

Through all this illusion, part of me recognized the self-deception it represented, but I shoved reasoning aside in favor of longing.

I even made excuses for every bit of Barak's past behavior. He had always loved me but been forced to pretend otherwise. Now that would no longer be true.

Near midnight the raucous celebration was just getting started. Shops, closed around suppertime, reopened. I could hear the voices of customers downstairs with the cobbler. A cool breeze sprang up, further tantalizing me with the smells of food.

When Barak came I did not want to appear anxious. To seem worried or nervous was too much like his little hen of a wife. Instead I would show Barak how I had been thinking of him.

Bathing in the dark, I anointed myself with perfume and donned a cotton nightdress.

Once that activity was past, worry returned, stronger than before: Where was he? Why didn't he come, or at least send word? Could he have changed his mind? Had his wife somehow discovered our plan?

Didn't he want me as much as I did him?

Loud jokes and boisterous laughter boomed up from the street. Young men whooped at a prank played on a comrade.

Eventually, despite the clamor, I dozed.

In the midst of a confused dream in which someone I knew well . . . but whose voice I did not recognize . . . was calling me, the bolt rattled. Instantly I sprang up, grasping the oil lamp as an impromptu weapon.

"Mary," a drunken voice slurred. "Whassamatter? Open the door. Hurry up!"

Groping my way in the darkness across the unfamiliar room I called out, "Who is it?"

"Who do you think? It's Barak! Open up." His fist hammering on the door panel added to the din.

"Barak, is it really you?" Despite all the times I had imagined, longed for this moment, I was apprehensive now that it had arrived. "Are you alone?"

"Alone? Are you crazy? Of course I'm alone. Mary, open this door. Will you make me wait all night?"

It was Barak! Eager! Impatient to hold me! Passionate!

I threw back the bolt and yanked open the door.

Lurching in, Barak almost knocked me over as he entered, then nearly dragged me to the floor by clinging to me to steady himself. His breath reeked of sour wine.

He grabbed at me, pawing me, tearing at my clothes.

Once more the image of Vara brought vomit to my throat. I cried out, "Barak?" and seized his face with both hands. It was bearded. No Roman officer wore a beard. It was Barak.

But it was not the Barak of my dreams. There were no gentle caresses, no loving kisses, no words of endearment.

There was just a gruff urgency as he pushed me down.

I felt sick, and this time it was no memory of Vara that sickened me.

He snapped, "What's wrong with you? Stiff. Stiff as a board."

I tried to speak to him then; whispered to him

words of love that I longed to hear. I told him my life had been hollow without him; that I had always wanted him and him alone.

He did not listen or respond. Impatient, urgent grappling was what he offered.

And then he slept.

It was early morning when I heard Barak's bare feet padding about the room. Gray hues were just beginning to lighten the space outside the windows.

Drowsily I murmured, "What are you doing, love?"

From a basin he splashed water on his face and toweled it briskly. "Early duty in the Temple. Got to go."

"Barak," I said, aching with disappointment, "I thought you . . . I thought we . . . can't we . . ." I stopped abruptly, afraid to finish the question, terrified of the response.

"Can't we what?" he demanded brusquely. His face wore a defensive scowl.

"Can't we . . . be together?" I sat up, tossing back the covers to entice him to return.

He stared at me vacantly with detached indifference. Pursing his lips he offered, "Tonight. Can't stay now." Slipping his tunic over his head he turned his back to me.

"Why not . . . stay?"

He snapped, "Things to do. Important things."

"More important than me?" I tried to make it a joke—keep the mood light—but my hurt came through in the trembling of my query.

"You'd be surprised," he responded without hesitation.

Drawing the covers up to my chin I asked, "When can I see you?"

"Told you: tonight. Be patient. Stay here. Do what I tell you."

"I'm hungry. The shoemaker said you'd bring food. I haven't eaten since . . . I don't know."

He cursed then. "I'll get the cobbler to bring you something. But listen: don't go out. Do you understand? Don't! You'll be safe here."

"Safe? From what?"

"You know what I mean." His eyes glinted fiercely.

He must mean Vara! He must have seen Vara in Jerusalem. That was it.

"So I must stay here . . . locked in here . . . all week?"

Barak shrugged with unconcern as he donned his sandals. "Or go home. If you don't care about seeing me, then just clear out."

"No! You know that's not what I mean."

He put his hand to the latch. "Then stay. But don't leave this room. I'll let you know when it's time to come out. But not before. Now I must go."

Opening, then slamming the door, he ran down the steps.

Chapter 31

At last it was *Hoshana Rabbah*—the last and greatest day of the feast. It was the end of the Festival of Tabernacles.

Perhaps it was a marker for the end of my life.

During my entire week's stay in the Holy City, Barak always arose before dawn and slipped out, leaving me alone over the shoemaker's shop until after nightfall. Only when it was safe and Barak would not be observed did he slip back to be with me.

The small amounts of time he devoted to me were not of giving nor even of sharing . . . they were all of taking. Barak was a man in a hurry: too busy to talk, too busy to see me, too disinterested to care.

If I asked him to embrace me he replied with irritation and fell asleep. His hold over me was such that if I annoyed him in any way he would threaten to leave and not return, and that menace was enough to silence me.

Now the week was ending, and I knew there was nothing but ashes between us. What we had was a matter of mere clinging to something that had no substance. Beyond this room there was nothing else except a great void into which I was afraid to step.

The stones on the shore awaited me, drew me, and repulsed me.

This morning, which I knew was an ending, I opened my eyes just in time to see the door shut after him as Barak left. Today in particular he had not wanted any conversation with me.

Would he even come back tonight? I wondered.

I scanned the chamber with a leaden sense of indifference. It was apathy borne of the inability to change the outcome. If I could make no difference, then what was left to care about?

His belongings, carelessly heaped in a corner, remained.

So he would be back at least once more.

Unless he sent someone else to retrieve them and to tell me he had urgent business elsewhere.

Even this studied lethargy I knew to be self-deception. If he came back again I would make another attempt to keep him. I would debase myself yet again to hold him. Once more I would tell myself he did love me . . . truly . . . if I could only once break through his reserve of self-righteousness.

One more time I would pretend.

Life was such a tangle of lies and half-truths I could not find the end of the ball of yarn to unravel it. I no longer knew what I believed, what I cared about, or who I was. No matter what I told myself I could be equally convincing in the opposite direction in the next second.

Each morning, as Barak's footsteps had retreated down the stairs, I wondered if he was going to the morning ceremony. Though I had not dared follow him to see it for myself, I remembered it from my childhood: A specially chosen priest, bearing a golden pitcher, was accompanied through Jerusalem's streets by a Levite honor guard, and by trumpets blaring and by singing.

At the Pool of Siloam, in the oldest quarter, just below what was still called King David's City, he filled the vessel. Then, with more music and dancing, the *cohen* ceremoniously returned the sacred vessel to the *cohen hagadol*, the high priest, on the Temple Mount.

Every dawn of the festival High Priest Caiaphas, dressed in his blue robes and golden headpiece, accepted the pitcher. The fringe of golden bells and pomegranates on his robe jingled as he poured out the water at the base of the altar of sacrifice. Upon his chest hung the array of stones—twelve in all—representing the twelve tribes.

My desperate connection to sacred stones and water and sacrifice was not lost on me, but I shook it away. I wanted to remain focused, for however long I could manage, on the pleasant scenes from my childhood.

All this imagery allowed the high priest to represent the nation's prayers for rain for the coming year. The Court of Priests was ringed by eager spectators.

It was said the outpouring of the water also symbolized the arrival of the *Ruach HaKodesh*, the Holy Spirit of the Most High, on his Chosen People. While the Levite trumpets blew the loudest blasts yet, the choir sang:

"With joy you will draw water from the wells of salvation. And you will say on that day, 'Give thanks to the Lord, call upon his name, make known his deeds among the peoples, proclaim that his name is exalted.'" [Isa. 12:3-4]

For six mornings I had spread my breakfast on the window ledge and watched the excited surge of pilgrims toward the ceremony. They called out *"Hosanna! Lord, save us!"* and reveled in the music and the spectacle.

But all that was nothing compared to this, the last and greatest day. For this day the palms all around the city would be stripped bare of their fronds.

For on this day, and only this once each year, the common men of Israel were permitted to dance around the altar of sacrifice. On this single annual occasion worshippers became intimately connected with approaching the Most High with their prayers, as if they were all of the tribe of Levi.

"Lord, save us!" they chanted as they waved their palm branches. *"Lord, prosper us!"*

There was a deep significance in all of this, though I had not thought of it for years.

With *Hoshana Rabbah* the fall holy days came to an end.

The New Year celebration was finished.

So too the Ten Days of Awe were long past.

Yom Kippur, the Day of Atonement, with its fasting and praying, and its vows of repentance, was but a fading memory. The high priest had entered the Holy of Holies on his once annual journey to the footstool of the throne of the Almighty.

All through the High Holy Days people greeted each other with "May you be inscribed for a good year!"

All that was over and done with, except that *Hoshana Rabbah* represented one last chance. It was a final opportunity to repent, to seek forgiveness from Lord, to petition the Almighty for reconciliation.

One last chance to have your name inscribed in the Lord's book of the redeemed.

"If you believed in that sort of thing."

"If you thought forgiveness existed anywhere."

"If forgiveness could be found for someone like you."

"Forgiveness? Not for you!" It was a lone voice of the ones in my head. While I had been with Barak, while I had been imprisoned in this chamber, they had been silent.

What was it about this day that brought them to challenge me again?

Fear of being recognized had kept me bound to the tiny room for days. Fear of Vara. Fear of my brother. Fear of an angry mob.

Today I rose up. I washed my face and braided my hair. Dressed in my best, plain white clothing, I went out to join the flood of pilgrims flowing through the streets of the Holy City.

Chapter 32

The Damascus Road led to the south entry of the Temple's Great Portico. Like a woodchip on a fast-rushing stream, I was borne on the surface of the crowd, amid flourishing palm branches. Under the viaduct connecting Mount Moriah with the western city, perhaps I, not part of the flow, but unable to escape from it, was being carried to my own destruction.

Shouts of *"Hosanna!"* rose up all around me like the fires of burning autumn leaves.

Bits of hymns drifted down like the first pattering of raindrops.

"Give thanks to the Lord, for He is good,
for His steadfast love endures forever.
Give thanks to God of gods,
for His steadfast love endures forever."
[Ps. 136:1-2]

The psalm went on to recount all the numerous occasions when the Almighty had shown favor to His chosen people: forming all of creation, freeing us from slavery, smiting our enemies, not abandoning us when we were at our lowest ebb.

It was comforting to believe in grace. It was pleasant to think that the Lord Almighty cared enough about me to offer undeserved kindness.

But I knew better.

There were some . . . like me . . . who were beyond grace, beyond mercy, beyond redemption.

And yet . . .

What did I hope to accomplish by joining the celebration this day? What did I seek if I did not believe?

If I could not hold onto the promises written in a book or sung in a hymn, what could I possibly find elsewhere?

I did not know the answer, but suddenly I felt as if I knew who did: Yeshua.

The Rabbi of Nazareth was in the Holy City. If I might only, somehow, speak to Him here. . . .

The morning air was sharp with a bracing chill and tangy with wood smoke. I tugged a shawl closer around my shoulders.

Once at the Temple steps the mass of worshippers was like a mammoth wave piling up as it neared a beach. The numbers pressed together as we mounted. The crest of the mighty human billow surged through the portico, past the archways, and spilled into the Court of Gentiles beyond.

Then as a wave reaches the shore, the throng spread out and slowed, its energy dissipated.

So had my enthusiasm at being part of the exuberant celebration. I slipped aside, out of the main current, and into a quiet eddy to reflect on what I was doing there.

Nearby light glinted on the helmets of soldiers. Anxious to keep order during the holidays the Roman governor must have ordered an extra display of Roman might. Guards were stationed all around the perimeter of the plaza.

Was Maximus among them?

Was Vara?

Just arriving was a family with four children. I tucked myself in close beside them as if I could become part of their group and escape detection. Stride for stride I paced beside the mother toting an infant, as a trio of wide-eyed children clung to her skirts. Her husband, perhaps anxious to join the men in the inner courts, darted ahead.

I said to the mother: "There's the Court of Women. Let me help you." Once within its confines I would be safe. No unbelieving Gentile . . . no heathen Roman . . . was permitted inside the boundary wall.

"The children," the woman said anxiously. "The crowd! I could blink and lose one of my babies."

Scooping up a toddler I balanced him on my hip and led the way. The mother thanked me and followed.

The Court of Women seemed already packed to overflowing. "No more room!" shouted a Levite at the entrance.

"Follow me," I instructed. I remembered another gate further around the side of the court. Perhaps there we could still gain admission. Squeezing through the press, I forged a way ahead for the little group.

We were in luck.

Just as we reached the entry the shofar blared, silencing the crowd. We could not go further, because just beyond us was the Court of Israel, only open to men. But from where we now stood we saw the elevated platform where the *cohen hagadol*, resplendent in his robes and breastplate, presided over the activities of the priesthood.

Fully ten thousand men jammed the terrace. All held palm branches as they waited expectantly for the conclusion of *Simchat Beit HaSho'evah*, the Feast of Water Drawing.

Still holding the child, I shepherded the others to the front so they could witness the event. Caiaphas gravely accepted the pitcher from a young *cohen*. The trumpets sounded. The high priest faced the altar.

The boy in my arms whispered a belief

common to this ceremony: "Tomorrow it will rain."

As Caiaphas poured out the golden vessel's water at the base of the altar the choir joined in the tune "Hosanna!"

"Save us, we pray, O Lord!
O Lord, we pray, give us success!
Blessed is he who comes in the Name of the
*   Lord!*
We bless you from the house of the Lord."
[Ps. 118:25-26]

As the last notes of the hymn drifted around the Temple courts on the cool breeze all sound died away.

I gasped at what happened next.

From the front rank of the men of Israel Yeshua stepped forward. Approaching the altar, His stride was confident and unhurried. As He lifted His gaze I saw His face. His arms outspread, He embraced all of Israel, like a shepherd standing before His flock.

His words, full of authority and power, carried easily to all parts of the crowd: "If anyone thirsts, let him come to Me and drink. Whoever believes in Me, as the Scripture said, 'Out of his heart will flow rivers of living water.'" [Yeshua in John 7:37-38]

In the confines of the Temple buildings and

walls Yeshua's words rang, echoing and reechoing with the sound of coming down from heaven and bouncing back up again. Near me someone murmured, "He's speaking of what the Prophet Isaiah wrote. He's calling himself the Messiah!"

I did not know about what the prophet wrote, or how the messiah would be known.

What I knew was that my heart was thirsty . . . my soul was parched . . . my spirit was dying for the gentle waters of forgiveness. Tears stung my eyes in affirmation. I wanted this living water of which He spoke. I wanted it so badly.

Who was He? What give Him the right to know the longings of my heart?

Stupefied, Caiaphas appeared to stumble and grasp the altar for support. The priests and the congregation made no sound; there was no immediate outcry against Yeshua.

Like a shepherd ready to lead His sheep to water, Yeshua stood before us all, but He might have been addressing only me. He offered to draw living water for me, and keep me in peace and safety while I drank my fill. The sun shone on Him, and for just an instant it seemed His face shone brighter than the sunlight, as if He contributed to its gleam, instead of the other way around.

Then with two steps Yeshua melted again into the throng and vanished.

The little boy squirmed in my arms. I had

forgotten he was there. The trumpets blew. The music, half-hearted and awkward at first, resumed.

My charge declared again: "It'll rain tomorrow."

Setting the child down beside his mother, I wiped my tears on my sleeve. How could I find Yeshua? When could I ask Him to give me this water? I did not merely want it for drinking, to satisfy my longing heart. I wanted to wash in it; be cleansed by it.

Posting myself beside the gate I scanned every face, waiting for Him to emerge. No one would stop me from speaking with Him this time—not Shim'on the Fisherman, not my unseen companions.

I would ask Yeshua for help, and He would not refuse. Hadn't I been part of His embracing gesture that enfolded all the assembly? Enfolded me, without preconditions?

But before I spotted Yeshua I saw Barak's ashen, angry face. He had seen me and was coming toward me. Raising my chin defiantly, I prepared my defense.

Then an unseen chilly hand gripped me by the neck. Beyond Barak was Vara. The Praetorian spoke with two priests and was not looking at me. But had he seen me?

My heart sinking, I covered my head with my shawl and fled. Racing from the Temple grounds, I did not stop until I regained the protection of the upstairs room.

Chapter 33

$\mathcal{I}$ waited for Barak to follow me back to the room.

Hours passed, and he did not appear. The long morning stretched into an intolerable afternoon and became an unrelieved evening. I huddled by the window, furtively peering out. Would anyone come for me, or had I run from shadows I alone created?

Perhaps Barak was so angry with me for disobeying his instructions I would never see him again. The holiday was over and he would return to his family, as I had always known he would. I had been a week's diversion for him, nothing more.

I had clung to foolish hopes before—Barak, Maximus, and lately, Yeshua—but there was no one who could save me.

I had no resources on which to draw: not inside me, where it counted. I had wealth enough. I could leave Judea and relocate somewhere else in the empire.

As quickly as such plans arose, I discarded them.

Somewhere I had left myself behind. On a road somewhere I had abandoned Mary and I would never find her again. No matter where I went, I would remain hollow inside.

I had squandered the coin of my life and the reckoning for all my past deeds was due. There was only one means of satisfying such a debt . . . and the payment awaited me on the shores of the Sea of Galilee.

Whether I slept or not, I can't say. In the upstairs chamber, with the shutters secured, all was darkness whether I closed my eyes or not. The voices had returned and haunted me waking or sleeping. No longer did they rail on me, accuse me, or belittle me. Now there was a soft hum of approval as I contemplated filling my pockets with stones. I would take one more stone from Jerusalem with me back to the Galil, I told myself. It would be fitting if the final weight added to my pockets had been trod by Barak himself.

Something jarred me alert.

Barak slipped in at the door and stood over me. I shrank back, fearful of being beaten.

"It was very foolish of you," he said. "You could have gotten hurt."

He spoke so kindly, so unexpectedly caringly, that tears welled up in my eyes. "I'm so . . . so sorry," I said. "But you're here. You're here."

"Of course. Didn't think I'd miss our night together, did you?"

He had not said "our last night." Could it be that our week together had won him back to me? Was it possible?

There was nothing different about the way he treated me before falling asleep, but I was so grateful for his presence I forgave him anything . . . everything.

Then the cock crowed and the gray light of dawn crept around the doorframe and shutters. I smiled to see the morning arrive, then was startled to see Barak awake and eyeing me strangely.

"Are you . . . you're awake. Must you leave so early today?" I asked.

He said nothing. In fact, he seemed to be listening for something in the street outside. His concentration was so apparent that I listened also.

Then I heard it: the creak of harness leather like soldiers use to bind on their armor.

Barak wore an odd smile.

Trampling footsteps pounded up the stairs and the door burst open. A quartet of Temple guards, accompanied by a handful of priests and Levites, tumbled in.

I shrank back, shrieking, trying to cover myself with the blanket. Fearful Barak would get hurt by jumping up to defend me I put my arms around his shoulders. "Wait," I urged.

He laughed, then.

Laughed!

Barak rose from the bed and yanked a tunic over his head.

"Woman," intoned the senior priest, "this man is not your husband. You are taken in the very act of adultery. You will dress—" here he tossed clothing to me—"and come with us." While the soldiers leered and the Levites frowned righteously, I struggled to comply.

"Barak? Barak, what . . . what?"

Without a backward glance at me he gathered his things, exchanged nods with the captain of the guard, and left.

"Barak!" I called uselessly after him. "Barak!"

Like being hit in the face with a fist the reality struck me: This had all been prearranged. Barak had betrayed me to the Temple authorities.

But why? Why?

My hair unbound, barefoot, and wearing only a linen shift designed for sleeping, I was dragged from the room and down the stairs. The shoemaker, hearing the commotion, appeared at the entry to his shop. When ordered to mind his own business, he retreated rapidly inside and slammed the door.

Priests in front, and on either side, and guards marching along at the back, I was the unkempt spectacle in the center of a moving diamond of shame. The senior priest led me by a rope tied around my wrists, past the curious stares of pilgrims and shopkeepers. When I tried to resist, demanding they "Stop! Wait!" the official cuffed me across the cheek and tugged me forward again.

We retraced the steps I had taken only the day before when a desire to see Yeshua had impelled me to go to the Temple. Now I was on the same journey again.

But from the street the Levites gleaned fist-sized chunks of paving stones and shards of broken pottery and discarded chunks of roofing tile. By the time we reached the Temple courts they had as many stones as their arms could carry.

Chapter 34

My feet slapped against the paving stones of Jerusalem. My breath left a trail of vapor behind me as if, step by step, bits of my life were being dragged from my body, never to be recaptured. I shivered uncontrollably, but no one offered me a cloak.

I did not ask foolish questions about what they were going to do with me. The formal accusation leveled by the priest and the weapons of execution in the hands of the others left no doubt about their intentions.

Nor did I ask why. I was to be made the focus of an object lesson. My apparel, my just-dragged-from-bed condition, and the jagged stones made the message clear to all onlookers. Barak had sold me—perhaps to save himself, perhaps for some other, unknown motive. My fate was sealed. In the corner of my thoughts where my invisible companions lurked I sensed satisfaction, as if at a job well done.

The only query intruding on my numb horror regarded where they were taking me. The Roman place of execution for criminals was west of the city, outside the walls at a place called "the Skull."

Stoning for blasphemy and offenses against the Almighty was done in a garbage dump, like the Valley of Burning.

I was being taken neither direction. It was to the Temple we were heading; that much was unmistakable.

Some detached part of me registered impressions of what I fully expected to be my last journey. The byways were nearly deserted, after the massive throngs of yesterday. The air was still: no trumpets called, no birds warbled, no pilgrims sang.

In the brisk atmosphere all objects around me had sharp edges and crisp outlines. The people, on the other hand—priests, guards, and curious bystanders—were blurred.

The smoke of the morning sacrifices rose in a thin, perfectly fixed, black thread into the sky. No matter how the streets turned or twisted, the column of incineration remained in view, as if that were indeed our destination.

Around me I saw all manner of expressions silently commenting. Some showed fear, others pity. Some exhibited the same quality of approval as from my now silent voices. Wealthy Pharisees, in expensive clothing and furs, folded their arms across their chests and nodded smugly. Such men would willingly cast the first stone at my execution.

As we went up the ramps and encountered more and more passersby there was a noticeable division of response: some turned back in alarm. Others joined the procession as if on the hunt for a wild animal and eager to be in at the kill. On such countenances I read excitement.

I was dragged upward through a tunnel at the south entrance to the Temple Mount. As we emerged from the shadows into the glistening sunshine of the courts I felt inexplicable gratitude for the warmth of the sun on my face.

A mob had collected around me. Perhaps a hundred actors and spectators accompanied me to this, the last act of the melancholy tragedy of my existence. Like a lone sheep surrounded by a pack of wolves, there was no escape. It was as if I could already feel the stones tearing into my flesh, gashing my face, crushing my bones.

I cried out for mercy! Mercy to die without the horrors I pictured. "Let me kill myself," I screamed. "Just don't do this to me. Not like this. Not this way."

No one replied. Perhaps they thought me mad, deranged with fear.

I was.

Across the way another throng had already gathered. Perhaps the news of my doom had been sent ahead so that participants had no need to tramp across Jerusalem. They were already in the arena, awaiting the arrival of the condemned.

Then, like the shaft of light that illuminated my steps when we came out of the tunnel, the two crowds parted. The sudden clearing gave me an uninterrupted vision into the heart of the other assembly . . . and of Yeshua in their midst.

The Teacher, who had been sitting, rose as if to greet me.

The two mobs coalesced into one, forming a ring around me. I barely noticed Vara, smiling smugly at me from outside the circle. My legs bloodied from being scraped across the stones of Jerusalem, I was flung to my knees literally at Yeshua's feet.

The *cohanim* who delivered me stepped aside so as to give Yeshua an unobstructed view but remained standing behind me as a wall of accusation.

"Teacher," one of the legal scholars asserted with an air of great accomplishment, "this woman has been caught in the act of adultery." [John 8:4] He seemed pleased with his own resourcefulness, as if expecting Yeshua to compliment him on his vigilance and his zeal.

The crowd gasped at the pronouncement, even

though no other explanation could possibly have made sense.

The staging of this drama abruptly made sense. I was to be the victim, but Yeshua was the target. The malice directed at me in the eyes of the upright and righteous was nothing compared to the palpable hatred they had for Him.

"Now in the Law," the chief spokesman continued, "Mosheh commanded us to stone such women." As if about to spring an amazing trap the scribe's expression grew crafty as he added, "So . . . what do you say?" [John 8:5]

Thus I was not to be the only sacrifice this morning. If Yeshua opted to show mercy and so disagreed with the Lawgiver, He would be accused of making Himself greater than Moses, greater than the Law. He would be subject to the same penalty as me, since blasphemy was also punished by stoning.

If Yeshua opted to enforce the Law, He would be no different than all the other ultra-pious, hypocritical, self-righteous upholders of legalism. If Yeshua did not object to my execution, all His teaching about love and mercy and forgiveness would be shown to be a lie. It would be the end of His popularity with the common people, who knew how they were despised by the Pharisees.

So would He sacrifice Himself . . . or me? Of course, His speaking up for mercy would not save me; it would merely add an additional lamb to the slaughter. That I would die either way was incidental to the trap.

Hopelessness settled on me like a heavy garment. I began to long for the end. Why torment me further?

Now all motion ceased. Not only was the air still, but all those atop the Temple Mount appeared to be holding their breath to see which path Yeshua would choose.

I saw Yeshua's gaze turn ever so slightly until it locked with that of Praetorian Vara. At that encounter I witnessed Vara's arrogant stare falter, then drop away. The Roman mumbled an aside to a priest, turned, and left, striding briskly as if to a more important appointment.

What would happen? Was Yeshua wise enough to see through their scheme?

There was only one escape for Him. He was in the midst of His admirers. All around Him were those who had been healed, or had been given a miracle, or who were hoping for His touch, or who admired His teaching.

If He called on them now, at this exact moment, the *am ha aretz* would support Him. If He denounced the Pharisees and the scribes and the priests as bad shepherds, leading the Lord's flock astray, the common people would agree with Him.

If He pointed out the trap laid for Him and told

His followers to do so, they would stone the priests and Yeshua would escape the trap. Of course as soon as He spoke openly against the religious authorities He would be branded a rebel and subject to the frown of Rome.

He could take to the hills, leading a desperate and ever-shrinking band of insurgents. Eventually they would all be hunted down and killed, but for today, He would escape.

Perhaps this latter scenario was exactly what the plotters had in mind. Perhaps this view of pushing Yeshua into open revolt explained Vara's involvement in the plot.

I saw all this clearly as I waited for the first stones to fly toward me. I had no expectation of escape for myself. I was guilty as charged . . . and I felt it. Whether Yeshua showed mercy, judgment, or rebellion, I was as good as dead.

What did it matter if the stones were in the hands of my persecutors, or in the pockets of my gown and myself wading out into the embracing waters?

Curiously, Yeshua did none of the expected things.

Stooping, He bent down. Stretching out His hand He smoothed the dust on the surface of the pavement. With His index finger He began to form letters in the dirt, as if the Temple court was a Torah school and He the instructor.

The chief spokesmen for my accusers looked

puzzled and then angry. "Did you hear the question, Rabbi? What is—"

A Pharisee, agitated at the delay, interrupted. "Sin is to be exposed and punished, according to the Law. What is there to think about, or to consider? The Law is plain."

A legal authority took up the refrain: "The Law says both must die. The adulteress and the man who—"

Another scribe hastily interjected, "We all know what it says, don't we? We just want to hear the Teacher from Nazareth explain His position in this matter. Well?"

Still Yeshua continued writing. Occasionally He glanced up as if registering a particular individual's features, then returned to His unhurried jotting.

Dusting off His hands, He stood and faced the crowd. The Pharisees and scribes who had pressed closer to see what He was writing fell back a pace.

Yeshua's steady, firm gaze moved slowly from eye to eye. Despite the trap He was in, He gave no sign of anxiety, nor of anger. "Let him who is without sin among you," He said, His searching stare piercing each man in turn, "be the first to throw a stone at her." [John 8:7]

I was mute, numb to all that was happening. Was He stalling for time to think? Had He given some secret signal for rescue? What was it again He had said, "Him without sin . . . ?"

Yeshua made no explanations, offered no commentary, did not elaborate. He neither railed at them nor pleaded. He cited no other rabbinic authorities; quoted no Scripture.

He merely laid down a challenge and waited. While His words still hung in the air, He stooped again and resumed writing—a picture of complete unconcern.

No one spoke. For a long beat, no one moved. None of their challenges were repeated . . . nor did He speak again. The jury had seen the evidence and had heard the charge from the presiding judge. *How do you find? What is your decision?* There is no such thing as judgment by committee. Each man must search himself and deliver the sentence of death as if he alone was responsible for taking my life.

Then from beneath the hank of hair hanging across my drooping head I managed to see an elderly Pharisee take a deep breath and shudder. He rubbed his eyes with both palms, as if in solemn prayer; as if a startling glare blinded him. Still without speaking, the Pharisee regarded Yeshua, then me, then the sun, then Yeshua again. I saw the stone he held drop from his fingers and bounce once in the dust. As he revolved in place a clear space opened around him and through it the old man exited from the circle and away from my view.

Next a pair of white-bearded Torah scholars

turned toward each other. One raised an eyebrow. The other cocked his head, then jerked it toward the stairs leading away from the courts. Both men let their weapons clatter to the pavement.

In ones and twos, then in greater numbers, beginning with the oldest members first, the execution party dropped their stones and departed.

One young Pharisee, fiery in his piety, grabbed a companion by the arm and tried to force him to remain. When his comrade shook loose, the angry one glared at Yeshua . . . then he also hurled his bit of broken pottery to the ground and stalked away.

That was the last of any resistance, though I saw this only through a haze of tears and unbelief. What was happening? Like ice melting in a fervent heat, the perfectly formed trap dissolved. My death was postponed.

I slumped to the ground, exhausted by the sudden release of unbearable tension. Chafing my wrists to restore circulation to my hands, I stripped off the rope that bound me. No one stopped me, though I glanced fearfully about, expecting the mob to change its mind again and rush back to finish us both.

Then Yeshua stood beside me. The force of His presence drew me to raise my chin and see Him . . . really see Him.

His hand sweeping around the empty circuit

where the throng of would-be executioners had stood He asked, "Woman, where are your accusers? Has no man condemned you?" [John 8:10, paraphrased]

Incredulous, I stammered, "No man. . . . Lord." [John 8:11, paraphrased]

With that admission the full weight of my sin flooded in. I had escaped a plot to ensnare Yeshua, but I was no less guilty because of that. Only Yeshua, sinless, had the right to cast the first stone. The one who towered above me might yet demand my life and I knew it. With bowed head I awaited His verdict.

In a voice overflowing with kindness and compassion and warmth He said, "Neither do I condemn you; go, and from now on, sin no more." [John 8:11, paraphrased]

His comment required no response from me. I would not have been able to offer one anyway. My throat was as swollen with emotion as was my heart with gratitude. In that instant I felt not just saved from death but set free! Freed from the oppression of all that had kept me bound: my self-will, my pride, my arrogance, my wicked plotting. More too, I was not just forgiven, I was liberated—freed from the despair that I could never be made new.

All the guilt I bore, that massive weight of conscience dragging me to make an end of myself, was removed.

Yeshua had put His life ahead of mine in order to save me. He had shown me mercy and taught me compassion. When He did not judge me, at that instant He also made it clear my sins were forgiven.

Not just some sins . . . all of them!

Just as the paralyzed man was completely healed, so too, I was entirely restored. I no longer had a crippled soul, but a shining new start.

Forgiven! I knew now I had desired it more than anything else possible, but I had not known what an enormous difference it would make immediately.

I felt the stones of oppression and guilt falling from my pockets just as stones of condemnation had fallen around the Temple courts. If He did not condemn me, then I could also forgive myself. Not excuse my crimes, not regret being caught, but repent and be forgiven.

Forgiven!

The voices in my head were not merely silenced; they were banished! And in their place the only voice I heard was Yeshua saying: "Neither do I condemn you. Go and sin no more."

I remained where I was, turning all these things over in my thoughts while Yeshua left with His disciples. Clouds scudded past overhead. Light and shadow chased each other over the sanctuary of the Most High. Clouds gathered over the mountains, and thunder boomed in the distance.

A single, plump raindrop struck my upturned face and rolled downward into my mouth. All around me the ground was littered with discarded stones. I smiled, smelling the sweetness of the promise of rain.

It was then that Maximus stepped from behind a pillar and into my view. I spoke his name.

"I'm here," he said. "I saw it all. I wanted to . . . but it's better this way."

"Yes, much. And Yeshua . . . you knew the truth about Him before I did."

"Yes," he agreed. "But we all reach that point on our own."

Extending one hand I allowed him to raise me to my feet. "Will you . . . help me get home, Maximus?" I asked.

His nod merged with the patter of drops as the rainstorm arrived in earnest. My arms extended above my head, I lifted chin and hands to receive the blessing of *forgiveness!*

Chapter 35

Family Home of El'azar, Marta, and Mary
Bethany, in Judea
First century, A.D.

Dearest Claudia,
   This, then, is the story of my desperate journey up to this moment. I was a lost lamb until Yeshua found me; hopeless until He offered me hope. The stones of my guilt weighed me down and pulled me beneath the stormy sea. I was condemned by all, including by my own heart. And then Yeshua pardoned me. The stones are cast down.
   Yeshua is coming here tonight and will stay in our family home in Bethany until He enters Jerusalem. The aroma of lamb fills the courtyard. I hear the shouts of people outside the walls, signaling Yeshua's approach.
   I ask myself what gift I can give to the One who has done so much for me. I have upon my writing table the alabaster vial of nard from the East, which you know I prized so highly from the old days. Even something of such value is not worthy to pay the debt I owe to Him. But I have nothing greater to offer.
   Maximus waits below to carry this testimony to you. His black horse is saddled. He will ride and

then return here. Return with Maximus if you are able. If so, you will meet Yeshua face to face and know I have written the truth.

If this is impossible, dear friend, because of your position in society, I will pray that you may find some other way to meet Yeshua face to face. Perhaps in Jerusalem over the coming days of our Passover celebration?

The time has come.

Claudia, now the world outside my gates begins to stir.

I hear the people. Along the highway, crowds of Passover pilgrims clamor and shout Yeshua's name as He approaches our house.

My brother, El'azar, calls up to me that I must come down to welcome the master!

Marta urges me to hurry!

I hear Yeshua's knock upon our gate!

His voice echoes in our courtyard, "Shalom, my friends! I have come for supper!"

I am certain tonight will be a night to remember.

Shalom until we meet again,
Mary

The Story of Mary Magdalene,
First Century, A.D.
Translated by
Moshe Sachar, Old City, Jerusalem, 1948

Dearest Rachel,
As I read the story of how lost and desperate Mary was, I am reminded of how strong and glorious her life was made by Yeshua's forgiveness.

In those first years of the church Mary and her brother Lazarus and sister Martha sold all their worldly goods and offered their riches to care for the poor. They administered charity to all in need, sharing the Gospel story first in their homeland. Mary, it is recorded, married Maximin (meaning "the Great")—one of the early followers of Yeshua.

The Legenda Sanctorum restates the ultimate fate of many of those first followers of Yeshua.

Fourteen years following the crucifixion and resurrection and the ascension of Yeshua the disciples were dispersed to many lands. Stephen had been killed, Paul was traveling the world, and the followers of Yeshua were expelled from Jerusalem. With the apostles at the time was Maximin, the former Roman centurion called

320

Maximus, to whom Peter entrusted with the life of Mary Magdalene by marriage.

In the dispersion, Maximus Maximin, Mary, her brother, Lazarus, her sister, Marta, and Peniel Cedonius, who was born blind and cured by the Lord, along with many other Christians, were herded by unbelievers into a boat and cast adrift on the sea. It was thought that they would all drown. By a miracle they landed on the coast of France near what is now Marseilles. None of the local people would give them shelter, so they took refuge under the roof of a shrine. When the local people came to their shrine, it is recorded that Mary Magdalene, no longer the "Bitter Sea," but calm and beautiful and serene, preached the Gospel and many were converted.

Legenda Sanctorum says, "All who heard her were in admiration at her beauty, her eloquence and the sweetness of her message . . . and no wonder that the one who had anointed the Savior could breathe forth the perfume of the word of God more profusely than others."

Epilogue

Rachel Sachar
New City, Jerusalem
November 14, 1948

It is 4:00 a.m. I have not slept since Eben Golah brought me Moshe's gift. How could I sleep when Mary's life began to unfold before me?

Caressing Mary's journal, I draw back the curtain and look toward the Temple Mount. The Jewish Quarter is so dark and empty. No light. I am sad for this desolate moment.

Yet now it seems to me it is as if all that ever happened within those walls two thousand years ago lives on.

I feel that Mary must be there still. I see the Pharisees confronted by Yeshua, turning away from her. They drop the stones and hide from the knowing gaze of the Messiah. I see Yeshua lifting her from the dust.

I am she. We are Israel.

My heart cries out, "Oh. Messiah! Come home soon to your broken people, my Lord!"

The moon breaks through the clouds. Silver light spills across the city where my friend Mary found forgiveness in the eyes of our Redeemer Yeshua two thousand years ago. He alone was without sin. He alone was worthy to cast the stone, yet He did not.

"Woman, who accuses you?"

"No man, Lord . . ."

"Neither do I accuse you!"

I am certain now that twenty centuries later, neither will Yeshua cast a stone at me.

Now I know Moshe is alive beneath the ancient city and I rejoice.

Moshe sent me this gift by the messenger Eben Golah so I would know I am not alone.

I am loved. I am forgiven. I am redeemed.

I remember the words written in Romans 8:1, which my dear friend Leah first shared with me while we were under siege in the Old City. I have memorized this truth, for it is my salvation. *"Therefore, there is now no condemnation for those who are in Messiah Yeshua . . . Christ Jesus."*

How many women, like me, are besieged by dark memories; held captive by the past? I long for all to know that such suffering of the heart and self-condemnation need not be! There is joy and hope within reach.

I know Mary well. I am filled with the certainty that even now Mary lives! The God of Abraham, Isaac, and Jacob is the God of the living, not the dead.

Mary is sitting at the feet of Yeshua, our Redeemer. He is standing now because He is marking the day that Israel was reborn as the fulfillment of the end times prophecy. He is coming again soon to Israel, and to this beloved city. Every eye will behold Him and every tongue confess that Yeshua is Lord.

I close my eyes now and can see Leah with Mary. There is no gulf that separates them, though twenty centuries have passed between. And Mama's there. And . . . so many other dear ones who perished from life at the hands of evil men.

How near I was to giving up, but I survived for some purpose: to marry Moshe; to become mother to a future generation born in Israel.

I wonder now, would anyone wish to read the story of how I have survived to this moment in my life? My children will one day, perhaps. My memories . . . so painful and yet . . . is not the burden of every soul too heavy to bear without hope?

Perhaps I am meant to draw courage from Mary's journal; ordained to remember what was and bear witness. Never again!

I stand beside Tikvah as she sleeps and I remember the night her mother died bringing her into the world. I pray this baby will never have to suffer as Leah suffered and as I. . . . Oh Lord, may this precious child meet you in this life and live her faith with purest joy.

My feet are cold. The fire in our little stove

burns low. I am too weary to make a cup of tea, so I climb into bed, determined that tomorrow I will begin the work of writing down the events of my life that have carried me to Jerusalem. With the courage of my friend Mary I will record of the path of Jewish suffering and salvation that have led me to this place. The survival of one Jewish life is the story of Israel. I am a daughter of Zion.

I lay back on the pillow and the baby moves within me. I understand what it would have meant if I had not gone on living in the darkest days.

I long to see Moshe again. Oh yes, to feel his arms around me. To look into his eyes and see his love. But also I will thank him for this gift . . . Mary's testimony, lighting the way from shame and judgment to redemption and new life.

Blessed are you, O Lord, who has let me live to see this day.

I am tired, but do not want to close my eyes. The presence of the Lord is so near and real . . . perhaps I will see Yeshua as Mary did.

I must sleep now.

The scent of lavender fills the room. I know He is near.

Footsteps approach outside.

Am I dreaming?

A soft rapping sounds upon my door. . . .

• • •

Old City, Jerusalem
Present-day

Shimon lowered the final page to see Alfie grinning broadly at him. The light of life had returned to Alfie's eyes. The gray pallor, which had been in the old man's face only hours before, was gone.

"Feeling better?"

"You know, I always love that story." Alfie sat up and adjusted his pillows.

"But . . . who was at Mama's door?"

Alfie sighed with contentment, still relishing Mary's tale. "What do you think, Shimon? I like best that part of the story . . . the last. Jesus takes her hand and all the evil chaps drop their stones and go away . . . you know?"

"Was it Eben Golah? At the door? He came back to Mama's flat?"

Alfie stuck out his lower lip, not wanting to discuss other matters. "Oh, Shimon. At your mama's door . . . you know. It was just your papa . . . and me too. We come out of the tunnels after six months. Out from under the Temple Mount. Broke through the Arab lines and then we come home to the little flat. Hungry."

"Hungry?"

"Hungry. It was a long way from the cavern through the tunnels and under the lines. We got lost and I had to dig some, too. Thought maybe we was gonna die in there. Then the angel stepped out of the wall and showed me. We was hungry when we got to your mama's flat. I was thinking about cake the whole way. Chocolate cake."

"Mama didn't write that part down." Shimon's gaze caressed his mother's handwriting. "She ended the story so abruptly. Didn't say who was at the door."

"Well, no. She couldn't."

"What do you mean?"

"This is how it was, see? Moshe knocks and waits. Wait. Wait. Wait. Finally Rachel opens the door, takes one look at your papa and gives a little scream. Happy like. Moshe hugs her and she hugs him and then we are all happy. Crying and happy. Tikvah wakes up."

"And then?"

Alfie laughed. "Then your mama is still holding on to your papa and he is kissing her hello." Alfie mimicked Rachel's voice in falsetto, " 'Oh, Moshe! Darling!' says your mama. And then your papa says, 'Rachel! Rachel! Rachel!' But I am not looking at them kissing. I am instead looking at how big little Tikvah has grown. I am picking up Tikvah and saying, 'Oh look! Tikvah is such a big girl!' Then your mama goes into labor. Boom." Alfie clapped his hands together. "Like that."

Shimon laughed and patted the manuscript. "And from there she never had time to write her own story."

Alfie snorted. "What do you mean?"

"Too busy raising all of us kids?"

"No. Not too busy."

"Too busy taking care of Papa?"

Alfie frowned. "No, not too busy . . ."

"You mean, she wrote it down? Her story?"

"Sure. She wrote it. For you kids."

"But . . . where?"

Alfie stretched and swung his legs out from beneath the blankets. "Where's my trousers?"

Shimon tossed the old moleskin trousers to the old man. "You sure you should get up?"

"Sure. Hungry. Come on. I'll show you where all the other books are. Your papa called the Zion. . . . mem . . . or." The old man got dressed.

"Mem . . . You mean, Zion Memoirs?"

"That's it. I like that word. It means something like light, I think. See? In Hebrew 'Or' means light. So Mem . . . or . . ."

"Memoir. My mother wrote her memoir?"

"Sure. The others too. The ones who could. If they lived long enough. Lots died, you know. But the others . . ." Alfie buttoned his shirt.

"Others?"

"Sure. And see, Mem is the middle letter in the Hebrew alphabet. Mem is the middle letter in the Hebrew word for truth, your papa told me. The only way to get to truth is to shine the light on it . . . so . . . yes. Your mama and the others wrote their stories . . . all like Mary did. They wrote their memoir. Truth and Light, I think."

Shimon's eyes brimmed at the giant's simple explanation. "Yes. I think you're right."

Alfie's strength had returned. He flexed his big hands and rubbed his palm across the stubble of his chin. "I need a shave, eh? Come on then, Shimon. I'll show you where the stories are. Your mama's friends. Your papa's friends too. Even Eben Golah. They all wrote down everything for you to read. Mem-or. Aunt Lori wrote, 'What I did in the Blitz.' Murphy wrote 'How we beat Hitler.' That sort of thing."

In awe of a new facet of Zion's ever unfolding story, Shimon followed Alfie down the hallway to Moshe's office.

"Your mama always said, 'Alfie, I think every person is a book, eh?' " Alfie glanced over his shoulder. "See? Shimon? Me too. I'm a book too. Your mama helped me. All about us . . . escaping and stuff. About the angels. I know their names, see. And I wrote down what is about to happen now too. Next year in Jerusalem . . . It's all written down. Bottom drawer." Alfie turned the doorknob and stepped aside, gesturing toward the bottom drawer of the bulging red oak file cabinet.

Shimon breathed in the musty smell of old

books and tobacco—his father's scent. For a moment he felt as though Moshe had just left the room . . . or that he watched from the shadows. "Alfie? But that drawer is jammed. I've tried to open it a dozen times."

Alfie lumbered past him and with one finger easily opened the drawer. A neat pile of manuscripts wrapped in brown paper and bound with twine were stacked in the deep file.

Shimon's shadow fell across the treasure. "How many? Who?"

"Oh, lots. Everyone you care about from when you was a small boy, eh?"

Shimon hummed with pleasure at the memories. "A dozen of Papa and Mama's friends at the supper table. We'd sit on the stairs and listen to you talk all night. The Blitz. The war. Israel."

"Lots more than that. Going all the way back . . . And you can read them to me like your papa used to . . . and we can eat something while you read. I'm feeling much better. Every time I hear that story and Jesus comes into the room . . . well, how can I be sick when Jesus comes to visit? Chocolate cake would be good. Also tea. Oh, your mama was such a cook!" Alfie rubbed his stubbled chin. "Eh, Shimon? The rest of the story. But maybe first, before the cake and before the tea and before the reading, I should take maybe a bath and have a shave. You think so, Shimon?"

*Soon afterward He went on
through cities and villages,
proclaiming and bringing the good news
of the kingdom of God.
And the twelve were with Him,
and also some women who had been
healed of evil spirits and infirmities:
Mary, called Magdalene, from whom
seven demons had gone out,
and Joanna, the wife of Chuza,
Herod's household manager. . . .*

Luke 8:1-2

About the Authors

BODIE AND BROCK THOENE (pronounced *Tay-nee*) have written over 60 works of historical fiction. That these best sellers have sold more than 20 million copies and won eight ECPA Gold Medallion Awards affirms what millions of readers have already discovered—the Thoenes are not only master stylists but experts at capturing readers' minds and hearts.

In their timeless classic series (The Zion Chronicles, The Zion Covenant, The Zion Diaries, and The Zion Legacy), the Thoenes' love for both story and research shines. The Thoenes also lead readers into stepping seamlessly into the world of Jerusalem and Rome, in the days when Jesus of Nazareth walked the earth. The A.D. Chronicles and the A.D. Scrolls tell the compelling eyewitness stories of those who met Jesus—and whose lives were transformed as a result—in their own words.

With The Shiloh Legacy and *Shiloh Autumn* (poignant portrayals of the American Depression), The Galway Chronicles (dramatic stories of the 1840s famine in Ireland), and the

Legends of the West (gripping tales of adventure and danger in a land without law), the Thoenes have made their mark in modern history. In the A.D. Chronicles and the A.D. Scrolls they step seamlessly into the world of Jerusalem and Rome, in the days when Yeshua walked the earth.

Bodie began her writing career as a teen journalist for her local newspaper. Eventually her byline appeared in prestigious periodicals such as *U.S. News and World Report*, *The American West*, and *The Saturday Evening Post*. She also worked for John Wayne's Batjac Productions (she's best known as author of *The Fall Guy*) and ABC Circle Films as a writer and researcher. John Wayne described her as "a writer with talent that captures the people and the times!" She has degrees in journalism and communications.

Brock has often been described by Bodie as "an essential half of this writing team." With degrees in both history and education, Brock has, in his role as researcher and story-line consultant, added the vital dimension of historical accuracy. Due to such careful research, the Zion Covenant and Zion Chronicles series are recognized by the American Library Association, as well as Zionist libraries around the world, as classic historical novels and are used to teach history in college classrooms.

Bodie and Brock have four grown children—

Rachel, Jake, Luke, and Ellie—and seven grandchildren. Their children are carrying on the Thoene family talent as the next generation of writers, and Luke produces the Thoene audiobooks. Bodie and Brock divide their time between London and Nevada.

For more information visit:
www.thoenebooks.com
www.familyaudiolibrary.com

Center Point Publishing
600 Brooks Road ● PO Box 1
Thorndike ME 04986-0001 USA

(207) 568-3717

US & Canada:
1 800 929-9108
www.centerpointlargeprint.com